TOGETHER
WE WILL
GO

Scout Press
An Imprint of Simon & Schuster, Inc.
1230 Avenue of the Americas
New York, NY 10020

First Scout Press hardcover edition July 2021

SCOUT PRESS and colophon are registered trademarks of Simon & Schuster, Inc.

For information about special discounts for bulk purchases, please contact Simon & Schuster Special Sales at 1-866-506-1949 or business@simonandschuster.com.

The Simon & Schuster Speakers Bureau can bring authors to your live event. For more information or to book an event, contact the Simon & Schuster Speakers Bureau at 1-866-248-3049 or visit our website at www.simonspeakers.com.

Interior design by Michelle Marchese

Manufactured in the United States of America

10 9 8 7 6 5 4 3 2 1

Library of Congress Cataloging-in-Publication Data is available.

ISBN 978-1-9821-4258-2
ISBN 978-1-9821-4260-5 (ebook)

TOGETHER WE WILL GO

A NOVEL

J. Michael Straczynski

SCOUT PRESS

New York   London   Toronto   Sydney   New Delhi

To absent friends, deeply missed and profoundly mourned . . .
a love letter written in the hope of understanding what
happened, and why, the day the road ahead suddenly
became inestimably shorter than the road behind.

INTRODUCTION

At 10:23 p.m. on 14 April 2019, a text file was uploaded to several commercial websites located within the United States. Because of its length and lack of publicity or provenance, the file went virtually unnoticed for several days, lost in the flood tide that is the internet, before being abruptly removed when the websites received court-ordered takedown notices at the prompting of the Utah State Attorney General.

The AG's office justified their actions by claiming that the document was necessary for an inquest into several deaths, and as evidence in any criminal proceedings that might come out the other side of that investigation. The filing also suggested that the document contained "dangerous ideas" that were a threat to the public well-being.

Both claims were met with skepticism by the online community, especially since the Utah AG's office figures prominently in the document, leading some to speculate that the takedown order was motivated by a desire to conceal their actions from public scrutiny. Nonetheless, the court order had a chilling effect on other sites that might have been willing to repost the material, and as of this writing it remains unavailable online.

In the belief that the public interest is best served by transparency, even—and sometimes especially—in the face of official pressure, steps were taken to ensure the document's release. Its publication in this volume is not intended to condone or condemn the actions described herein, but rather to encourage debate and discussion in the public sphere. It contains journal entries, emails, texts, voicemails, and real-time transcripts that deal with issues of controversy that some may find disturbing.

Discretion is advised.

Everyone says first-person narratives are bullshit, that there's no suspense because you know that whoever's talking can't die by the end of the story, otherwise who's writing it? Well, by the time you read this I'll be dead, along with maybe a dozen others, so I guess the joke's on you.

That's called the narrative hook, like when Alfred Hitchcock talks about putting a bomb under a coffee table so the audience knows it's there but nobody on-screen does, and they're talking about golf or who's screwing who or some other shit that would normally bore the life out of you but you're going nuts because you *know* that thing's gonna go off any second and then it's blood and guts and brains as far as the eye can see . . . or that Stephen King story that starts with a woman shoving a gun in her purse and she walks around with it while she's shopping and getting coffee but you know sooner or later she's going to use it on somebody so you keep reading because you want to know when and where and how but mainly who and why. Grab 'em by the nuts and run like hell.

Difference is: this is *real* death, and lots of it.
Can't wait.

––––––––––––––––––––

From: Mark Antonelli MDAntonelli@gmail.com
To: Rick Lee RickLee@retailtransitsales.com
Subject: Re: Bus pickup

Rick:
The mileage thing will not be a problem, thanks. Just need to get it
and go. Will follow up via text.

Rick Lee RickLee@retailtransitsales.com wrote:

> Hey, Mark—
> I'm still cleaning it up a bit—the last owners weren't exactly gentle.
> As tour buses go, this one's a bit old and frankly she needs a lot
> more work than I can get done in the time required. The four bunks
> are as clean as they're going to get, ditto the toilet in back. Biggest
> worry would be the bearings. Mileage wise they'll need to be
> replaced at about 10K or you're going to have problems.

––––––––––––––––––––

The latest rejection:

Dear <u>Mark Antonelli</u>:

Thank you for submitting your novel to Eagle Publishing. Unfortunately, it does not meet our editorial needs at this time,
and we are returning the manuscript. We wish you the best of

luck in placing the book with another publisher, and thank you again for thinking of us.

Sincerely,
Tim Dunn
Editorial Assistant to Donna Lyons

I should rephrase: not the latest rejection. The *last* rejection.

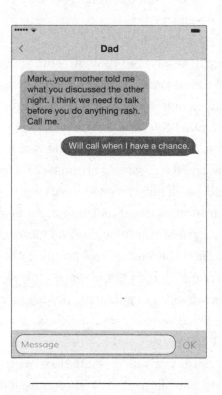

Draft three of the release form. Part of me wants to keep tinkering with it, but I'm out of time. It'll have to do. Art is never finished, only abandoned.

Congratulations! You're one of the few to decipher the invitation hidden in the Personals section of HomepageAds.com and show up on time. You have officially joined the weirdest cross-country party ever. Our destination is San Francisco. Upon arrival, we will ditch the driver, find an appropriate seaside cliff with an amazing view of the ocean, then just as the sun kisses the horizon, we hit the gas and drive out of this world.

In return, you agree to the following terms:

1.) You are serious about killing yourself. No tourists or last-minute backsies.

2.) As the price of admission, you will write your story, upload it to the Wi-Fi hotspot on the bus, and periodically update it. It should include your name, age, background, your reasons for wanting to check out early, and any other salient information. The name of the portable server is getmeout-ofherenow, and the password is boom427. Once you log in and create a username, you will have the option of linking the system to your email and text accounts to provide a real-time record of your thoughts and messages leading up to the Big Day. The system uses an app called RightWrite, which is great at fixing grammar and intuiting punctuation and conversations, and automatically backs up the files to an off-site cloud server. There are iPads on board for those with small cell phones and big fingers. You can choose to keep your entries private or share them with others on the bus. And no, I won't peek without permission.

3.) In order to ensure that nobody's relatives try to block distribution of the material, you agree to relinquish all claims to everything described in Section 2, which will be uploaded to the internet at the end of our journey. Consider it the world's longest suicide note, a collective Last Will and Go Fuck Yourself. Nobody ever tells the truth because they're afraid of what people will think of them, but since we'll literally be speaking from the grave, you can finally tell everybody in your life what you really feel, no holding back.

4.) If at any point we get pulled over by the police, you will not discuss the purpose of our trip, and you acknowledge that any drugs or other contraband found on your person belong to you and are not the property of anyone else on the bus.

5.) You absolve myself and everyone else on the bus of any liability, civil or criminal, that might be incurred during our trip. This includes accidents or a decision on your part to check out prior to finishing the journey. You alone bear legal responsibility for whatever you do to yourself while you're on the bus.

If you agree to these terms, please sign below and use the fingerprint scanner on your phone (or one of the bus iPads) to confirm your ID. Then take a screenshot of the agreement and upload it to the bus server.

If you do not agree to these terms, get the fuck off the bus.

_____

Dad

Mark...your mother told me what you discussed the other night. I think we need to talk before you do anything rash. Call me.

Will call when I have a chance.

It's been two days. Still no word. I don't want to bring the authorities into this but I will if I have to unless I hear from you soon.

I understand. Will call Friday night.

Message | OK

Transit Sales

Hey, Rick, I really need the bus ready to go by Friday morning. Can you make this happen?

Yeah, if it's an emergency I can put the pedal to the metal. How's 11:30 Friday AM?

Perfect, thanks.

Message | OK

From: Mark Antonelli MDAntonelli@gmail.com
To: Dylan Mack DylanMack@dylanmackservices.com
Subject: Re: Job Inquiry

Hey, Dylan—

Not a problem, totally understand. Meet me tomorrow morning at 11:30 at Retail Transit Sales, 21327 Via Capri Road, Miami. I'll be coming in from Kendall, so if I'm running late with traffic, check in with the owner, Rick Lee. He'll walk you through anything you need to know about the bus. Would love to be on the road by noon-thirty latest. Will have the letter in hand, signed, sealed, and notarized. See you then.

Dylan Mack DylanMack@dylanmackservices.com wrote:

> I have to be honest, Mark, while I need the money, this job is a bit more complicated than I bargained for when I answered your Help Wanted ad. I did some research and the laws about assisted suicide vary a lot by state, and we'll be passing through some of the riskier ones. I take your point that we won't be doing anything while we're in those states, and that I'll be getting off before the end, but for my protection I'd like a notarized letter saying that I'm only working for you as a driver, that anybody who gets on the bus is doing so at your invitation, not mine, and that I'm not involved in any way with what happens later. I'm just there to drive the bus, period, end of discussion. If you can do that, I'm in.

Username: AdminMark

Five Miles North of Miami.

I was still switching over the last of my files to the cloud server, creating the admin account and getting the hotspot online as we pulled out of the parking lot. Hard to believe we're actually on our way.

We've got about three hours before our first stop, so I may as well get the confession-ball rolling.

My name is Mark Antonelli. Twenty-nine. B.A. in Creative Writing from Eastern Florida State College, which means I have zero qualifications for any job that pays actual money. My mom works as a paralegal and my dad used to be a security guard until a few years ago, when he got a job at an insurance company and his boss was also the pastor of an evangelical church and next thing you know Dad goes full-tilt Born Again and holy fuck has *that* been a shitstorm.

I was an only child, so my folks piled all their expectations and unrealized hopes onto me. I had to get A's in every course or face the consequences. Nothing physical, they weren't violent, but I would've preferred a punch in the mouth to *Your mother and I are very disappointed* or *You hurt us when all we wanted was the best for you*. Anger, yelling, *anything* would have been better than that soft-walled death sentence. Nothing I did was good enough. At twelve, I started showing signs of depression, so they put me on Prozac, then Zoloft. I hated what the meds did to me, so I learned how to hide what I was feeling. Smile and the world smiles with you. Frown and they stick needles in your arms. No thanks.

I first started having suicidal thoughts in high school, and spent most of my junior year researching ways to kill myself without it *looking* like I killed myself, because when that happens, everybody makes it about *them* and what *they* said and what *they* did or didn't do and *ohmygod if only we'd read the signs, we could've prevented this.* When I die, I want it to be about me, okay? That's how I found out that a lethal dose of potassium is both hard to trace *and* slow-acting, which would give me time to ditch the evidence. Took a while, but I finally got my hands on enough to do the job, and held on to it for months, waiting for the right moment.

To kill time (so to speak), I started writing a journal, just for myself, so I could express what I was feeling. The more I wrote, the more I discovered that I *liked* it, so I began writing poems and short stories that were good enough to impress my teachers and they told me to keep going.

I don't think they had any idea what *keep going* actually meant at that point of my life, but it was enough to make me ditch the potassium, which to be honest wasn't as big a gesture as it sounds since I knew I could always get it again. I just needed to see myself tossing it down the toilet as a symbol of *I've got this,* you know?

By the time I graduated high school, I'd pretty much convinced myself that I was going to be okay.

Then my dad said, *If you expect somebody to give you a job as a writer, you have to get a degree.*

And that's when it all went to shit.

I wanted to say, *Nobody just* gives *you a job as a writer the day you walk out of college like some kind of goddamned Cracker Jack prize and they don't even give* those *out anymore because some stupid kid choked on a plastic toy soldier thirty years ago . . .* wanted to say, *I'd be better off spending those years hitchhiking across the country or building shelters in South America than sitting in a room for the next four years listening to some guy who's never sold a thing in his life tell me how to write.*

But I didn't say any of those things. I nodded and smiled and deferred and agreed and enrolled and took notes and tests and Adderall and wound up right back on the Potassium Highway. Because like everybody else in my demographic, I fell for the Big Lie.

If you're over thirty and reading this, you don't understand that the road between Get a Degree Avenue and Here's Your Job Boulevard broke down a long time ago. But that's not your fault. You don't understand because you *can't* understand, because that's not the world you lived in.

The Civil War was stupid lethal because the generals weren't living inside the war they were fighting; they were living in the *last* one. During the Revolutionary War, muskets were shit. You had to get up close, *closelikethis* if you wanted to hit anything. So when the Civil War came along, the generals used the same tactics they'd used in the Revolutionary War: they ordered their soldiers to line up in rows, elbow to fucking elbow, so close to the enemy they could see each other's teeth before opening fire with weapons that were a hell of a lot more accurate than muskets. They fought the *next* war using the strategies of the *last* one, and six hundred thousand soldiers died because of it.

So when our parents said, *Go to college and get your degree so you can get a job*, we did it even though we know it doesn't work that way anymore because we wanted to make you happy, because we wanted to believe what *you* believed, that the rules still applied, that you walked out of college with a degree in one hand as a recruiter shook the other, offering a job and a salary and a desk and maybe a pension plan that they'll take away before you get to actually use the goddamn thing but hey, it's the thought that counts, right? But that's not true anymore. We will never, *ever* have the same opportunities you did. Full-time jobs are fading fast, replaced by part-time jobs where you get paid shit money to work long hours that are constantly being shifted around so there's no stability, no benefits, and no backtalk or you're fired, and there's nothing you can do about it. And the American Dream of owning a home someday? How? With what? Everyone I know who graduated college came out $50–80K in the hole for student loans they'll never pay off, which by the way also shoots down their credit rating, so there's no savings, no loans, nothing to invest, nothing to buy a home with, and the planet is frying and in thirty years most of us will end up climate refugees, so yeah, there's *that* to look forward to. And in return we get shit upon from On High for living at home or not having ambition or putting experience ahead of owning stuff because in case you weren't paying attention *we can't fucking afford anything.*

And that's why you don't understand. Not your fault. Not your paradigm. It's just what it is.

So when I graduated with a degree in writing, my parents expected me to start making a living as a writer *rightdamnitnow.* What followed instead was seven years of part-time work and full-time rage, sending out short stories and novels and *This doesn't suit our needs* and *Come back another time* and *Sorry we can't help you* and *Get the hell out.*

After a while I stopped kidding myself that the writing thing was ever going to work out. So what was left? Spending the next thirty years of my life flipping burgers for minimum wage and making up the rest with food stamps and welfare? Going back to school so I could come out with another useless degree, crushed by more loans that I'll never repay and a credit score that'll keep me from renting anything bigger than a litter box for life? No.

Looking down the barrel at thirty, I finally accepted once and for all that there was nothing I could do and nothing I could write that would change things, so I said fuck it, I'm outta here.

That's why I'm doing this. *That's* why I used the last bit of cash I socked away after college, my I-can-live-on-this-for-a-while-if-everything-else-goes-to-shit emergency fund, to buy an old, beat-up tour bus off a government surplus website.

Because the only good writer is a dead writer, right?

This is the notice I uploaded last week to the Personals section of HomepageAds.com:

> If you can't carry this weight anymore . . . if you want it to stop, REALLY stop . . . then you'll understand what this ad is about. I'm not here to talk you out of anything. That's BS and we both know it. So let's do this right. One big party, one last drive, flat-out, right to the edge and no coming back. Looking for 10–12 people who GET what this ad means and can commit to seeing it through. If that's you, respond with a text number. Burner preferred. Don't want or need to know details. Will get back to you ASAP with a pickup address.

The notice went live two days ago in every big city between here and San Francisco. Once I had enough convincing responses, I pulled down the ad so the police couldn't find it or, if they knew about it, trace it back. Everything after that will be done in texts, the language vague enough to be safe, but clear to anybody who's ready to check out. It's funny how we can dog-whistle this stuff with each other when we decide it's over.

First stop is Orlando, because fuck Disney.

Dylan keeps circling the pickup location, worried that this is a setup, that the cops are waiting for us. I tell him it'll be okay. Not sure I trust this myself. But there's only one way to find out.

She was waiting on the corner when we pulled up. Five two, thin, pale, with light brown hair. She was pulling a pink suitcase and when she got in she said her name was Karen and I gave her the release form. She read it over several times, like she was buying a car, then signed and uploaded it. As we took off, I peeked at the server long enough to see a last name—Ortiz—then logged out until and unless she says it's okay to look. Since then she's been sitting in the front seat without saying a word. As far as I can tell, she hasn't started writing her story or anything else—she's just staring out the windshield, purse wrapped around one arm, the other resting on her suitcase. When I offered her a beer from the locker, she just shook her head, eyes locked onto the view outside.

So far, not exactly a party.

When we stopped to get something to eat, Karen went ahead of us, still silent, still pulling her suitcase.

"I think we ought to ditch her," I told Dylan.

I figured he'd be all over the idea. Instead he shook his head and said, "No."

Since meeting him for the first time back in Miami, I've come to the conclusion that Dylan's one of those guys who always seems to know more than you think. He's a big guy, about six four and stocky, with a sandy-colored buzz cut, the kind of guy you'd expect to be big and loud and trying to dominate every conversation, but most of the time he just lies back real quiet, until you've pretty much forgotten he's there, then he drops in the most unexpected comments. That's how I found out he did two tours of duty in Afghanistan, which explains his *The Army Made Me Build Up All These Muscles So I Could Destroy Things But Now That I'm Home I Don't Know What to Do With Them So I'll Let Them Go a Little Soft Around the Edges But Keep the Rest Around Just in Case There's Trouble* body type. After his discharge, he came back to Florida to do odd jobs and spend two weekends a month playing poker in the casinos. He thinks he can make a living at it someday. He's probably right.

So when he vetoed the idea of ditching Karen, I asked him why.

"Mark, *look* at us. We're two guys picking up people who don't want to live anymore and nobody would miss, driving a beat-up old bus that looks like a goddamn rape/murder van. She's probably scared shitless. Yeah, she *says* she wants to die, and maybe that's true, but you can bet your ass she doesn't want to get tortured on the way."

"So why'd she get on the bus?"

Dylan glanced ahead to the restaurant, where Karen was talking to the hostess. "I don't know, Mark. Maybe she *wants* to believe this is really what you said it was, and maybe she doesn't have any-where else to go. All is know is what I saw in the mirror when she was staring out the window. She's lost. I don't think I've ever seen anybody that lost. I think we're her last chance to get out clean. But she's scared."

"So what do you want me to do about it? Tell her I'm safe? Like *that'll* work. It's just what a serial killer would say."

"Then let's be honest about it and tell her we can see she's un-comfortable, like maybe she's having second thoughts or she's not sure about us, which is understandable. Before she got on the bus this was just an idea, but now it's real and that's a big jump and we want her to feel safe, so after dinner we'll leave on our own, drive around for a while, then circle back. That way we won't be able to see where she goes if she decides to split, and she'll know we're not trying to control her or force her into anything. If she wants to come with us, she'll be here when we come back. If not, not."

"Okay," I said, "but if this was a casino, I wouldn't bet on her sticking around."

Update: Two hours later.

Now I understand why Dylan bets smarter than I do at the casinos.

Username: Karen_Ortiz

My name is Karen Ortiz. I'm 26. Mark said I should feel free to write about my family, but there's not really much to say. We were pretty ordinary. Craziest thing I ever did was get on this bus, so I guess it's never too late to lose your mind lol. We lived in Jacksonville, Florida, before moving to Orlando a few years ago. I went to an okay high school, got asked to a couple of dances, tried out for cheer and debate. First kiss at sixteen. That's also when the pain started.

At first I thought it was just a really rough period but the pain didn't go away, it just got worse. I could feel it in my stomach, arms and legs, then all the way into my feet and fingers. I couldn't sleep because I couldn't find a position where I didn't hurt. I cried all the time. When our doctor couldn't find anything wrong, he said I was faking it to get attention.

Finally my dad took me to a specialist who did an MRI and a bunch of other tests and said I had pain amplification syndrome related to arachnoiditis. It means there's a short circuit between my brain/spinal cord and the rest of my body that creates a feedback loop of constant agony. The pain signal bounces back and forth like two mirrors facing each other, getting stronger each time it's reflected back. If I don't move at all the pain is bearable, but if I shift position in a chair or touch something or someone touches me, it's just awful. Screaming-level awful. If you ever got a charley horse, or pulled a muscle so bad you couldn't move, that's what it feels like but instead of staying in one place it spreads out into the rest of your body until you're one huge ball of pain and it goes on and on for hours or days.

Rather than calling it arachnoiditis, I started calling it the Spider, because at night when I'm trying to sleep it's like I can feel it laying eggs in my spine, chewing on the nerves in my body and eating me alive from the inside out. My periods became blackout painful and kept me in bed for days at a time, constantly crying. It got so bad that my parents agreed to let me get a partial hysterectomy, which helped with the pain and I could never survive having a kid anyway.

One of the hardest parts—other than everything—is that once we figured out what the problem was, nobody knew how to deal with it, or me. When somebody at school gets sick, people can say *Oh, I'm so sorry* or *Hope you feel better soon* because sooner or later you will. But when they know it's never going to change, they can't keep saying *I'm sorry* or *Tomorrow you'll be better* because they know it's not true, so after a while they say nothing at all. Nobody comes to sit with you at lunch, or invites you to parties (which I couldn't go to anyway) . . . you can feel everyone looking at you, but they never come close.

After graduating high school, everyone I knew went on to college but I hardly ever left home. I spent most of my time in my room, half-asleep from antidepressants and painkillers, trying to take online classes, sleeping or watching television and trying not to move. The doctors kept saying, *You have to hold on, there are some new treatments coming.* But they never showed up.

When I turned twenty-one and a bunch of my former friends graduated college, I decided to do the same, but different. See, there's a distinction between suicidal *ideation* and suicidal *attempts*, SI versus SA, as doctors like to say. Suicidal ideation was when I'd think about how much easier it would be for me and everyone else if I was dead, but I wasn't ready to actually do it until the day I was in bed watching online as everyone I knew from high school walked onto the stage and picked up their diplomas, jumping around and yelling and throwing their caps in the air and I said that's enough, you know, it's just *enough* and I graduated from SI to SA by chowing down on sleeping pills, except I didn't do it right and ended up getting my stomach pumped, then spent six months getting outpatient psychiatric treatment. They put me on more meds. I slept a lot. Watched more TV. After a while I couldn't tell if I was sleeping, dreaming, watching TV, or dreaming about watching TV.

Nothing made the pain go away. So a year later I tried to kill myself again. I just flat-out attacked the Spider. I could feel it crawling through my arms and legs and I snapped and grabbed a knife and started tearing into my skin but the amplified pain was more than I could handle and I passed out. Woke up in the hospital, my arms tied to the bed, leading to more observation, more treatment, more meds, and more depression.

After that, I kind of shut down. I don't remember much of the last few years. I've never traveled. Never had a boyfriend because I creep out the boys; they don't know how to talk to me and they're worried they'll hurt me if they kiss too hard, so whatever mental boner is required for more than that goes limp. I've never had sex, never even had an orgasm until I realized I can't climax from outside stimulation alone. It took a dozen tries before I could get a vibrator deep enough inside to fix the problem. At first I was afraid of passing out from the pain and having my folks walk in to find me sprawled over the bed with a buzzer in my bush, but eventually we became good friends.

The rest of the time, it's just me and the Spider, waiting for the right moment to walk off the earth together.

When I saw the notice on homepageads.com, I thought this might be a good way to see some of the world before I leave it. I like the idea of being with people who've made the same decision I have, who understand that when I say I want to kill myself I'm not acting out or being dramatic, that I'm not saying something *bad,* just something inevitable, and won't try to talk me out of it. There's something nice about being just one more rider on a bus that's taking us all to the same place.

I was a little nervous when I got on because Dylan's a big guy, and Mark looks like somebody's twitchy, resentful ex-boyfriend, short and skinny with a pinched face under a big tangle of curly black hair. Whenever I glanced over at him, he looked like he was thinking about something very serious and I couldn't tell if he was having some deep writer thoughts (at least he *said* he's a writer) or working out where to hide my body once they were done with it, but so far they seem safe, so I think I made the right choice.

To be honest: I'm scared. But I'm also more alive than I've been in ages, which is kind of ironic considering why I'm here. So I guess we'll see what happens.

I don't mind dying. I want to get it over with so I can finally kill the fucking Spider. But like Dylan said at dinner, I just don't want to be murdered.

Different things, you know?

AdminMark

When I first came up with the idea for this road trip, I knew the only way it could work was by keeping a low profile. Just stick to the map, pick up whoever's waiting to be picked up, then get the hell out of town. Nobody makes a scene, no trouble, no police.

I don't think Dylan got the memo.

By the time we crossed into Brunswick, Georgia, we'd been driving for almost nine hours. I hadn't gotten much sleep the night before, worrying if the bus would be ready in time, so I was tapped out and we decided to call it a day. Simplest thing would've been to sleep in the bus, but if everything goes the way it's supposed to, pretty soon there'll be too many of us to crash out at motels without drawing attention. Since there's only three of us for now, I told Dylan to pull over at a Motel 6.

Karen went in first while Dylan and I locked down the bus. We'd just finished up and were heading for the motel when we passed this fat guy in an old denim jacket and a Metallica ball cap standing by his car in the parking lot, yelling at his girlfriend. He was right up in her face, drunk out of his mind, saying she was stupid and a whore and he ought to punch her face in. She was crying, tears and snot running down her face, saying she was sorry for whatever the hell she'd done to piss him off, but that only made him madder. Then he slapped her, hard. Backhanded the shit out of her, *whap!*

And Dylan stopped. Stared at the guy. Eye-fucking him.

The guy felt it. Shit, he'd have felt a look like that on the other side of the planet.

"What're you staring at, asshole?"

"A coward," Dylan said. "Only a coward hits a woman."

Shit, I thought, *we don't need this.* "C'mon, man, let it go."

The guy pushed his woman back against the car and started toward Dylan. "You mouthing off at *me*, you prick? You saying I'm a coward?"

"Hey, if the yellow fits, right?"

"I'll kick your ass, faggot!"

He swung at Dylan, but D leaned out of it, smacked his arm from behind as it went past, then shoved the guy back against the car like he wasn't even trying, like he didn't *have* to try.

But now the guy's even more batshit angry and he came back at Dylan all out of control, fists swinging like a big fat pinwheel, but Dylan got under the swing and hit him in the stomach so hard so fast the only way I knew he hit him *twice* was by the sound the fat guy's gut made when he got hit, all floppy and slappy as the air got knocked out of him.

He backed up for another swing, but D punched him in the face and he went down like the house that pancaked the witch in *The Wizard of Oz*.

And of course now the girlfriend gets all up in D's face, yelling at him and telling him to mind his own business and now it's just going to be worse and who the hell does he think he is, anyway?

Then she helped Shamu into the passenger seat, climbed in behind the wheel, and drove off, tires spitting gravel.

Once the taillights had blinked out around the corner I looked over at Dylan. "You know we're gonna have to get another motel now, right? Because he's either gonna call the cops or come back with some friends."

He nodded. Shrugged. It's what he does when he doesn't know what else to say.

"Why the fuck did you do that?" I asked.

"Had to," he said, and that was that.

We turned as Karen came up behind us. "Good thing I checked to see where you were before I put down my credit card." It was the most she'd said at one time since getting on the bus. "You're right, we should go."

Twenty minutes later we checked into an Embassy Suites up by Dock Junction. As he headed off to his room, Dylan promised it wouldn't happen again.

But I'd seen his eyes when it all went down. Whatever's in there, wrapped around his brain like a snake, it's not going away tomorrow or the next day, and it doesn't give a shit about promises.

Karen_Ortiz

From: Mom TracyOrtiz@mountainview.com
To: Me KOrtiz2019@simrose.com
Subject: You okay?

Karen, I just got a call from Sheryl who said she went by your apartment but you weren't there and nobody's seen or heard from you in a couple of days. She said there was mail and a package on your porch that looked like it had been there for a while. I tried calling but it kept going to voicemail so I wanted to leave word here in case you were out of cell reach or you'd lost your phone (again). I don't need to know what you're up to or where you are, I just want to make sure you're all right, so if you get this or any of my messages, give me a call so I know you're okay. You know how I worry.

Love you.
Mom

AdminMark

When I was in junior high, too old for a babysitter but bound to get into trouble if I was left alone, my folks took me with them on a trip to New York. As my dad and I checked in at the front desk, my mom waited outside by the car, watching the porters to make sure nobody stole anything, because apparently she thought that was a thing. As my father signed us in, the desk clerk said, "Do you have any baggage?"

"Yeah," he said, and nodded toward the entrance. "She's outside with the luggage."

Yeah, my dad turned into kind of a jerk, but he could be funny when he wanted to.

Also, persistent. Viz:

📞 PHONE   8:27 AM
MY NUMBERS   DAD
Missed Call and Voicemail

📞 PHONE   10:13 AM
MY NUMBERS   DAD
Missed Call and Voicemail

📞 PHONE   1:23 PM
MY NUMBERS   DAD
Missed Call

Karen_Ortiz

To: Dr. Tom TPowell@RidgeMedical.org
From: Me KOrtiz2019@simrose.com
Subject: Checking In

Hey, Dr. Tom! Long time no email!

I wanted to touch base because I thought of you earlier today and realized that I never thanked you, or at least never thanked you enough, for what you did for me. You were the first doctor who ever treated me like I was an adult who could understand what you were saying, and that I didn't need you to make the truth soft. You didn't lie to me. I hated it but I needed it.

You worked so hard to try and help me. I hope you won't think this is silly, but sometimes I thought of you as Samwise Gamgee climbing up the side of a mountain with your bare hands to kill the giant spider and save me. (Obviously I was playing the role of Frodo for purposes of this story, and yes, I've seen the movies a *lot*.) Of course I knew you wouldn't be able to kill it no matter how hard you tried, but I never blamed you because this isn't a movie, and not everything works out in the end.

But that's not why I'm writing.

I wanted to tell you that I appreciate everything you did for me, every battle you fought, every truth you told, every time you let me cry in your office and never tried to stop me or look at your watch like you had somewhere else to be. You loaned me your courage when I didn't have any, like training wheels that kept me going until I could find some of my own. That meant so much to me. You have no idea. I'm proud to say that a little piece of your courage is still with me. Guiding me.

No matter where I go, or what happens in the future, I want *you* to know that *I* know you did everything you could. Thank you.

Be well.
K.

AdminMark

Savannah, Georgia, was a no-show, so we kept going north. By the time we rolled through Hardeeville, in Jasper County, South Carolina (and seriously, *Hardeeville?* Were all the good names taken?

Twenty bucks says any kid who went to *Har-Har-Har*deeville High School spent the rest of his life saying he went somewhere else because that's the only way he would *ever* get laid), Karen had become more loquacious, which is Creative Writing 101 speak for *She pulled the pink suitcase out of her ass*. I think she finally accepted that we weren't going to kill her, or that if we *were* going to kill her we'd at least wait until we found someplace with a nice view, and Hardeeville definitely wasn't it, so she could afford to open up a bit.

At first it was just casual chatter—the weather (sunny but not too hot), how long I thought it might take us to reach San Francisco (ten days *mas o menos*) and where I got the bus—but eventually we started talking about what brought us here. She said it was chronic pain, but didn't go too deep. She was surprised to find out Dylan wasn't there for the same reasons as us, and asked why.

"Think about it," he said. "If you're trying to get from Point A to Point Z, the last thing you want is somebody at the wheel who might decide 'fuck it' and drive into oncoming traffic at Point C."

She laughed and said it was a fair point. It was the first time she'd laughed since she got on the bus, and I got the sense she doesn't do it easily or a lot. Then, like she realized she'd shown more of herself than she intended, she went back to her laptop.

Karen_Ortiz

To: Mom TracyOrtiz@mountainview.com
From: Me KOrtiz2019@simrose.com
Subject: From Karen

Hey Mom.

Sorry it's taken a while to get back to you. I wanted to be sure I understood what I was getting myself into before talking to you about everything. Now I do, so now I am.

I don't think I need to tell you what this email is about. We both know this has been coming for a long time. We've certainly talked about it enough, especially this year with the Spider growing bigger and badder than ever.

Don't worry about me. I'm with friends, if you can believe that. They actually understand what I'm going through, and why I've made this decision. We're going someplace beautiful, and I think going there together will make things easier.

I left the key to my apartment under the penguin on the front side window. I went through and labeled everything so you'll know who gets what, and put the smaller bits that might get lost in Tupperware containers with Post-It notes on top.

OCD to the very end, right?

I think you know that this isn't your fault, that there was nothing you could've done to change things or stop me from taking this next step, but it's important for you to hear me say it one more time, so it'll stick.

The hard part for you, beyond the obvious, will be Dad. He won't understand. He never has, really. He always thought he could fix everything, and even though he never said it out loud, I think he felt like he was a failure because he couldn't fix me, which was why he went down that bad road for a while. I'm glad he came back and I don't want him to go down that road a second time because of me, so please do what you can to make sure he understands. This is my choice and nobody's fault.

I love you both so much, and I'm sorry to have been such a burden for so many years. I probably should've done this a long time ago. I guess I was just afraid. But I'm not afraid anymore.

Tell Chuck he was the best brother anyone could have asked for, and I love him more than a fat kid loves cake. That may seem weird, but he'll understand what it means when you say it.

Don't try to find me. There are no footprints to follow, and I won't send any more emails until I get where we're going in case Dad tries to get the police to check the cell tower info or trace my phone. I'll let you know where to go to take care of things once I'm ready to step off.

I love you, Mom, so very much.

Please be at peace, because I am. Finally.

All my love—
K.

AdminMark

Karen closed her laptop, looked up for the first time in almost an hour, and said, "I want to go to a strip club."

Dylan almost drove off the road.

The first time she starts a conversation on her own, and *that's* what she says? What's weird is that there was a lightness to her voice, as if a weight she'd been carrying around for a long time had suddenly and for the very first time been lifted off.

"You want to do *what?*" I said.

"A strip club. I've never been to a strip club. It's on my bucket list, along with getting drunk. Just once."

"Yeah, but . . . right now?"

She shrugged. "May as well, I mean, I'm almost out of bucket, right? Besides, I'd be too shy to go in with a big group. Better to do it now when it's only the three of us. Is there a place near here?"

I checked the map. We were about to cross into North Carolina and this part of the world was known more for churches and titty bars than fancy strip clubs. "Might be something in Charlotte, but by the time we get there it'll be almost ten and they may close early on a weekday."

"I wasn't planning on moving in," she said. "I just want to go long enough to say I did it."

Half an hour later, we rolled up to Lace Cabaret, an industrial-looking building at the ass end of Pineville Road. The parking lot was full of pickups and older model sedans bearing Confederate flag decals and *Fuck Liberals* license frames. I told Dylan maybe we should try someplace else, but then he pointed to a car with a bumper sticker that said *My Other Vehicle is a TARDIS* and I figured we'd probably be okay.

The guy at the cash register was surprised to see a woman with us, but our money was good, so he buzzed us through a heavy fire door covered in photos of dancers and posters announcing upcoming parties. Inside, a long L-shaped bar ran along two walls, with couches, tables, and chairs lined up on the other side. The main runway ran straight down the middle of the place, with a couple of smaller stages tucked into opposite corners. Curtained doors led off to private rooms where the real action took place. A handful of strippers (I wonder if *a handful of strippers* is like *a murder of crows*) prowled the club or sat with customers, encouraging them to buy overpriced drinks or step away for lap dances.

Huge speakers painted the same matte black as the walls blasted country hip-hop across the club, and I didn't even know that was a thing until we walked in the door and heard "Baby Got Back" sung with a twang under steel guitars, which totally weirded me out. I don't think the dozen or so guys in the club had *any* idea where that song came from, but they weren't here to critique the music.

Then again, neither were we.

Dylan headed to the bar to buy the first round while Karen and I tucked into a table near the runway, where a brunette in a red bra and panties was making love to the pole. Most of the tables had one customer each, with the rest sitting on worn sofas or clumped up in Pervert Row at the edge of the stage, which provided the best vantage point for any free-floating labia that might wander into view. Seven one-dollar bills were crumpled up on the runway. Slow night for tips.

"Strip club's kind of old-school, isn't it?" I said.

"Like I said: bucket list."

"What else is on it?"

She ticked them off on her fingers: "Skydiving. Riding in a limo. Riding a camel. Seeing the sun go down in Paris."

"Not likely to hit many of those on our way to San Fran."

"That's why we're doing this one. Taking what I can get."

Then, I noticed a guy at another table staring at Karen, his hand down the front of his pants. When he caught me looking at him, he pulled it out like he was just scratching an itch and went back to watching the dancer.

As Dylan returned with the drinks, one of the strippers came out of the dressing room and headed toward us: thirties, blonde, with a set of silicone-enhanced bolt-ons that stood up so straight they looked like they were pissed off at somebody. Angry titties. There's a band name in there somewhere.

"Hi, I'm Nikki," she said with a slight drawl, could be Texas or Louisiana. "Y'all just get in?"

"Two minutes ago," Dylan said. By now the other strippers had noticed fresh meat in the place, and seemed annoyed that Nikki got to us first. New arrivals meant we hadn't spent our money yet, and there's always a rush to get what's there to be gotten.

She draped an arm around Karen's chair. "Hi, sweetie. We don't get many pretty ladies like you in here. Buy a girl a drink?"

"Sure. How much?"

"Bossman says we're only supposed to have water, so it's five plus a tip if you're so inclined."

Karen handed over ten bucks and Nikki went off to get the water. Dylan raised his glass of beer. "To Karen!"

I seconded. Karen smiled like she hadn't been toasted before. An item for the bucket list she hadn't even known was there.

Nikki came back with an unopened bottle of water that she kept beside her the whole time, leading me to wonder how many times that bottle had been resold. Dylan and I had already worked out our cover story, so when she asked where we were from and why we were in town we said *Chicago* and *On vacation*. Not that I think she was really listening to the answers, just marking time until she could say—

"Anybody want a dance?"

"What's the fare?" Dylan asked.

"Twenty per song, twenty-five topless, thirty nude. Should have a two-for-one blue-light coming up pretty soon if you want to wait a bit. VIP is one hundred for fifteen minutes, nude."

I was trying to decide whether or not to go for it—normally it wouldn't be a problem, but having Karen there made things a little awkward—when she said, "Let's do a VIP."

Nikki smiled and brushed Karen's hair away from her face. "Love a woman who knows what she wants. You good now or you want to finish your beer?"

"Now," she said, like she might change her mind if she waited.

Nikki led her away by the hand, pausing only to throw back a wink at us. "Don't you worry about your friend, babes, she's in good hands. Until then, any of these bitches come poaching my territory, you tell 'em you're all mine."

The other strippers must've gotten the message, because for the next few minutes nobody else came by our table. While we were waiting, Dylan pulled out a folded piece of paper where he'd written down some of the issues he was having with the bus. "She's grinding like a sonofabitch on inclines. Might be the bearings."

"Yeah, Rick said the same thing. Should last long enough to get us where we're going."

"You're the boss," he said dubiously, and glanced back at his list. "Still pulls to the right. Air conditioner doesn't travel back very far, so unless you're planning on just picking up lizards, you're gonna get complaints about the heat."

Then he straightened suddenly and looked past me. I swung around in time to see Karen race past in tears, heading for the door.

I started to say *what the hell*, but D was already in motion, hurrying after her. Soldier reflexes.

I started to follow him out when Nikki came up behind me, pulling her bra back on. "Is your friend all right?"

"What happened?"

"I don't *know*," she said. "Everything started okay . . . I do a little air-dance to get things going while I undress . . . I touched her face . . . everything was fine . . . then I turned around and sat on her legs and—"

She shook her head, visibly upset, and for the first time I noticed that she was wearing a blonde wig that had come slightly askew, revealing close-cropped black hair beneath. "I can tell when someone's enjoying the dance because they relax into me, but she tightened up. I asked if she was okay and she said yeah, so

I kept going but it just got worse and when I turned around she was crying. I said, 'What's wrong, sweetie?' but she didn't say anything, she just got more upset. Then she pushed me off and ran out, cursing a blue streak and yellin' something about a spider . . . I thought maybe she got bit by something in the booth, or she was mad at me."

"It's okay. You didn't do anything wrong, she's just had a long day," I said, and hurried out the door.

I was halfway to the bus when I saw Dylan standing in the parking lot with his arms around Karen. As I got closer I saw that he wasn't actually touching her, just surrounding her with his arms. She was crying, her face up against his chest.

When he saw me, he shook his head, his eyes saying, *It's okay, I got this.*

I nodded and continued on to the bus. They stood out there for a long time. I could see she was talking to him, but I was too far away to hear anything she said.

And he never took his arms away until she was ready to go.

From: Rick Lee RickLee@retailtransitsales.com
To: Mark Antonelli MDAntonelli@gmail.com
Subject: What the fuck?

Mark—

I don't know if I should even be writing this, but you seemed like an okay guy, so I hope what just happened is some kind of mistake.

When I came in to open up the shop this morning, two plainclothes cops and a guy who said he was your dad were waiting for me.

They questioned me for about an hour. How did I know you? What was the job I did for you? When was the last time I heard from you? Did I know anything about why you wanted the bus? Were there any special modifications made?

I told them the truth: you brought in the bus to get worked on, put down a deposit on your card (maybe that's how they found me?), and paid the rest in cash. I said I finished the work, installed the server bay, you picked it up on Friday, and that's the last time I saw you or heard from you. Which is the truth. I think they believed me but it's cops, who the fuck knows.

I gave them the VIN for the bus and the license plate, but unless they put out a national alert it probably won't do them much good without some idea of where you are, so it's all on you, Mark.

They didn't tell me what's going on or why they're asking about all this, but these are serious guys, so if you're doing something you shouldn't, you need to knock it off and call them and straighten it out, tell them I've got nothing to do with it. Because we both know that's the truth.

I don't want to lose my shop because of whatever you've gotten yourself into. So do the right thing.

Rick

AdminMark

When the work on the bus was almost done and I knew this was really going to happen, I told my mother what I had in mind because she Gets It, she knows how important this is to me. My dad, not so much. So when I said, *Don't tell Dad about this,* I should've either said it louder or been less stupid, because she tells him everything.

Once he turned all Born Again, my dad got more and more extreme; we argued all the time about abortion, gay rights, weed, suicide, you name it. So when she told him what I was going to do, he probably went batshit crazy and called in some of the cops he knew back when he worked security. I can only imagine what he told them. *He's fallen in with secularists who are using him for their own agenda, convincing him to put himself at risk to help kill people who are sick and need God and you have to stop him before this gets out of control, so release the kraken!*

Rick's right about one thing, though. We haven't broken any laws yet, so as much as my dad is probably raising all kinds of hell, there's no legal grounds to put a multi-state alert out on us. Besides, the police are probably too busy chasing terrorists, bank robbers, illegal aliens, and the latest asshole to shoot the hell out of a [ ] school [ ] church [ ] fast-food restaurant [ ] concert [ ] military base [ ] newspaper [ ] sporting event or [ ] other (please check whichever mass murder is most relevant at the time you are reading this) to get too upset about us.

But I don't want to take any unnecessary chances, either.

My original plan was to keep going north on 81, through Maryland and DC to New Jersey and New York, then head west. But there are a bazillion traffic cameras all over DC with license plate recognition software; if we're not already on-camera somewhere, we sure as shit would be by then.

So I told Dylan to jump onto surface roads for a while, head northwest, then take the 79 to Pittsburgh, where I had a shitload of emails from people interested in getting on the bus. At first I thought, why so many in Pittsburgh? Then I found out that Pittsburgh is ranked number eleven in suicides in the U.S. How fucked up does your city have to be that it can't even make it to the top ten list of something like suicide? Even Miami and Jacksonville made it to seven and nine respectively, which is why I figured we'd do more local pickups before leaving the state, but we're coming up on spring break and I guess everybody who was gonna kill themselves already did it to free up rental space for the party crowd, which if you think about it is pretty neighborly of them.

I don't like having to miss New York . . . there are some clubs I really wanted to hit on our way out . . . but 'tis not to be. Besides, if somebody in New York wants to kill themselves, they've totally missed the point of being in New York. On the other hand, if you're living in New Jersey and want to kill yourself, you're being redundant and should do it someplace pretty. That's why there's a shit-ton of fences all over Niagara Falls to discourage jumpers who want to experience death-in-beauty, not death-in-a-really-depressing-part-of-town-so-why-the-hell-not?

If you're in New Jersey and you're reading this and you're offended, I'm sorry, but it's the truth and everybody knows it. If it was any *more* the truth, it'd be on the license plates. *Welcome to New Jersey* on top and at the bottom, *Seriously, Just Kill Yourself.*

———————————

Karen_Ortiz

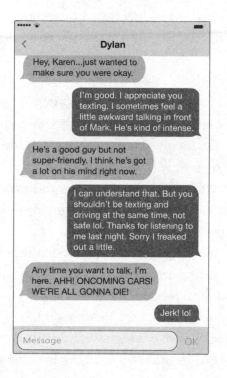

Dylan

Hey, Karen...just wanted to make sure you were okay.

I'm good. I appreciate you texting. I sometimes feel a little awkward talking in front of Mark. He's kind of intense.

He's a good guy but not super-friendly. I think he's got a lot on his mind right now.

I can understand that. But you shouldn't be texting and driving at the same time, not safe lol. Thanks for listening to me last night. Sorry I freaked out a little.

Any time you want to talk, I'm here. AHH! ONCOMING CARS! WE'RE ALL GONNA DIE!

Jerk! lol

AdminMark

It was a little after nine when we finally reached Heinz Field in Pittsburgh. I chose this spot for the next pickup because there isn't a game tonight, which means minimal security, no traffic, plenty of room for the bus, and lots of ways to get out in case there's trouble. I told the next two scheduled riders to wait around the corner on North Shore Drive near the Three Rivers Heritage Trail. Lots of joggers out even this late at night, so if anybody asks I can always say I'm out for a walk.

I hate being this paranoid, but Rick's email kind of got to me. If nobody stops us in the next few days, I can relax and feel confident that we're clear of trouble. Until then, best to be careful.

Update: Before I could head out, Dylan switched up the plan.

"It's probably safe," he said, "but maybe I should go, just in case. Nobody knows I'm involved with this or what I look like, so they won't be watching for me."

"I thought you just wanted to drive the bus and not get involved."

"It makes sense, that's all. You don't want me to go, totally great, I'll stay on the bus."

I let him go, checking my watch as he stepped off the bus. I figured it wouldn't take more than about ten minutes for him to get to the rendezvous point, pick up the newbies, and come back.

Twenty minutes passed.

I was sitting in the driver's seat sweating bullets when out of nowhere someone banged on the side of the bus and a woman yelled, "Open up, police!"

I was about to shit myself when Dylan came in with this embarrassed grin on his face. "Wasn't my idea, Mark—swear to God I didn't know she was gonna do that."

The next one up the stairs—in her emails, she said her name was Lisa Rousseau—couldn't stop laughing. "Your face! Dude, your face! Best! Thing! *Ever!*" She threw her arms up and spun around in front of me. "Woooooooo! Party!"

She came out of the spin and opened her bag to let me peek inside. There were bottles of Molly and salvia, two baggies of shrooms, and enough weed to stock a dispensary. Then she snapped it closed and put her face right up to mine, all green eyes, olive skin, and freckles beneath a waterfall of curly red hair. She reminded me of a girl I dated in college whose family came from Spain. *Basque*, I thought, *gotta be.*

"Still mad?" she said, her voice low and sexy. "Because you can't have any treats if you're still mad."

Before I could answer, I noticed the guy standing behind her at the top of the steps.

He was blue.

Seriously. Blue. Blue skin with round blue fingernails, like an alien. Not a deep Smurf blue, but lighter, more like a robin's-egg blue, particularly around his lips, but his hair was wheat-blond and cut short.

"Eisenmenger syndrome," he said in the tone of someone who says it all the time, as in *Let me explain this before things get awkward so you don't have to ask.* "I have a hole in my heart between the left and right ventricles, which makes some of my blood flow the wrong way, away from the lungs, so it gets deoxygenated, causing cyanosis, meaning my skin doesn't get much oxygen, which is why it's kind of blue. It also causes pulmonary congestion, arrhythmia, and fatigue, so I walk slow, which is why we're late, and sometimes I faint."

Then he grinned at me, but I could see in his eyes that he was tired, that this was a guy who was *always* tired. "Tyler Weston," he said, and held out his hand.

I shook it. It was cold. I didn't react. He seemed to appreciate that.

"Ohmygod, you're right," Lisa said, as though there had been some debate about the subject, "you *are* blue! I couldn't tell outside. That's so amazing! Blue is a god color, because there's blue sky and blue water and blue eyes and blue gems like sapphire, turquoise, and aquamarine but no blue people, because God keeps that color for herself unless you count the people in that movie, what's the name, the one with the blue people, everybody saw it, you must've seen it but what was the *naaaame—*"

"*Avatar?*" Karen said, and glanced at me like *Holy shit, does this one come with an off switch?*

"*Avatar*, right! That movie was such a spiritual experience! It makes you understand that everything has meaning, but meaning can also be a trap, you know? Sometimes we start with the story of us, the meaning of who we are and how we got here, like religion or spirituality, and we see everything that happens to us through the lens of that meaning. Other times it goes the other way, we start with all the things that happen to us and we make stories about it until meaning comes out the other side, so blue is meaning *and* story and that's amazing!"

Tyler had no more idea what the hell she was talking about than the rest of us, but she hugged him anyway. "From now on, *you* are my good luck charm!" she said, then turned and *whooped!* her way down the aisle.

"I got to the pickup spot an hour early," Tyler said, "because I didn't want to risk missing the bus. She was early too."

"How early?" I asked.

"Fifty-eight minutes," he said, and the look on his face said everything we needed to know about that hour.

"Is she high?" Karen asked.

"I don't think so," Dylan said. "I think she's just really hyper."

"Swell," Karen said under her breath.

"*Whooooooooooooo!*" Lisa yelled from the back of the bus. "Where's the disco ball?! C'mon, this place needs a disco ball, let's go buy one!"

"We should probably take off," Dylan said. "Stadium security might swing by soon."

I hesitated long enough to debate whether or not I should boot Lisa out the door before deciding she might make for some interesting dynamics. "Go for it."

Dylan climbed behind the wheel, coaxed the engine to life, and we lurched out of the parking lot.

"Hey!" Lisa called, holding on to the back of one of the seats as the bus bounced onto the main road. "There's a bar I know near here—we should go, last call, right?"

"Not a good idea," I said. "If they know you, we can't risk being seen with you in case the police come around asking questions."

"Okay, then let's go to *another* bar—we can pick one I've never been to before. Come *onnnnnn*, you promised us a party bus!"

I looked to Dylan, who did his usual smile-and-shrug routine. "It's been a long drive, it's still early, and I could use a drink."

"May as well," Karen said resignedly. "I was looking for an excuse to get drunk just once, knock down another item on my bucket list, and I guess she just walked in the door."

"Okay, fine," I said, agreeing to the stop not because Lisa's little stunt had put me in need of getting hammered beyond the limits of human endurance, but because *Karen* wanted to do it. I made my decision *entirely* for her benefit.

Officer.

Dylan picked a little no-frills sports bar on Noblestown called the Ugly Dog Saloon, and everybody piled out except Tyler.

I poked my head back inside the bus. "You coming?"

"Next time. I should probably fill out the passenger information while I'm still fresh."

Clearly, Tyler is a diligent kind of guy.

As we crossed the parking lot, Karen leaned into me, nodded toward Lisa, and whispered, "If she pounds down enough tequilas, maybe we'll get lucky and she'll pass out."

She didn't. I've never seen anyone drink that much and not die. She even put Dylan under the table. We closed down the joint at two, and even then the owner had to chase down Lisa to get the microphone back because she was *still* singing karaoke half an hour after he'd turned off the machine.

Bottom line: Lisa's bugfuck, but she's a shit-ton of fun, and it's not like we're going to have to live with her for very long.

Username: TylerW1998

My name's Tyler Weston. 22. 5'10," 175 pounds. B.S. in Computer Science from University of Pennsylvania, not far from where I grew up in Glenside. Diagnosed with Eisenmenger syndrome when I was four. Like every other kid, I liked to run and jump and climb on things, except half the time I'd pass out. At first the doctors thought there might be something wrong with my brain that was causing seizures, but the tests came back fine. Then the blue started to come onto my skin, and they realized what they were dealing with.

You know when you've been sitting for a long time, and you stand up too fast, and everything kind of goes sideways for a second? That's how it is for me 24/7. When I was a kid, the hole between the left and right sides of my heart was smaller, and the doctors might've been able to repair it but the procedure was way expensive and my folks were independent contractors so they didn't have the cash or health insurance, and even if they did, it would've been considered a pre-existing condition, so yeah good luck with that. They weren't sure I'd even make it past junior high, because with ES just about anything can kill you.

I survived by teaching myself how to breathe deep and hold it hard to push oxygen into my system. I started carrying a small oxygen bottle in my backpack, and any time I felt that sideways thing coming on, I'd sit down and breathe pure O2 until it passed. Instead of panicking, I learned how to be really clinical in my thinking at a very early age, and that saved my life more than once.

That's how I got into computer science. Coding, information technology, programming logic, discrete structures . . . it's all about sitting at a keyboard and being really still and quiet while you try to figure out how to solve the problem. There's not a lot of excitement in computer science, but that was fine by me, and I got good at it. Designed several algorithms to assist in code security for the university's IT system. Even got paid for some of it.

I didn't have many friends growing up because hello, blue, so I didn't date much. Only reason I made it to prom with a girl from social studies class was because she was afraid I'd fall over dead if she said no. Had another date in my freshman year at UPenn. I think she was trying to show how open-minded she was, but when she took my hand and it was cold, she shrieked. Literally. She didn't mean to. Spontaneous reaction. So yeah, no second date on *that* one.

Never thought I'd get laid, but a year later I met this girl who seemed to like me and said she wasn't bothered by the blue or the cool skin, and we had sex on our second date. Later, when she didn't call or return my texts, I found out that the only reason we got together in the first place was that her friends dared her to fuck me because they wanted to find out if my dick was blue. And no, I'm not telling you.

I started looking for full-time work after graduation, which was also when the ES got a lot worse. I'd wake up in the middle of the night and couldn't breathe, like I'd been hit in the chest by a steel fist. My folks got me an appointment with a specialist who said the hole in my heart had gotten bigger, too big to operate on even if we had the money, and that the techniques I'd used to stay alive had only added to the problem. By forcing O2 through my lungs into my bloodstream, I'd increased the congestion in my right ventricle and now it was like a lot of people in a big room all trying to fit through the same tiny door at the same time and everything gets jammed up. No blood in, no blood out . . . next thing you know, boom and you're on the floor. The only way we might be able to fix the problem is with a heart *and* lung transplant, but even if we could find donors with the right blood type at the same time for both organs, I can't even *imagine* what that would cost.

The last time we went in for a follow-up exam two years ago, I overheard the doctor talking to my folks and he used the two words I've been dreading ever since I knew they existed: palliative care. *There's nothing more we can do . . . Our best guess is he has six to twelve months left . . . All anyone can do now is try to make whatever time he has left as comfortable as possible.*

Hoping to extend that window, I took everything as slowly as possible, slower than I'd ever gone before. I watched each step as I took it and applied for small, low-stress consulting jobs that let me work from home. Some days I didn't go much farther than the front mailbox but it got me past the one-year mark.

In my spare time I got really good at hacking.

My first big one was the night I got into the scoreboard of a Steelers game during a live broadcast and dropped in five minutes of footage from *Night of the Living Dead.* You probably heard about it on the news. Yeah, that was me. And those roadside safety signs in Virginia that started showing warning messages that read WARNING ZOMBIE APOCALYPSE IN PROGRESS? That was me, too.

I like zombie movies. Zombies are the only ones who move slower than I do. Which is why I don't like the idea of fast zombies. They're not canonical with the George Romero movies and I can't outrun them, and that's just not fair.

After a while, even going slow wasn't enough. I was dizzy all the time, and every night that steel fist came back to pound the shit out of me. In theory I have maybe six months left, but I could literally fall over dead at any time. So when I saw the Homepage ad, I did what I always do: I ran the numbers. Six months imprisoned in a hospital or hospice, suffering until I die, versus one last chance to have some fun, even if it means cutting whatever time I have left down to almost nothing.

It wasn't much of a choice. So here I am. And here I'll be. Until I'm not.

I don't know if this is the right place to put this—I didn't see any other tabs for personal information, and to be honest the on-line interface Mark's using wasn't thought through very well—but if anyone should ask after I'm gone, I'd like my headstone to read:

Here Lies
TYLER WESTON
Because Frankly, He's Exhausted

AdminMark

After we closed down the bar, I checked in on Tyler. He was already asleep in one of the bunks at the back of the bus, so Karen (who crossed *getting drunk* off her bucket list at the cost of spray-painting the bathroom with everything she'd ever eaten since the age of twelve), Lisa, and I got rooms in a skeezy-looking motel down the street while Dylan crashed in one of the other bunks. He was so drunk a real bed would've been wasted on him.

I got to my room, fell flat on my face on the bed, and passed out. For an hour.

Then Lisa began pounding on the door. *"Maaaaaaaark! Open the dooooooooooor!"*

I didn't want to get kicked out because of the noise, so I let her in. I couldn't tell if she'd kept the party going in her room or if she was just really hyper, but she was pacing back and forth like she couldn't stay in one place for more than a minute. She'd sit down, stand up, walk around the room, then sit down again, talking non-stop the whole time but none of it had anything to do with me, so as soon as I could fight my way into the word tornado I asked why the hell she woke me up.

"Is your room hot?" she said. "My room's hot. I can't sleep it's so hot." Then she glanced in the bathroom. "You have a tub! I don't have a tub, just a shower."

"Bigger room," I said, desperate to go back to sleep.

"I'm gonna take a cold bath," she said, and before I could stop her she stepped out of her clothes in one move—and seriously, how the hell do women do that, one minute they're dressed, then they pull something in the back and it's all skin—and climbed into the tub.

"Oh my God, that's so much better," she said as the water rose. Then she smiled up at me. "It's a big tub. Might even be room for two."

Every male reading this knows there are two brains, the Guy Brain and the Smart Brain, and they're always fighting it out. The Guy Brain wanted to get in there and fuck her brains out. The Smart Brain knew that if I got horizontal I'd probably fall dead asleep; that even if I managed to stay awake the water was so cold I'd never get it up; and that I'd made a vow before starting all this that any women on the bus were off-limits. If I met someone outside the bus, then yeah, fair game. But passengers? No.

That decision didn't come out of virtue. I don't have that gene in me, or at least I've never seen it. But I'm in charge of this expedition, and if I start screwing around it'll flip the dynamics upside down and blow up my whole reason for doing this. Everybody else can do what they want, but I have to stay out of it so I can focus on the big picture.

I also have a Philosophy of Phucking: never fuck anybody crazier than you are, and Lisa was one hundred percent batshit crazy.

So I shook my head no and aimed the rest of me for bed.

"What do you mean, no?" she yelled. "I'm naked! I'm wet! Fuck me!"

She was still complaining as I collapsed onto the mattress and closed my eyes.

I fell asleep to the sound of water splashing.

When I got up a few hours later, she'd already gone back to her room. I went into the bathroom to piss and found that she'd thrown my toothbrush in the toilet and written STUPID FUCK-ING DICKFACE in red lipstick on the mirror.

Yeah: batshit crazy.

From: Mark Antonelli MDAntonelli@gmail.com
To: Tyler Weston BigBlue@BigBlueGuy.com
Subject: Re: Server Info

Hey, Tyler—

I appreciate the offer re: security but the current version is already configured and working fine and I don't want to mess with it. Besides, we won't be in any one spot long enough for anyone to get a bead on us, so I think we'll be okay. But I'll definitely download the voice recognition app. Could be a good addition to everybody's options.

That said: please don't muck around in the system. I got it just the way I want and don't want to redo everything if you put your finger in the wrong socket.

Tyler Weston BigBlue@BigBlueGuy.com wrote:

Hi, Mark . . . I don't want to be intrusive, but when I uploaded my price-of-admission story last night, I noticed that you're using an old version of DeathCryption. The current version (4.2) is better and more secure. I can install it if you want, it's real easy, takes about five minutes. Or I can give you the link and you can do the install if you'd rather not share admin.

Also, it occurred to me that some of the others who get on the bus might not be the best at typing on notepads, or they might feel awkward writing about themselves. There's a dictation app I've used before, Speech Awareness Audio Recorder, that has a really simple interface, with voice-recognition software that can identify who's talking, and doesn't take up much space. Just click record and it'll auto-transcribe the whole thing to text, then store the .mp4 file when you hit stop. I've attached the latest version if you want to give it a shot.

Thanks again for pulling this all together. I've felt really alone since making my decision to end things. It's good not to feel that way anymore.

From: Mark Antonelli MDAntonelli@gmail.com
To: Lisa Rousseau lisarousseau@ccop.edu
Subject: Re: Chipping In

Hey, Lisa—

While installing some new software, I glanced at the server log and noticed that you hadn't written anything yet in the "My Story" folder, or even logged on. So I wanted to fire over a quick reminder that it's important for everyone to contribute to the cause. Write what you can when you can. Hope this doesn't ping and wake you up, know you had a long night.

All Best—

Stupid Fucking Dickface

 Hi, I'm Audio Recorder!
Tap the icon to start recording.

VOICE 1: Testing, testing . . . just seeing if this app works. One two three four five six seven.

EDIT VOICE? Y/N   Y

ENTER VOICE 1 NAME: MARK ANTONELLI

VOICE 1: Is this working now?

INCREASE MICROPHONE VOLUME TO ASSIST WITH VOICE IDENTIFICATION.

MARK ANTONELLI: Is this better? Good. Okay, I think we're locked and loaded.

VOICE 2: Who wants some music?

VOICE 3: No, Dylan, come on, some of us are trying to sleep.

VOICE 4: How about something low?

VOICE 3: No. Later.

VOICE 5: I think we should stop for pork chops. Who wants pork chops smothered in onions?

VOICE 2: I do. Or how about liver? Fried liver and onions.

VOICE 3: Fuck all of you.

EDIT VOICE? Y/N   Y

ENTER VOICE 2 NAME: DYLAN

ENTER VOICE 3 NAME: LISA

ENTER VOICE 4 NAME: TYLER

ENTER VOICE 5 NAME: KAREN

TYLER: Hey, Mark, is that the voice recognition app? Did you get it working?

MARK ANTONELLI: Yeah, just a second, let me—

END RECORDING

Username: LIsa

My name is Lisa Rousseau, I told you that part already, 24, WTF, why are you bothering me with this shit stop sending me stupid emails asdfkaldiflmh12345 whatever leave me alone I'll finish this later fuck.

Karen_Ortiz

Vengeance is mine, sayeth the daylight.

The only thing I wanted at the bar last night was ten minutes when Lisa wasn't talking. Well, she's not talking now, that's for sure. She's SO hungover, OMG, just crashed out against the window with her coat over her head. Every once in a while she sits up a little, squints out from under the coat, then goes back to sleep again.

I know I shouldn't be enjoying her distress, I'm pretty hungover myself, but payback can be pretty funny sometimes. I don't even know what she's doing here or if she's even halfway serious about this. Seems to me like the only people who'd want to kill themselves are the ones who have to put up with her.

On the other hand, Tyler seems interesting. It's like he knows everyone is staring at him because of how he looks, so he's always smiling. That way they won't feel they're bothering him by staring. Or maybe he just likes to smile. Either way, he seems really nice, if a bit shy.

It's funny how we're breaking into high school cliques, the Sickos versus the Wackos. Tyler and I (the Sickos) get along like he's my older brother even though he's actually a bit younger than me, and Lisa (Wacko) definitely has her eye on Mark. Dylan is kind of in the middle. As the driver, he belongs nowhere and everywhere. After the incident at the strip club, I thought maybe there might be a thing between us, but I don't know if that's a good idea. I think he'd care too much, and I don't need or want that right now.

I didn't get on the bus to start something.

I got on the bus to end something.

Stick to the program.

To kill time I went online and browsed Pinterest until we reached Cambridge, Ohio, one of those big/little towns that went to sleep a long time ago and nobody bothered to wake it up. Lots of old, red-brick buildings with flags on every corner and handmade posters announcing Homecoming for the local high school (Go, Bobcats!), craft fairs, scheduled meetings of the Chamber of Commerce, and who won the latest Spirit of Community Award.

We got lunch at a little restaurant on Dewey, then split up to stretch our legs and check out the area. Even walking slowly hurts, something else I have in common with Tyler, but if I don't do at least a little every day I start to pull back from the world, so I headed toward a clutch of little shops. Some of them were cute, others more industrial looking, selling used clothes, hardware and toys, things that once belonged to someone who decided one day that he didn't want them anymore and sold them to the store so they can sell them to someone *else* who'll have them for a while then lose interest and sell them again.

Maybe everybody in town should just get together once a year and swap everything they have, I thought. *It'd save time and sales tax.*

By now the Spider was awake and crawling around my nerve endings, looking for something to bite, so I was about to head back when I noticed a sign across the street for The Museum of Cambridge Glass.

Might be pretty, I thought. *Five minutes then I turn around.*

The Spider said nothing, its mouth too full of me.

The museum was a rainbow of shapes and colors: glass vases and plates and bowls and ornaments and candle-holders and dishes and perfume bottles and Buddhas and doorknobs and wineglasses in lime green and purple and red and blue and clear crystal that fractured the light into a million colors that shifted every time you took another step. When I was a girl, my dad had an old kaleidoscope that he kept on the mantel in the living room, and I loved to look through it, turning it so I could see the patterns change. Walking through the rows of colored glass felt like I was looking out of the kaleidoscope instead of into it.

"We've added a new exhibit."

I turned to see an older woman standing by the gift shop. "Paperweights. They're part of the Elizabeth Dengenhart Collection. We don't get to show them very often, so you came on a good day." She pointed down the center aisle. "Row seven."

"Thank you," I said, and went where directed more out of courtesy than interest. What could be so amazing about paperweights?

But they were beautiful. Hundreds of glass spheres containing butterflies and flowers and swirls of color like little galaxies. Others were shaped like crystal hammers, owls, cats, purses, tiny glass shoes, and figurines. I smiled as I walked down the row of glass cabinets, taking in their beauty. Not just beauty, *trivial* beauty. A paperweight was designed to do one thing: keep pieces of paper from blowing away. Literally a thing to put on top of a thing. You could use a rock to do that, or your keys, or a pen, or a million other mundane everyday items. Instead, someone decided to create little moments of beauty to do the simplest, smallest job in the world, because why *shouldn't* that be beautiful?

For some reason, that thought made me ridiculously happy.

By the time I got back to the bus, everyone else was already on board, waiting for me. "We were starting to get worried," Dylan said, and grinned at me. "You okay?"

"I'm good," I said.

And I was.

AdminMark

D says we're about an hour out from our next pickup in Alexandria. I had a bunch of responses from Ohio (not surprising because Ohio), but I picked Alexandria because a) it's a village—population 531—and I've never been to an actual village before, b) during the Civil War, it was a stopover on the Underground Railroad, which seems appropriate given what we're doing, and c) it's in Licking County, and seriously, how many times in life do you get to park your ass in the middle of a place called Licking County? Okay, yeah, it's the logic of a sixteen-year-old, but you'd do the same thing just so you could say you'd done it.

The village is so small that the only landmark I could use for the pickup is the Alexandria Public Library, which should be closed by the time we get there. The downside is that the bus is really going to stick out in a place like that, and there aren't a lot of places to duck-

and-dodge if anything goes wrong—just houses, churches, and a couple of parks—but I haven't heard any more from Dad since we jumped off the main highway, so we're *probably* okay. Besides, the emails from Vaughn Richmond were the smartest, the best-written, and for sure the longest I've gotten from anybody, and it'll be nice to have someone who can really make use of the server.

We parked on College Street (no college in sight, just an elementary school), one block up from Church Street, where there are two churches, Baptist and Methodist. So at least one person on the village planning council understood what a church was, but they were apparently a little confused when it came to higher education.

Dylan volunteered to go out again and make contact, explaining that he used to live in a small town like this back in Wyoming (which was kind of a surprise and the first time he's mentioned it), so he'll know what to do if anybody starts asking questions. I said okay because it made sense, but honestly, I think he just enjoys playing spy.

————————

Update: Dylan's been gone almost half an hour. I don't like it. How long does it take to walk three blocks, say "Hi, are you coming?" and then walk back?

Forty minutes. Tried to text him, but I can't get a signal. Lisa keeps saying we should go, but we can't. Not without D.

I relaxed a little when I saw him come around the corner and wave. *We're good.*

Then I saw who was with him.

Updating the Update: After the pickup we stopped at the Rusty Bucket Tavern in New Albany for burgers, pizza, and complaints.

"This is bullshit," Lisa said when I walked past her on my way to the bathroom. "I came for a party, so I say we dump his sorry ass right here." She's pretty pissed, but it's hard to take her seriously knowing that she'd throw *any* of us under the bus—or out of it—if the mood hit her.

So I'm going to let him stay, at least for now. Karen thinks he's cute, and Dylan's totally cool with it. I have no idea what Tyler thinks, but then I don't know what he thinks about *anything* because he's got one of those faces you can't read. Also, frankly, the blue keeps throwing me off.

Lisa said I should've figured it out from the name alone. How was I supposed to know? Vaughn sounded hipster to me.

All I *do* know is that from now on, before we pick up anybody, I'm going to ask more about their age than "Are you over 21?"

Hi, I'm Audio Recorder!
Tap the icon to start recording.

VOICE 6: My name is Vaughn Richmond. Age sixty-five. Born March
  third, nineteen fifty-four. Hang on, just a—
EDIT VOICE? Y/N Y
ENTER VOICE 6 NAME: VEUGHN
VEUGHN: Goddamn it—
EDIT VOICE 6 NAME: VAUGHN
VAUGHN: Okay, that's better. Vaughn Richmond. Sixty-five years old.
  Born in Davenport, Iowa. Five foot eight, a hundred seventy-five
  pounds. Gray hair, but I guess that's not much of a surprise. Most
  days my health is fair to middlin' as my mother used to say. Other
  days not so much. Right-handed. Don't know if that matters, but

Mark said I should talk about anything that came to mind. Brown eyes. Probably should have put that higher on the list, up by hair color, but I don't know how to edit this and I'm not gonna mess with it now.

Feels like I'm filling out a job application. Is that really the only way I can think of myself? Age, weight, height, special skills?

Special skills. None to speak of, really. Except I can talk people's ears off. Spent fifteen minutes before I got here telling Dylan about Alexandria, which is a ten-minute town on the best of days.

Widowed. Going on a year now. Her name was Carolyn. Most people would shorten that to Carol or Car, but she preferred the way it sounded at full length, so everyone including me called her Carolyn. She was a good woman who kept me out of a lot of trouble I might otherwise have gotten into. Kept me grounded. Kept me safe.

What else?

This would be one hell of a job application, wouldn't it? What's your preferred salary range? What can you do for our company? Do you have referrals from former employers? What brings you here today?

Why do you want to kill yourself?

Truth is, I don't really have much choice. But that's a long story, too long to tell here. Maybe later, if I can tell it at all. Guess we'll have to see.

It's a pretty night, though. Cool wind coming in from the west. This far out in the middle of nowhere there aren't many decent hotels, and Dylan was pretty tuckered, so rather than keep searching we pulled over for the night. Dylan, Mark, and the girls took to the bunks, leaving the seats to Tyler and me. Came outside to record this because I'm still pretty wide awake. On my best days I don't sleep as much as I used to, and to be honest I'm kind of excited about all this. When I was a kid I loved reading books about folks going off on big adventures and what they ran into along the way. Now for the first time I'm on one of those myself, and my heart's going a mile a minute. Feels like the road might just grab me and take me off somewhere if I step too far from the bus.

Still, morning comes early, so I should probably go on back inside and try to get some rest. Hope this recorded okay. More when I can.

END RECORDING

LIsa

Two in the morning. Crazy Lisa's finally gone to sleep and now it's just me. God, she makes me—what, crazy? So we're both nuts?

No. At least not literally. I mean, I'm not schizoid or whatever they call it, it's not like there are a bunch of different personalities in here, it's not Crazy Lisa and Quiet Lisa *and* the Sandman *and* Randy the Meat Puppet. There's just the two of us, the same person but with different minds, I guess. That's what being bipolar/manic depressive is all about.

I got *that* diagnosis when I was fourteen and my hormones were all over the place, which is also when the hypersexuality kicked in and Crazy Lisa started fucking everyone in sight. Quiet Lisa kept hoping that some of the older boys (or the men) would say no, that they'd see I was too young and out of control, and try to help me instead of screwing me. But none of them ever did. Chick comes onto a dude, he gets all excited, like he's some fucking sex god, so he has to slam it in because he's too full of himself to take the ten seconds to figure out it's got nothing to do with him and everything to do with me being completely out of my head. Except for the guys I scare off, like Mark. I don't blame him. I'm scared too. Been scared ever since the world flipped upside down and everything stopped making sense.

And *that's* why I'm here, Mark (if you're reading this, you said you wouldn't but I don't trust promises). I'm tired of being scared and out of control. Tired of being zoomed from Lithium to Epitol to Depakene, Loxapine, Haldol . . . one drug cocktail after another and they don't work and my hands are constantly shaking and I sleep all the time or I can't sleep at all. Tired of the endless crying and yelling. Tired of hurting people when I don't mean to or they don't deserve it or shit even when they do deserve it like My Stepmother the Bitch because I still hate myself afterward. Tired of feeling useless and stupid and not being able to hold down a job, which means I'm constantly borrowing from people or selling my clothes just to get by, then I end up blowing it all on new clothes when I'm manic because Crazy Lisa thinks that will solve everything and she's brilliant and somehow she'll figure out a way to make a million dollars by Thursday but it never happens because she's Crazy Lisa. Tired of fucking total strangers and each time it's never enough and an hour later I need to fuck again and if he's not up to it I find somebody who is and I think it's something like a hundred guys in the last couple of years and the only lucky thing about *any* of it is I didn't get any STDs that couldn't be fixed. Even managed to avoid the herp, and given some of the dudes who didn't tell me they weren't strapped until after they came because I was too blurred out to care, that is about as close to a miracle as I will *ever* get.

When I'm not all hypered, I spend most of my time sleeping or lying in bed for days, feeling useless and stupid and judged, drowning in credit card bills for things I didn't want and don't need and can't return and all my friends keep saying *why can't you just control yourself* like I actually have a choice, and thinking all the time about hurting myself or killing myself.

But you can only think about that stuff for so long before you finally go, okay, that's enough, fuck it, let's do this thing. But when I told my friends I was gonna do it, they just laughed. They figured it was just Crazy Lisa being Crazy Lisa, all dramatic and over-the-top, so they just said whateverrrrr and oookay and waved it away. They didn't want to get into it and they for *sure* didn't want to call the National Suicide Prevention Hotline at 1-800-273-8255 (and yes I memorized the number) because they were afraid of being embarrassed if it turned out I was just bluffing, which of *course* I was because as everybody *knows* and everybody always *tells* you, people who are really going to kill themselves just *do* it, they don't talk about it, so the ones who *do* talk about it are just looking for attention.

And you know what? Maybe that's true sometimes. But it's not true *all* the time. Some of us tell you we're going to kill ourselves because we're serious, not because we're looking for attention, we just want to say *Goodbye*, or *I love you*, or *You've been a really good friend and I'll miss you.* And some people—people like *me*—say it because we want to make goddamn sure that when you find out we actually *did* it, you'll remember *exactly* where you were and what you were doing when we told you what we were gonna do. We want to bookmark the moment in your brain so that while you're busy pumping out tears on the outside you'll know on the *inside* who you *really* were the day we told you the most intimate and important thing we've ever told anyone . . . and you shrugged and laughed and looked away.

So yeah, me and Crazy Lisa, we're just tired of it. *Both* of us.

At least we finally agree on something, right?

TylerW1998

In addition to writing introductions about why we're here, Mark asked if we could journal the journey, if that's not redundant, talking about what we see and feel and experience, so here we go. And yeah, I probably could've just gone straight into this without a long preamble, but OCD is the language all programmers learn before they ever get to coding. There are some people in this world who, if you ask them what time it is, will give you a history of the watch, and apparently I'm at least six of them.

I was able to breathe a little easier last night than the day before. I think sleeping sitting up in the bus seats helps a little, so I may stick with that. Besides, the bunk beds in the back are pretty tight, I've always been a little claustrophobic, and they're right next to the bathroom (more like a porta potty with delusions of grandeur) and I'm very sensitive to certain kinds of smells.

Of everybody on the bus so far, I think Karen is the most interesting. She doesn't talk much, so when she does say something, you pay attention. When someone talks or yells all the time, after a while it doesn't mean anything anymore, it's just background noise and you tune out. But if most of the time you're quiet, when you finally do let loose everybody looks up, like holy shit, now what do we do? That's how Karen is. She doesn't say a lot, but when she does, we pay attention. Which is maybe the point.

After leaving Ohio, we stopped in Indianapolis to pick up a new rider, but nobody showed, which pissed off Mark, so rather than stop for the night at a motel he told Dylan to keep going to the next stop in Cloverdale, which turned into *another* no-show.

By this time we were way in the middle of nowhere, no cities, no towns, no hotels or motels anywhere nearby, just miles and miles of miles and miles, and everybody was bushed, so we pulled into a "scenic rest stop" that looked out over nothing but scrub and dry grass.

After Dylan killed all the lights except the personal lamps, Lisa crawled into one of the bunks and pulled the shade. I figured Karen and maybe Vaughn would do the same, but they stayed in their seats, like they were too tired to sleep, if that makes any sense. We were just these little islands of light, staring out at the low hills, and I noticed that Karen looked like she wanted to say something. She'd open her mouth like she was about to make a comment, frown, purse her lips, and try again a second later. Karen's one of those people who says one thing for every ten things she thinks and I guess she had to run through the other nine before she found the one she liked and started talking about her experience in the glass museum back in Cambridge: what she saw, and what she felt about what she saw.

"It was just one of those little moments of perfect beauty," she said at the end. "You know what I mean?"

"Yeah, I do," Dylan said. He was still sitting in the driver's seat, turned so his arm was draped over the back as he leaned against the side window. "Had one of those during my senior year in high school. A bunch of us were staying with a friend whose family owned a beach house in this little town called Cayucos, halfway between LA and San Francisco. Literally a one-street town. One night we were sitting on the beach, just hanging out and talking and smoking weed, and it was warm and I must've dozed off because when I looked up, everyone was back inside and I was all alone. I was about to get up when I saw something that knocked the breath out of me. The moon was huge, the way it gets when it's real low, and it was just barely touching the edge of the horizon, creating this ribbon of moonlight that came all the way down the water to where I was sitting. It was like the moon was melting into liquid light. I put my head down low to the water until I could see it coming almost all the way to my face, and when I touched the water, it was like I was touching the moon."

"So you were stoned," Mark said, because sometimes he's a dick.

"No," Dylan said. "The weed had pretty much worn off by then. It was just a simple thing, it was just the moon, but it was the most amazing thing I'd ever seen. Even though it was cold and I was shivering, I didn't want to go inside. I just lay there on the sand, grinning like an idiot until the moon dropped below the horizon and the light went out. I can see it in my head right now like I saw it then. Just beautiful."

"How about you, Mark?" Karen asked. "Any moments of perfect beauty?"

"Nothing that's worth anybody's time," he said, arms crossed over his chest as in, *I don't want to talk about it.*

"Why don't you let us decide if it's worth our time?" Vaughn said.

"Hello?!" Lisa called from behind the shade. "Trying to sleep back here!"

"It's not like we have anything else to do," Dylan said, ignoring the orc in the back of the bus. "We can't even get a cell signal."

Mark sighed like he'd just been asked to donate blood. "Okay, fine. So during my junior year at college, I was dating this girl named Tracy."

"Nobody cares!" Lisa called out.

"Fuck off," Karen yelled back. "Keep going, Mark."

He crossed his arms tighter. "I was taking animal biology to meet my science requirements, and for homework one weekend we had to go to the zoo and monitor different animals, writing down everything they did for a four-hour period. Each of us was assigned a different animal: zebras, chimpanzees, sloths . . . I got stuck with geckos.

"So when I went to the zoo that Saturday, Tracy came along to keep me company. But it turned out that the only geckos they had were the nocturnal kind that spend their days sleeping. I mean, yeah, sometimes they'll lick a leaf, or turn around to the sun, but the rest of the time there was just nothing going on.

"But I still had to write it all down, so I'm sitting on this low wall by the lizard cage, and it's hot, and after a while we're both sleepy and Tracy leans against my back because there's nowhere else to lean. And she falls asleep like that, her arms around me from behind, her head on my shoulder, and . . ."

He frowned and looked off. "I know it sounds stupid, but as I sat there in the warm sun, with her asleep against my back, it was just kind of perfect, you know? I could feel her breath on the back of my neck, real slow and soft, and I didn't move even though I was cramping up because I didn't want to wake her, and I thought, y'know, for all the shit that's going on in my life, for this one moment, everything's okay, everything's good, everything's beautiful.

"So like D said, it wasn't like this big moment, or a revelation, or looking at some painting and having it blow the back of your head off, it's just . . . I was *happy*, and it was perfect, you know?"

After that it got quiet for a bit, then Karen looked at me, and I knew it was my turn in the barrel.

"Up until a year ago," I said, "I used to cosplay as Sage Eregon at a local anime convention."

"Who's Sage Eregon?" Vaughn asked.

"It's from an online RPG."

"What's an RPG?"

"Oh, fuck me," Lisa said from the bunk.

"RPG stands for role-playing game," I explained. "In this case, it's a video game called *Brighthaven.* Sage Eregon is a master-level necromancer and he wears a mask with a veil over his face, so you only see his eyes. I found a pretty good replica of his outfit online and cosplayed him at cons because when I was behind that mask, nobody saw the blue. Yeah, people stared, but they weren't staring at *me* because I was different, they were looking at everybody who was in costume. *Oh, look, it's Sage Eregon, cool.* I got to be just *some* guy instead of *that* guy."

"Love that," Dylan said.

And now there were just two of us left to speak up.

"Lisa?" Karen called. No reply. "Lisa, come on. You ever had a moment of perfect beauty?"

And from the bunk came a stream of curses and insults so loud, so profane, but so intricately constructed that all we could do was listen in absolute no-kidding awe, like if Notre Dame Cathedral was made entirely of fucks, and it just blasted through the bus, line after line assembled in waves so breathtaking that it would've made even the best coder in the business kill himself and *it just kept going*, rolling and roiling and filling the bus like a big black cloud until we could barely see each other.

It. Was. Amazing.

When she finally stopped, I wasn't sure if we should applaud or bury her in the desert with a stake through her heart to keep her from rising again.

"Now, that," Vaughn said, breaking the silence, "*that* has just become my moment of perfect beauty!"

And everyone laughed. Even Lisa.

Karen_Ortiz

We hit Chicago around noon and were scoping out the area for the next pickup when we found a clean truck stop with showers and OMG did we need it. The water was so amazing and hot that Lisa decided to stage a revolutionary Occupy Shower movement and refused to come out and I'm getting texts from Mark saying where the hell are we and we need to get going to the next pickup point or we'll be late, and the lady in charge of the women's showers has people waiting to use them and Lisa won't leave until she's practically dragged out of the stall trailing fingernails and we finally *do* get back on the road and we *do* make it to the address on time but Mark and Dylan take one look at the guy, decide that he's got a weird vibe, and ditch him.

Meanwhile Lisa looks like she got in a fight with a feral raccoon which is pretty much what happened when that lady came after her, and I just realized that the more time I spend around Lisa the less I use punctuation. I don't think she ever met a comma she liked.

By now we were desperate for something to eat, but just as we walked into this little Italian café on the South Side Lisa flipped out when she saw a poster on the door for Virtual Daylight, an EDM festival going on tonight in Union Park. I've never been to a rave but apparently she's seriously addicted and put it to a vote. Based on what happened in the shower I was going to vote no just on principle until I found out that Barnbirds and Yucca Flats were going to be there. It's the first tour for both bands in almost two years and it turns out most of us are fans, except for Vaughn, who needed us to explain what a rave was and that EDM stands for electronic dance music. He never seems embarrassed to ask about this stuff, if anything he's very cute about it and I think he's slowly winning over the others.

At first Mark "We Need to Keep Moving" Antonelli was against the idea, but Dylan reminded him (again) that this isn't supposed to be an express. If we were in a rush we could just buy a plane ticket to San Francisco to end things, or stay home and do it there. We signed on to have some fun on the way out, and if we're not doing that then what's the point? I don't understand why Mark's such a pill sometimes, it's like he's running from something.

The only problem is going to be cost. Virtual Daylight is one of the biggest festivals in the Midwest, and they sold out months ago. We'll have to find someone scalping tickets, and those can go for a ton of money.

Lisa said no problem, she could carry the cost. "I have three bottomless credit cards and I'm not afraid to use them."

So I guess we're doing this.

 Hi, I'm Audio Recorder!
Tap the icon to start recording.

MARK ANTONELLI: Okay, well, this isn't going as planned but totally as expected.

LISA: You're not helping and stop recording this, what the fuck.

VOICE 7: Look, if you can't pay I got to find another buyer—

LISA: The cards are good.

VOICE 7: FeePay doesn't agree. Nothing I can do. Sorry.

VAUGHN: What did you say the tickets cost?

VOICE 7: I don't have time for this.

VAUGHN: I'm just asking.

DYLAN: He said two hundred fifty a ticket. Some of us have it, some don't.

KAREN: It's okay, let's just go.

VAUGHN: I can cover it.

TYLER: Vaughn.

VAUGHN: How much does FeePay charge for its service?

VOICE 7: Ten percent. Why?

VAUGHN: Ten percent of fifteen hundred total means you're losing a hundred and fifty bucks. How about we pay for the tickets in cash and you knock down the price to fourteen hundred? We pay less, but you end up with fifty dollars more.

MARK ANTONELLI: Vaughn, you don't have to do this.

VAUGHN: It's okay.

VOICE 7: You've got the cash?

VAUGHN: I can get it.

VOICE 7: Okay, you get it, we're cool.

DYLAN: I'll go with you.

VAUGHN: Dylan.

DYLAN: It's safer if we're doing cash, that's a lot of money.

VAUGHN: Okay. We'll be back in five.

MARK ANTONELLI: Listen, I was thinking, how about once we get inside, everybody journals about the festival in real time? You can use the voice app—

KAREN: Seriously? You're giving us homework?

MARK ANTONELLI: Well, you're getting in free.

LISA: You're getting in free too, Mark, I didn't see you reaching for your wallet.

MARK ANTONELLI: Look, nobody has to do anything they don't want to do, so if you're not into the journal thing, that's fine, just thought it would be—

LISA: Here they come!

(LOUD NOISE)

END RECORDING

Hi, I'm Audio Recorder!
Tap the icon to start recording.

UNIDENTIFIED MUSIC. LAUNCH LYRICMASTER?   Y/N   Y

SONG FOUND: CLUSTERFUK, "DRY EYES." DOWNLOAD?   Y/N   N

MARK ANTONELLI: Okay, so Barnbirds opened the festival and since we were late getting in we missed a few songs at the start, but most of those were from their new release, they hit all the good songs in the second half.

One of the security guys said there's seventy-five thousand people here tonight, and they expect a total of two hundred K over the weekend. We're packed in tits to backs and balls to butts. Frottage paradise. Chicks in rompers, cat-ears, corsets, capes, G-strings, bras, veils and bigfoot fuzzy boots. Guys in glow-in-the-dark tiger shorts, unicorn hoodies, ballet costumes, ninja masks, raver-swing jackets, and for some reason I'm seeing a lot of panda onesies in the crowd. Must be some new anime thing.

I used to think raver costumes were just another kind of cosplay, like dressing up to look like Thor or Scarlet Witch or one of the guys from Mortal Kombat, but when I said that to a girl I was dating last year, she reamed me a new one. She said cosplay is dressing up to look like someone else. Raver wear is about dressing up to look like your real self, the one you can't let out anywhere else if you want to get a job or a degree. So it's kind of like they're wearing the inside on the outside. You've got death-metal fairies and—

LISA: Hi! What are you doing?

MARK ANTONELLI: I'm—

LISA: Dance with me!

MARK ANTONELLI: I'm in the middle of—

LISA: You can do that later! Dance with me!

MARK ANTONELLI: In a minute—

VOICE 8: Excuse me, is this your drink?

LISA: Oh, hey, sorry, here, let me—

VOICE 8: I almost tripped over it.

LISA: Thanks.

VOICE 9: Why aren't you dressed up?

LISA: I am! I'm dressed as a living dead girl!

VOICE 9: You look normal to me, but cool.

VOICE 8: Hey, as shitfaced as I am right now, we're all living dead, right?

VOICE 9: Living dead Delta Gamma Epsilon!

LISA: Frats!

VOICE 8: Fucking A! All of us, man. Came down in a group.

MARK ANTONELLI: Screw it.

END RECORDING

Hi, I'm Audio Recorder!
Tap the icon to start recording.

VAUGHN: Not sure what I should say about all this. It's pretty loud. Didn't realize it was a costume party. Normally this wouldn't be my kind of music, I like classic rock and jazz, but what I'm hearing is not bad. Funny thing is I had several young women come up and ask how I got in here and was I lost? Probably think I wandered out of an old folks' home and I've got Alzheimer's and there's a bunch of people out looking for me. When I said I was fine, just here for the music, they smiled so big, just lit right up. They said their folks hated their music and could they take a picture with me to put on "Insta," I think? I said sure and we all laughed as they took the photo. They were about as surprised by me as I was by them, and that's what made it fun. I've wasted so much time being scared of stuff like this.

Think I'll move a bit farther back from the speakers, though. I have perfect pitch hearing, but if I keep standing here I don't know if I'll have it much longer.

So much time. Now so little.

END RECORDING

Hi, I'm Audio Recorder!
Tap the icon to start recording.

KAREN: Can I just say how much I'm loving this? The worst thing about the Spider is that it stops me from going out and doing things because moving is pain. But right now I don't have to move. I don't have to do anything. I can just stand here and let the music wash over me. The bass roars through my body like I'm not even here. I can feel it in my bones. My skin vibrates where the music touches it, like if I close my eyes, I AM the music. One big, bad, beautiful wall of sound.

Lisa! Hey, Lisa! Are you okay? Over here!

Shit, I lost her. Hey, excuse me, did you see where those guys were going?

END RECORDING

Hi, I'm Audio Recorder!
Tap the icon to start recording.

TYLER: So I've been listening to Clusterfuk ever since they came out with Lost Road two years ago. Everybody's been saying the band stalled out, but I just saw Jimmy Rose pull out a Gibson custom limited edition electric guitar and those things retail for at least five grand. He didn't have one on his last album or any of the concert videos, so if he's confident enough to bring it on the road, that means he's cool if it gets smashed up by accident and that is not the sign of a band that's stalled out.

I don't know if my phone mic is sensitive enough to pick it up, but they've been playing "Vizion" for the last ten minutes, which is only a four-minute song so they've added a lot of new lyrics. I wonder if they're going for a Grateful Dead thing, adding more to the songs as they go.

VOICE 10: Oh my God, I love how you got your face blue, it looks so natural.

TYLER: Thanks.

VOICE 10: How'd you do it?

TYLER: Born that way.

VOICE 10: Cool.

TYLER: So would you like to get a beer or—

KAREN: Tyler, hey, have you seen Lisa?

TYLER: Not since we came in. Why? Is she okay?

KAREN: I'm not sure, I saw her with some guys and—

END RECORDING

Karen

> Hey Mark, is Lisa with you?

Not now, no. Saw her about ten minutes ago.

> I think she's in trouble.

Why?

> I saw her walking with three guys, and she looked totally out of it. They were practically carrying her.

You mean like the other night?

> No, this looked different, like she was drugged. Meet me by the food tent.

Message — OK

AdminMark

I called D and gave him the info while Karen, Vaughn, Tyler, and I started searching for Lisa.

We found them behind the porta potties behind the main tent. Lisa was unconscious on the ground and they were just getting her skirt up when they saw us coming. We yelled as loud as we could and they started to run.

Then Dylan came out of nowhere and launched himself at them like something out of a goddamn comic book. He threw the guy who'd been on top of her into a wall, then punched another guy right in the face. So now instead of scaring them off, they're drunk and in for the fight. Karen grabbed the third guy's hair and yanked him back as Vaughn pulled off his belt and swung at him, hitting him hard across the face with the buckle. Then the first guy got back up and came at me, and I grabbed a plastic chair and hit him in the head as hard as I could.

Dylan threw Lisa over his shoulder and yelled "Go!" We ran for the exit as they came after us, two of them on their phones, calling for backup.

We'd just reached the parking lot when Tyler went down, breathing hard. He couldn't talk but waved for us to keep going. Vaughn and I ran back to get him, which slowed us down, and I guess their buddies showed up because now there were six of them coming at us hollering, "Gonna kick your ass, sonsofbitches!"

Then Karen moved like I've never seen her move before, running up alongside Dylan and yelling, "Keys!"

"Right pocket!"

She fished in his pocket, came up with the keys to the bus, and took off. She was crying hard and I thought it was because she was scared, but when I caught her eye I saw that she was in pain, like a lot of pain, but she kept running anyway. She got to the bus and opened the doors and we piled inside as Dylan jumped into the driver's seat, gunned the engine, and took off. The shitbags chased us halfway down the parking lot, throwing beer bottles and empty garbage cans and anything else they could get their hands on, then we hit the main road and kept going.

I shook Lisa, and her eyes fluttered open a little. "Lisa, it's Mark, can you hear me?"

She nodded, but didn't respond.

I shook her again, pushing against whatever they'd given her. "Lisa! Stay with us. We're getting you to a hospital."

"No!" she said, slurring her words. "No hospital! They'll find me."

"Someone should check you out—"

"No! I'll be okay! No hospital! Promise me!"

"Okay," I said, though I didn't like it. "I promise."

Then she closed her eyes and passed out again.

Tyler knew first aid, because of course he would, so while we looked for a place to crash he checked her pulse and respiration every few minutes until we reached an Embassy Suites. Some of us still wanted to get her to a doctor, but Tyler seemed pretty sure she'd be okay.

"I'm not a doctor," he said, "but I've spent a lot of time in hospitals and I've been through this before with friends. She's way out of it, but her vitals are solid and she can come out of it when she has to. I'll put her in my room and sleep on the couch so I can keep an eye on her. If she goes south even a little, I'll dial 9-1-1, so either way she'll be safe."

I nodded, relieved but still pissed, not just at what those assholes did to Lisa, but because they were gonna run as soon as they saw us coming until D threw the first punch and got their backs up so they *had* to come after us.

We need to discuss this.

TylerW1998

Midnight. Finished checking Lisa for the third time. Her heart rate was a little slow earlier and I was getting concerned, but now it's back to normal. I woke her up enough to check her hand-eye co-ordination and ask if she knew her name and who I was. She was groggy but answered correctly and seemed more clearheaded than before, so I made sure she drank more water without throwing up, tucked her in, and went back to the couch.

I'm glad I was able to help because it's the only thing keeping me from feeling like a completely useless asshole.

When the fight started, everybody jumped in except me because I was afraid that if I started in on these guys my heart would pick that moment to give out. I'm not afraid of dying, I've been over that a long time, but if I went down during the fight they'd have to leave me behind or stick around with me being dead and the police would shut down the bus and I'd ruin everything for everyone.

So all I could do was stand there with my thumb up my ass as everyone else did the fighting, even Karen, who can barely handle the pain of walking across a room. And Vaughn! Holy shit! He whipped off his belt and wrapped it around his fist in one move, swinging this big metal horseshoe-buckle like a fucking ninja, and took one of the guys down so hard he's gonna be bleeding for a week.

And I did nothing. I couldn't even make it out of the parking lot. I couldn't breathe, couldn't walk . . . I was so bad off they had to pick me up, and the whole time Vaughn's carrying me with his right arm, he's got that belt in his left hand and his pants keep slipping down, so he has to run *and* carry me *and* keep pulling up his pants so he doesn't trip.

I slowed them down so bad that if it wasn't for Karen, we never would've made it out of there in one piece.

Once Lisa's on her feet, maybe I should just get off the bus at the next stop, find a bridge somewhere, and jump. It'd be easier for everybody.

AdminMark

Nine a.m., and this happened.

From: Jay Ellis JEllis@charterpublishingpartners.com
To: Mark Antonelli MDAntonelli@gmail.com
Subject: In Regard to "The Long Road"

Dear Mr. Antonelli:

My apologies for the delay in replying to your email and the attached proposal we received last week. As you can imagine, given the subject matter, I had to run the material past the rest of the editorial staff here at Charter as well as our people in Legal and Business Affairs.

On the one hand, we find the subject matter intriguing and timely. On the other hand, for obvious legal reasons, we cannot be seen as condoning or in any way encouraging you in the actions described in your proposal. When and if the manuscript is completed, it will be necessary for our attorneys to review the book before giving any consideration to its publication in order to assess whether or not there could be the potential for *ex post facto* litigation.

As you state in your email, the release forms signed by all parties should help mitigate the risk of publication, but they can still be voided if it can be shown that they were signed under false or misleading pretenses, not to mention the many legal issues involved with the journey itself.

There's much that I can't say in regard to your proposal, so let me just say this: *if* the project is completed as described in the proposal, *if* no illegal actions occur during the process of gathering material, *if* this produces a completed manuscript that can be submitted for examination by our editorial staff, and *if* all legal concerns can be satisfactorily addressed, we would be open to the possibility of publication.

Your proposed journey is equal parts dangerous and fascinating. It could be useful, prescriptive, and of great value to readers in similar situations. It could also be seen as promoting actions that society deems inappropriate, or of trivializing the subject should the treatment be too light. If you condone, you lose; if you condemn, you also lose. How you navigate those diametrically opposed positions is something that I suspect even you do not yet know, but are hoping to determine along the way.

I will not say best of luck for all the obvious reasons.

I will say only to be careful.

Regards,
Jay Ellis
Editorial Director
Charter Publishing Partners, Ltd.

Karen_Ortiz

I was crying last night when I told Mark that I wouldn't be joining them for breakfast, maybe not lunch either, that I was in a lot of pain because of what happened at the festival and I really needed to sleep. He said it was probably safer to stay off the road for a while anyway.

So I walked/crawled/staggered down the hall to my room and collapsed on the bed, feeling like every inch of my body was being ripped apart. I had to bury my face in the pillow to keep from screaming. You don't know what it's like. It's the worst agony in the world. I doubled up on painkillers but they barely did anything, all I could do was lie there and cry and hurt, God, it hurt so much. I must've blacked out to escape the pain, because the next thing I remember is waking up on the floor an hour later.

The pain also woke up, like insects under my skin trying to bite their way out. I climbed back into bed and dropped sleeping pills on top of the painkillers, but it was still almost dawn before I finally fell asleep. Didn't wake up until two thirty. Everybody was texting to check on me. I replied to a couple but let the rest go so I could order in some soup and tea and toast because that usually helps me stop shaking but in this case, yeah, not so much.

I need a real meal, I thought. *Bacon and eggs would be wonderful, but it's too late for breakfast and I don't know if I can hold it down right now anyway.*

It was almost dark by the time I was strong enough to step outside.

So of course the first person I saw was Lisa.

She came over to ask if I was okay, and even though I knew that what happened wasn't her fault, that she was the one who got attacked, I was angry and in pain and I wasn't thinking right and I totally lit into her.

"What the fuck is *wrong* with you?!" I yelled. "You *never* let somebody touch your drink or hand you a cup at one of those things! That's the rule, you *know* that!"

"I do! I'm sorry!"

"Don't fucking *I'm sorry* me, Lisa! You were out of control! You didn't give a shit what happened to you or us, or—"

"It wasn't on purpose, none of it was! When I get like that, I don't go that far!" She was crying and yelling, not at me but at herself. "It's like there's some part of me that thinks she can't be hurt, that she's too smart to get roofied, so when he handed me the cup the front of my brain didn't even think twice and the whole time the back of my brain is screaming, *What are you doing?!*

"I'm not stupid!" she said, fists balled up and crying hard. "When I get manic it's like I can't see something dangerous when it's right in front of me, or I just don't care! I mean, shit, nobody else does, so why should I? And I'm sorry you're in pain and Tyler got screwed up! I'm sorry about *all* of it! It's tearing me apart and I can't stand being in my own skin anymore and if there's anyone who can understand what that feels like it's got to be you or I am completely fucking alone here!"

"You're not alone, you asshole!" I said, and I realized I was crying too. "None of us are! That's the whole reason we're *doing* this! So we don't *have* to be alone, so we can rely on each other! We *do* care about you!"

"Bullshit! I've seen the way you look at me. I piss you off!"

"Oh, hell yeah. Hugely. Like all the time. You're a jerk, but that doesn't mean we don't care."

"I'm not a jerk!"

I just stared at her.

"I'm *not*," she said, and laughed. "I'm just fucked in the head, that's all. I'm nutty as squirrel shit."

Now it was my turn to laugh. "Squirrel shit?"

"My aunt used to say that. Well, she said squirrel poo, but I think squirrel shit is funnier."

"It is," I said, and I could feel my mood softening. "Look, I'm sorry I yelled. I didn't mean to get angry, I'm just tired and sore and we were all scared for you—"

"I know . . . and I'm sorry, I really am, and thank you. Mark said you were the one who saw me and figured out something was wrong. If you hadn't stepped up—"

"I'm just glad we were able to find you. You should've seen Vaughn. He went full-scale road warrior on those guys."

"I heard, and I feel so bad now about giving him such shit."

"Are you all right otherwise? They dosed you pretty hard."

"Yeah, I'm okay. Tyler was great. I started calling him Nurse T. He thinks it was either roofies or GHB. Still got a headache, but it's nowhere near as bad as it was."

"Good, I'm glad."

She backhanded the tears from her cheek. "Can I at least buy you breakfast? Make up a little for last night?"

"They're only serving dinner, and your card's maxed out, remember?"

"Not a problem. I stole one of Mark's cards the night I slept in his tub. Stupid jerk hasn't even realized it yet."

So we went inside the hotel restaurant and split a Cobb salad with extra egg and bacon.

TylerW1998

Once I was sure Lisa was going to be okay, I ducked out for breakfast around nine, then came back, checked her again, and crashed hard. When I woke up, it was almost five and she was gone. I changed and went outside and found Vaughn sitting at a concrete patio table in the courtyard.

"Hey," I said. Not the smartest conversation starter, but it's all I had. "Nice day."

He nodded back at me. "It is, indeed," he said. "I checked the weather and it looks like clear skies for a while, maybe a little rain later tonight, so driving conditions shouldn't be too bad as long as we get going soon." I get the feeling that deep inside, Vaughn's one of us "history of the watch" people.

"Have you seen Lisa?" I asked.

Vaughn nodded. "She's in the restaurant with Karen."

"Should we go in there and break it up before somebody gets hurt?"

"No need. They were having a bite together and laughing. So either they patched things up or one of them is an alien imposter and needs to be turned over to Homeland Security."

"Well, I'll keep an eye out for tentacles," I said, and the smart part of my brain jumped in front of the stupid part of my brain before it could say *especially the hentai kind* because no way was I going to try to explain *that* one to Vaughn.

Instead I started to apologize for being totally fucking useless during the festival fight, but he waved it away like it was nothing, wouldn't even let me finish.

"You know what I've decided?" he said. "I've decided most people are morons."

"Okay, maybe a bit broad—"

"The reason they're morons is they spend years, decades, hell, their whole lives regretting or apologizing for things nobody else even remembers. They carry those things around like bags of sand that keep them from going to all the places they could've gone and *would've* gone if they hadn't been so busy thinking about the goddamn sand.

"You want to go around hauling sandbags, that's your business, but don't do it on my account, because I never thought twice about it. We're in this together, we do what we can when the moment comes that we have to do it."

Then he smiled in this kind of embarrassed way and shook his head. "Damn, sometimes I sound old even to me. But I'm not. I'm not that fucking old. I've just given it all a lot of thought."

"Is that why you kicked in the money to get us into the festival?"

He shrugged. "I had it, they didn't. Not a big deal."

"I'm just surprised you were carrying around that much cash."

He looked at me for a second, like he was making a decision. Then I guess he must have made it because he stood and said, "You want to see something I'll bet you've never seen before?"

He led me into the empty bus, reached under his seat to pull out one of the two suitcases he'd brought on board, snapped open the latches, and pulled out a bag slightly bigger than a shaving kit. Unzipped it.

Inside, shoved in tight, were stacks of hundred-dollar bills bound with rubber bands. Given the size of the bag, I clicked through the numbers and came up with a figure somewhere between fifty and sixty thousand dollars.

"Aren't you worried somebody'll steal it?"

"Nope. Besides, under the circumstances it's not like I'll need it to live on during my yes-okay-*now*-I'm-that-fucking-old age. Hell, technically it's not even mine."

That part caught me by surprise. "What'd you do? Rob a bank?"

"Something like that," he said. "Point being, I had the cash to spend, so I spent it and I'm glad and I'll do it again if sufficiently provoked."

Then he saw the rest of the group headed our way, zipped up the bag, and put it back in his suitcase. "On the other hand," he said, "I'd rather not have Lisa find it and use it to buy the world's biggest ball of string."

"So why'd you tell me?"

"Because I trust you, and if anything happens to me before we get where we're going, I want to make sure this ends up with someone who'll do the right thing with it." He shoved the suitcase back under his seat, then gave it a little kick for good measure. "I like the way you think, the way you talk to the others and look after 'em. My wife used to have all these terms for different sorts of people, like she was some kind of street-corner zoologist: users, losers, takers, martyrs . . . bunch of others . . . and saviors, guys who spend their lives looking for birds with busted wings that they can save. A savior, that's you."

"Thanks."

"Don't thank me," he said. "That was the kind she had the least patience with. Said it was self-indulgent. As for the fight, like I said, don't give it another thought. Yeah, it got messy, but it's the kind of thing that makes you feel alive, you know? Which is pretty funny, considering the circumstances."

"I bet *that kind of thing* must've happened to you a lot over the years."

"No, not really," he said, and left it at that as the others piled back onto the bus.

AdminMark

We hit the pickup point in Des Moines, Iowa, well ahead of schedule. I'd gotten emails from about half a dozen prospects in the area, but since a lot of people have flaked out on us I emailed everyone to say we'd be doing group pickups to make sure at least one or two show up and we don't waste time chasing our tails.

While everybody else got out to stretch their legs, I took Dylan aside to talk about what happened at the rave. I reminded him that this wasn't the first time he'd come out swinging in a difficult situation, and that we could've gotten out with a lot less trouble if he'd played it cool. He can't keep pulling this shit because it puts everybody at risk.

He promised he'd do better going forward, but I'd heard that before and it wasn't enough for me anymore. I wanted to understand *why* he kept doing it so I'd know for sure whether or not he was going to keep *on* doing it despite his promises. At first he didn't want to explain, but I kept after him and though it was really hard for him, he finally told me the whole story.

I can't go into details about it because it's uber-private and I never had him fill out a release form. I didn't even think about it, which was my mistake; I figured he's the driver; the story is everybody *else*. Should've known that would change once we got on the road. I could ask him to sign one now, but a) it's kind of late in the day, b) I don't think he'd sign it, and c) if he said no, it's not like I could find another driver to step in at this point and I don't want to back myself into a corner. So all I can do is take his word for it when he says he'll try to be more mindful when the urge hits him to Hulk out at *exactly* the wrong moment.

The main thing is: I get it. I understand. Shit, if I'd been through something like that, I'd react a hell of a lot worse. I'd never get over it.

Gotta go. Newbies should be here any time now.

Hi, I'm Audio Recorder!
Tap the icon to start recording.

MARK ANTONELLI: Hey, hi, what's your name?
VOICE 11: Theresa . . . Theresa Caldwell, I wrote you—

MARK ANTONELLI: Okay, yeah, but who's this?

VOICE 12: Jim Atwater.

VOICE 11: My boyfriend.

LISA: Fuck me.

MARK ANTONELLI: This isn't a passenger bus.

VOICE 11: We know.

MARK ANTONELLI: Nobody should be on here unless they intend to—

VOICE 12: We are, both of us!

VOICE 11: My father said that if we didn't break up he was going to dis-inherit me and call the cops on Jim because he's black and I can't take it anymore and neither can he and we're done, okay, we're just done with people and this world and my family and—

LISA: This is bullshit.

VOICE 12: Hey, you can't judge us, we're just as serious as you are.

LISA: Talk to the wrist, the hand's not listening.

TYLER: It's a valid point.

KAREN: Tyler, come on.

TYLER: I just don't know if we should be judging how serious other people are or their reasons for—

DYLAN: Mark, we should go, I don't want to stay here too long, we're exposed.

MARK ANTONELLI: Okay, we'll sort this out later. Here's the release forms, grab a seat in the back and sign them. Who are you?

VOICE 13: Theo. Theo two two five seven at gmail dot com.

MARK ANTONELLI: Last name?

VOICE 13: None. Just Theo. I travel light.

MARK ANTONELLI: Right, here you go, sit wherever you want. You?

VOICE 14: Shanelle Rose. Shanelle at—

MARK ANTONELLI: I got you. Go on in. Anybody else?

DYLAN: Not that I can see.

MARK ANTONELLI: Okay.

DYLAN: Wait, hold on, we got one more coming.

VOICE 15: (INDISTINGUISHABLE)

MARK ANTONELLI: Open the door.

VOICE 15: Thanks.

TYLER: Dude, take a breath, that backpack's bigger than you are.

DYLAN: Are you okay?

VOICE 15: Yeah. I'm Zeke. I'm on the list.

MARK ANTONELLI: Right. Here. Okay, that's the last of them. Let's go. Jesus Christ.

END RECORDING

LIsa

This is the second time I've tried to write about what happened at the festival. I spent most of my first attempt blaming Crazy Lisa, writing about how she's acting out and getting more and more reckless. Sane Lisa never would've let someone she didn't know handle her drink, but Crazy Lisa did it because like I told Karen she thinks she's *way* too smart to fall for something like that so the drink *couldn't* be drugged and even if it is there's nothing left to lose, so why the fuck not? And everybody had to pay for her choice.

So yeah, that's what I said and that's what I wrote, and it's bullshit. I need to accept that there *is* no Crazy Lisa and no Sane Lisa, no Loud Lisa and no Quiet Lisa, there's Just Lisa. Having "her" to blame for my stupid choices made it easier to live with whatever shit followed. It's the lie that helps me keep going. Well, we're heading for the end now and I don't want to keep lying anymore.

The truth is that *I'm* fucked up. *I'm* making bad choices. *I'm* out of control. Not her. Me.

Don't die with a lie on your lips, Just Lisa.

If we're going out, let's do this right.
Let's do it clean.

Username: VaughnR

I've never been very good at typing, especially on iPads. My fingers are too big for these things, but it's late, everybody's tired or pissed off about the newcomers, and I don't think they'd appreciate me talking back here.

I've decided I want to clear up a few things for the folks I leave behind so they'll understand why I'm doing what I'm doing. Though on reflection, if they're going to read this after I'm gone, shouldn't that sentence be in the past tense? "Why I did what I did" instead of "what I'm doing"? It's the kind of thing Mark would ask. He seems to like questions. Don't know what he thinks about answers. Maybe I'll ask him.

Anyway.

Carolyn and I were born and raised in Davenport, Iowa, just across the border from Illinois. It's a funny border because it runs down the middle of the Mississippi River instead of along the shoreline. Turns out there are little islands in the river and fingers of land that stick out into the river from either side, so the surveyors drew a line down the middle of the river and parceled them out to one state or the other. So when you swim to the center of the river you're technically nowhere. Swim a few feet east and you're in Illinois. Swim west and you're in Iowa.

This is what passes for a good time in Davenport.

Carolyn came from a nice part of town called Red Hawk, right up near the golf course. My dad worked as a plumber, and my mom waitressed four nights a week, so all we could afford was a small place farther south in Five Points, on Telegraph Road just down from Locust Street, and no, I'm not making that name up. As neighborhoods go it wasn't much, just a handful of old two-story houses, rusted-out cars parked on the street for months at a time, and a smidge of grass just off the main road. In high school my friends and I used to hang out under an old bridge on Telegraph where it hit Pacific, smoking and talking about what we wanted to do when we grew up. We'd travel the world, seeing amazing places and doing amazing things. *Live dangerous, die young!* we'd yell out as one, then smash our Coke bottles against the bridge wall and ride our bikes down to the river to look across at Illinois, thinking about Chicago and everything else on the other side of that dark muddy water.

I'd just started my senior year in fall '71 when Carolyn transferred to our school after her family moved into the area. Her father picked Five Points to set up the main office for his new company because real estate was a lot cheaper than in Red Hawk. She was in my homeroom and three other classes, and I thought she was the most beautiful girl I'd ever seen. She wasn't fond of this part of town since it wasn't as nice as she was used to, so she wasn't looking to make a lot of friends, just get in and get out. But like I said, we were in four classes together and I wanted to meet her, so I started taking better notes than usual. That way I could help out if she forgot hers or didn't take any. Sure enough, she came up short one day and I jumped in to help. After that, she seemed to come up short on her class notes a lot, and we began spending time together.

When we started dating, I told her about how I was planning to leave Iowa so I could go to college out of state and study to be an architect. I'd filled out applications for Berkeley, NYU, University of Chicago, and a few other places. Probably could've gotten in, too. I had the grades, and I was able to convince a few contractors around town to use some of my designs for local stores, so I could include pictures with the application. My dad took a photo of me holding the blueprints next to a storefront I designed, and I was smiling so big I thought my face would break. I still have the photo, but don't know what happened to the designs. Lost, I guess.

The downside to being an architect is that unless you're lucky enough to be in a big company, it's all freelance work. It's less like having a regular job and more like being an artist. If people like your paintings, they buy them; if not, you starve. If businesses like your blueprints, they buy them; if not, well . . .

It was a risk for sure, and Carolyn saw that right off. What would I do if it didn't pan out? What if I invested all that time and money into a degree and nobody wanted to buy my ideas? I could end up nowhere. I could fail. She didn't want that, my folks didn't want that, and I sure as heck didn't want it, but I didn't see any way around it until she talked her dad into giving me a part-time job at his company. Clearview Brite Boards produced long fascia boards used in interior design. They were made of pressed fiberboard that on the outside looked like expensive wood or marble depending on what kind of finish you wanted. They were light, easy to cut, and once they went in, they shined up great.

She said it was a good opportunity because I'd still be (sort of) working in the construction business, but with a regular paycheck and a chance for advancement. Yeah, there was a downside, since taking the job meant I couldn't go to college out of state, and the local college didn't offer any classes in architecture, but I could still work up designs on my own time.

Carolyn, I should mention, wasn't a go-to-college kind of gal. She had plenty of money through her father, and back then it wasn't a big deal for women to prefer being a wife and mother to pursuing higher education, assuming you met the right match, and we were both pretty sure we were the right people for each other. But I'd have to stick close to make the relationship work.

We all do what we do for the same reason: it seemed like a good idea at the time, so after high school I started taking classes at the local JC and working for her dad, first in shipping and invoicing, then sales fulfillment. But it wasn't all just office work. When I said the patterns we used to reproduce the look of marble weren't right, he let me redesign the paint system, and it made a big difference. Did the same for the wood boards too, so the grain looked like real grain and the knotholes looked like real knotholes. It didn't have a huge effect on sales, I don't think most people pay much attention to grain, but I've always been a detail-oriented kind of guy, and I got a lot of satisfaction seeing my designs on there.

Carolyn's dad was a level-headed and practical guy who used to say "Better to be safe than sorry" so often that I had it printed on T-shirts for both of us. He thought that was pretty funny, so he'd wear it to the office under his work shirt and whenever anybody did something stupid on the manufacturing line, he'd pull his shirt open like Clark Kent and say "See! Right here! Better safe than sorry!" The line guys always got a kick out of that.

One day we had a meeting with some folks who were starting up a new construction company in Los Angeles. They were looking to place big orders for a contract they were bidding on to construct a bunch of office buildings and apartment complexes in Beverly Hills and West Hollywood. They were making the rounds and getting budgets to make sure they could do the job for the money they were asking for in case their bid went through.

Carolyn's dad didn't like dealing with new companies in speculative situations where the order might not even come through, so he left it to me to take them out to lunch and walk them through inventory, prices, stock, and the rest. They were very LA, real showy, not the sort we were used to seeing in Davenport. When they asked what I did when I wasn't doing what I was doing, I said I was interested in architecture and the head of the company invited me to send him some of my stuff. I figured he was just being friendly or softening me up to try and get a better deal, but I sent him some of my blueprints anyway, assuming that'd be the end of it.

They called back on a Wednesday a few weeks later to say they were close to making their deal, but the guy in the Architect II position, who does smaller designs that the lead man doesn't have time for, had left to take another job. They felt that some of the designs I'd sent them were in line with what they had in mind, and if I came on board in the Architect II position, it'd save them a lot of time training someone to see things their way. They had to move fast because they were supposed to submit the final bids in two weeks with all the positions locked and loaded, so they'd need a firm yes or no by that Friday. If I wanted the job, I'd have to be on a plane to LA first thing Monday morning. I asked my folks what they thought I should do, but they didn't know architecture as well as I did, and said it was up to me.

Carolyn and her father understood how I might find the idea exciting, but there was an awful lot at risk. This was a new company that hadn't done any previous work, applying for a contract they might not get. And that Monday a bunch of buyers were coming in for a contractors' convention in Des Moines and I'd already said I'd be there to help with sales and logistics.

"If you put all the reasons to do it on the left side of a page," her dad said, "and all the reasons *not* to do it on the right, it seems to me the right side is a lot longer than the left side."

I really wanted to give it a shot, but Carolyn helped me see that he was right: the situation was just too uncertain to take that kind of risk. Besides, even if they got this contract, there was no guarantee they'd get another one later. Most new construction companies go out of business inside a year. I could end up quitting my job and moving to LA only to find myself out of work in six months with no prospects and no guarantee that her dad could hold my job open.

So that Friday, I called and said I appreciated the offer but would have to decline. They were very kind and understanding about it.

I didn't give the conversation a lot of thought after that, as there was plenty to do and never enough time. Six months later, Carolyn and I were in her folks' kitchen stuffing envelopes with invitations to our wedding, when her dad's copy of *Construction World* came in the mail. It's kind of the bible for contractors, so I flipped through it while Carolyn and her mom took turns looking at photos of bridal gowns.

Dead center of the magazine was a two-page article about the guys from LA. Their company had not only scored the big deal they were hoping for, they'd gotten two more contracts for a shopping mall in Culver City and a medical plaza in Woodland Hills.

Over the next few years they went on to become one of the biggest companies in Los Angeles. If you want something that doesn't look like everything else, these are the guys you call.

But at the time, none of us knew that things would go this way, so it was still the correct decision.

Not everything is meant to be, right?

Better safe than sorry.

AdminMark

Funny how fast group dynamics change when somebody new enters the circle. Lisa had just started to calm down when Theresa and Jim got on board and now she's back up to ninety. Totally pissed. And I can sort of understand it. Everything about the newbies says Death Tourists, like they're just acting out and not as serious about this as everybody else. Lisa refers to them as *TheresaAndJim*, one word without a breath in between because they're always together.

They're not even trying to engage with the others, which makes them feel even more like outsiders.

Theresa's one of those people who seems nervous all the time, super thin with long auburn hair she combs straight like a curtain and is constantly peeking past it to see if anyone's looking at her. Of course the more she does that, the more we're all looking at her and the more nervous she gets. Jim seems like a nice guy, maybe too nice to be with someone who is clearly high-maintenance. He's always talking low and reassuring her and getting her sodas or munchies from the cooler when she could just as easily get them herself. And she's constantly holding his hand but not in a romantic way. Some people hold the other person's hand like they want you to know *She's with me*, all protective, while others want you to know *I'm with her*, because they're proud or maybe showing off a little. With Theresa, it's like *I'm holding your hand to keep from falling off the earth*, which is weird.

So yeah, I can see where Lisa's coming from, and I'm not sure she's wrong, but for now I'm going to let them stay and see what happens. They still haven't entered anything into the group chat, which is a requirement for staying on board, so I can always use that as grounds to boot them out if things get too tense.

As to the other newcomers . . . I'm not sure what to make of Theo, but I suspect that's kind of the point. Shanelle is super friendly, an easy laugher full of energy who won everybody over in five minutes. Zeke seems okay, but my antennae are up. He's pale and way skinny, with a backpack twice his size, a beat-up old army jacket, and a tangle of blond hair that doesn't seem to know which way it wants to go. First time he smiled and I saw his teeth, it was the smile of a meth addict, but for now he seems straight and friendly and funny in a goofy, almost shy kind of way, so he may fit in fine with the rest of the group.

And just when I finally started to fall asleep, *this* showed up:

Karen

> Hey Mark, you awake?

> I am now. What's up?

> I just looked over to the seat where the new guy - Zeke? - was sleeping and I think he has a cat with him.

> You're shitting me.

> Do I look like I'm shitting you?

> You're sitting six seats ahead of me, how can I tell? Okay, I'll deal with this in the morning when we hit the next rest stop. Jesus. A cat. Seriously.

> I know.

Message   OK

Username: IamTheo

Most of my friends put their preferred pronoun in their Instagram bios—he/she, him/her, they/their—but I respond to any and all of them. I like to think of it as collecting pronouns: the more I get, the more fun I'm having. To get the obvious out of the way, because that's apparently important to people, I think of myself as post-gender. I was trying to figure out how to explain that because sometimes it's a paragraph and sometimes it's a term paper depending on who I'm talking to, and I have no idea who will be reading this in the aftermath. Then I noticed that one of my fellow passengers has a cat with him, and that's perfect.

When you visit a friend and find they have a cat, you just see it as a cat in all its pure catness, it doesn't require further definition. You'll probably get a name, and if you ask, whether it was born male or female, but even after you have that information you still don't think of it any differently. It's not a He-Cat or a She-Cat or a They-Cat. It's just a cat. And unless the cat's name has any gender-specific connotations you'll probably forget pretty fast which gender it was born into.

My name is Theo, and by that logic, I am a cat.

What I was or was not born into has nothing to do with how I see myself. It's not about going from one gender to another, or suggesting that they don't exist. Some of my friends say that the moment you talk about gender you invalidate the conversation because you're accepting the limits of outmoded paradigms, but I'm not sure I agree with that. I just think gender shouldn't matter.

If you're a man, aren't there moments when you feel more female, like when you're listening to music, or your cheek is being gently stroked, or you see a spectacularly handsome man walk into the room? If you're a woman, aren't there moments when you feel more male, when you have to be strong in the face of conflict, or stand behind your opinion, or when a spectacularly beautiful woman walks into the room? Well, in those moments, you are all of those things, so why deny that part of yourself?

For me, it's not about being binary or non-binary. It's about moving the needle to the center of the dial and accepting all definitions as equally true while remaining free to shift in emphasis from moment to moment. It's about being a Person, not a She-Person or a He-Person or a They-Person.

There are three parts to this: how I see myself, who I'm attracted to, and how I'm seen by the world that I have to live in. The first I can manifest on my own, the second is what it is, and I have no control over the third. So I live and thrive in the space between them.

So I'm just Theo, which could be short for Theodore, or Theodora, or anything else that fits. And yes, I have a last name, but it has not been kind to me so I left it behind. Technically it remains on documents because it's a legal identifier, but it doesn't define me; it has no more to do with who I am than my social security number.

When you go into a clothing store, you don't just go to the "one size fits all" rack. You look for clothes that fit your waist, hips, legs, chest, and neck, clothes that complement your form and shape, and reflect not just how you see yourself but how you want to be seen by others. If it's still not quite right, and you can afford it, you get the clothes tailored to fit exactly who you are.

That's what I'm doing. Post-gender is one term for it. Another might be tailored gender. Maybe bespoke gender. But definitely not one-size-fits-all. The world doesn't get to decide what best fits who I am and how I choose to be seen. I do.

So rather than let the world define me, I've chosen, in an admittedly grandiose sort of way, to define myself. Unfortunately the world does not always take kindly to self-definition. *You're all unique*, we're told in school, but as soon as we try to *be* unique the world insists that we have to conform, to act like everyone else or face the consequences. Not to put too fine a point on it, this world sucks. So a few years ago, to preserve what little remains of my sanity, I began writing stories, just for myself, about a world that is better than the one I was born into. Fairer, gentler, and more decent; honorable and just; a place of clear streams, blue skies, and silver cities, free of cruelty and meanness of spirit. A place where the bullies and the hurtful can never find me.

Viewed through the lens of those stories, this is not a bus and we are not driving on a road. It is a ship with golden sails taking me across the sea to the great cities I have created with my thoughts, where I can simply be who I *choose* to be. A place where I will finally be free.

And it will be beautiful.

LIsa

From: Debbie Rousseau drousseau@aol.com
To: Lisa Rousseau lisarousseau@ccop.edu
Subject: Washing my hands of you

I was cleaning the front room and found the note you left for your father. How selfish you are. How destructive. Mean doesn't even begin to describe you. Cruel, maybe. Assuming this isn't just another of your "moments" of acting out, do you have any idea what this is going to do to him? Of course you do. That's why you're doing it. It's not enough that you kept hurting him when he was just trying to help—you want to hurt him even more by letting him know what you're going to do and then making sure he can't save you, because you know that's what he's going to want to do. Not that you WANT to be saved. Not that you CARE about him or me or anyone but YOURSELF. You never have. Selfish.

That's what suicide is, you know. It's selfish and self-indulgent, the easy way out for you, but the hard way for everybody else. You never gave a single goddamn thought to how this will affect the people who will have to clean up your mess and keep going after you're dead, because it's all about YOU, because you always MAKE it all about you. It's what narcissists DO. I said that three years ago when I married your father and saw the kind of person you were then, and it's even more true now.

Well, I want you to know that I'm not going to show him your note. I'm going to burn it. I don't want him to sit here frantic and upset waiting for the news about how and when and where you died. You don't deserve the chance to say anything to him, not after what you've done and what you're doing.

You want my advice, not that you've ever taken it? If you really are going to kill yourself, do it someplace where the body won't be found, so your father will never have to know what happened and the rest of the family won't have to put up with the scandal. And if he does find out about it, me getting rid of your note will save him the burden of thinking he could have done anything to stop you.

Don't bother to respond. I'm blocking your email address as well as your number on both our phones, so you can't call or text him—not that you will because you're too much of a COWARD.

Do whatever you're going to do. I really don't care anymore.

Username: SunnyShanelle

Hi, my name is Shanelle Rose and I just turned 21 last June. Glad to be here! What a crazy and beautiful idea!!! I can't wait to get to know everybody better before we do the Big Jump together!

Last year, my therapist asked me to write a short essay about my past and why I started hurting myself. So if it's okay I'm going to copy and paste that here, just to get things going. I'm looking forward to the journaling, though. That should be fun!

Okay, here goes!

I was born in Middleton, Wisconsin, which is about twenty minutes west of Madison. My dad was a welder for a company that made custom cars, and my mom worked sales at Macy's during the day and sometimes waitressed at night when we needed to fill in the gaps.

We moved from Middleton to Fitchburg after an incident with some white guys who ran a gas station down the street from our apartment. My dad didn't talk about it much, but it was enough for him to pack us up in the middle of the night and move out. He said that even the worst part of a small town would be safer for a family than any of the nicer parts of Middleton. Even so, Mama didn't let me hang out with other kids until I was old enough to go to school, and if she could've kept me home even then, I think she would have.

There were only a few black families in Fitchburg, so on my first day of school Mama said there might be some problems because I probably wouldn't look like anybody else in my class. She was right, but not for the reasons she thought. From across the street, in a hat or a hood, you couldn't always tell I was black. But you could for sure tell that I was fat.

Before I started going to school, being fat was something I never really thought about. My dad was a big guy, had to be to push around all that steel he worked on. Mama used to say that she wasn't fat, she was big-boned, and just had more bones than anybody else, which I believed because at that age I didn't know how many bones people were supposed to have. Gramma? Big. Grampa? Big. Runs in the family. Well, waddles. My dad used to joke that when we joined hands for dinner prayer, we looked like an eclipse.

"If anybody says anything about your color, you just smile and keep on walking," Mama said as she dressed me in new clothes for the beginning of first grade. In the pictures, I'm wearing a pink pullover sweater and jeans with glitter-butterflies on the back pockets. "You got a sunny disposition, baby girl, and that'll get you through anything bad and bring lots of good people to stand with you on your side."

We'd had this talk many times, so I was ready, I was prepared, I knew exactly what I should and shouldn't do if anybody gave me a hard time for being black.

What we never talked about was what to do when the other kids called me fat, which they started doing the second I got off the school bus.

"Fatty!" one of the boys yelled as I started up the sidewalk. "Hey, fatty-fat-fat!"

Other kids picked it up, yelling "Fatty!" until the teachers hustled everyone inside.

I refused to cry about it until I got home, then I just let go as my mama held me and rocked me back and forth. She went with me to school the next day to talk to the teachers, and they said they'd put a stop to it.

But it kept right on happening anyway. Worse yet, the other kids started going after my mama for being fat, too. Which is how I got into my first fight.

"They had it coming," Mama said when I was sent home early. "Don't worry, baby girl, kids like these have no attention span. Give it time, they'll get tired of picking on you and find somebody else."

It was the right thing to say.

It just wasn't true.

There's a lot of good about growing up in a small town where everyone knows everybody else from way back. But there's also a lot of bad, and the worst is that once they decide who you are and what you are, that's *all* you are, ever. When you're the fat girl or the ugly girl or the poor girl at five years old, it doesn't change when you hit twelve or fifteen. It's who you are, and anybody who wants to treat you different has to fight their way through years of *you're not hanging out with HER, are you?* Kids are cruel, they move in packs, and who you are is all about who's in your posse. Nobody wants to get second-hand fat all over them, or second-hand ugly, or second-hand poor. Easier to stay in your own pack.

Starting in fifth grade, we did Valentine's Day cards for class, but I never got one because, as one of the other girls told me, "Nobody sends hearts to chubbies." I pretended I didn't care. Then in seventh grade, as the cards got passed around, there was one with my name on it! I was so excited to think that somebody liked me. But when I opened the card, there was a picture of a hippopotamus with APRIL FOOLS! written on the other side.

After that, I begged my parents to move somewhere, anywhere else, but we were stuck where we were.

I tried losing weight. I'd go days without eating until I was ready to pass out, but every time I looked at the scale, nothing changed. So I gave up and began eating more. If they were going to call me fat, I might as well go for it.

I wasn't invited to parties or dances. Nobody called to say, *Hey, let's go to the mall.* Things might have been a little better if I was white, because it seems like everything is, but to be a fat black girl in a small town that was 99.99999% white folks? Forget it.

High school was even worse, because it was the same kids from elementary, but now older and meaner. Some of them broke into my school locker and smeared everything with dog shit. Other times, girls would trip me during gym so I'd look stupid when I fell, then yell that a whale had beached itself on the racquetball court. They'd wait in the hall and follow me, making fun of me and knocking my books out of my arms and pinning me against the wall or pulling my hair until I cried.

Girl bullies are worse than boy bullies. If a boy beats up another boy, he gets bruised or maybe it goes too far and he breaks an arm and then the cops get called and the bullies wind up in a lot of trouble, so they usually don't go that far. Still, it's all on the outside. Girl bullies are just as hard on the outside, but they also know how to hurt you in all the soft places on the inside, where you thought you were safe.

Halfway through my junior year, I couldn't take it anymore. I don't even remember what set me off, or if it was any one thing.

I think it was just the All Of It that finally tipped me over, and I was tired and I was done and when the bell rang for lunch I went home while I knew my parents were out working and swallowed every pill I could find in Mama's bathroom.

I woke up later in the hospital with my dad and mama. She was crying, and he had this stone-statue look on his face, real hard, like one of those Easter Island statues, but his eyes kept leaking the whole time. After that they took me out of class for a while and I saw a therapist twice a week. The teachers said they'd make sure that nobody in school heard about the suicide attempt, but when I finally came back, the first girl I saw, one of the worst bullies, knocked my books away and said, *Oooh, drama queen, gonna kill yourself. Next time, call me and I'll make sure you finish the job, bitch.*

I couldn't get out of there fast enough. No prom date, no corsage, and graduation was just a party with my dad and mama and some of our relatives who came into town for the day.

Anyway, that's as far as I wrote for the therapist. I need to get some sleep now, but I'll write more as soon as I get a chance. I hope I'll fit in with everyone. If it helps, I have a sunny disposition!

 Hi, I'm Audio Recorder!
Tap the icon to start recording.

MARK ANTONELLI: Hey, Zeke, got a second?

ZEKE: Yeah, sure. We're not getting breakfast?

MARK ANTONELLI: In a bit. I wanted to talk to you about something first.

ZEKE: You recording this?

MARK ANTONELLI: Just want to get clear on a few things.

ZEKE: Okay, cool, cool.

MARK ANTONELLI: Someone said you've got a cat in there.

ZEKE: Yeah, Soldier. You want to see him?

MARK ANTONELLI: No, you don't have to—

ZEKE: I fixed my bag up for him special, put holes in the sides, see, and a place where he can lie down.

MARK ANTONELLI: It's just that we can't have pets on here, Zeke.

ZEKE: The form didn't say that.

MARK ANTONELLI: No, but it's common sense, I mean, once we're gone, there won't be anyone to take care of anybody's pet and that's cruel, so—

ZEKE: Here he is. Say hi, Soldier.

MARK ANTONELLI: Is he okay? He looks—

ZEKE: Yeah, I know. And no, he's not. But he's got spirit, don't you, pal?

MARK ANTONELLI: What's wrong with him?

ZEKE: Kidney disease. Way advanced. Blood levels are like off the scale. Spent pretty much the last of my money finding that out.

MARK ANTONELLI: Is there anything you can do?

ZEKE: Nope. I mean, if we'd found it earlier and I had a ton of money, maybe we could've done a few things, but by the time I got him in, it was too late.

MARK ANTONELLI: Does he ever try to get out of the bag?

ZEKE: Hey, that's funny! Let the cat out of the bag. Nah. He's a good cat. And you know, with the sickness and all, he's basically like a rag doll, so he doesn't move around much. He never saw much of the world, so I figured we'd take one last road trip together, show him what's out there.

MARK ANTONELLI: I'm sorry.

ZEKE: It is what it is, man. I was kind of hoping we'd have more time, but from what the doctor told me to look for, I think all we have is about a week, maybe less.

MARK ANTONELLI: How will you know?

ZEKE: The same way I always know what he's feeling. It'll be in his eyes. Anyway, that's why we're here. One last ride, then we go out together, right, Soldier?

MARK ANTONELLI: If you're saying you want to kill yourself because your cat's going to die—

ZEKE: No, man, that's not it.

MARK ANTONELLI: Because everyone else here is serious, this isn't some kind of—

ZEKE: It's not, I swear to god, okay? It's not that. I'm not, like, what's the word? Frivolous. I'm not frivolous. Or stupid. It's just, I got some bad habits, okay? Heroin, meth, ice, crack, uppers, downers, I'm not a drug bigot, I'm open-minded. If I can shoot it or toot it, I'm there, you know? I've gone off the shit lots of times, and I can get by for a week or two, like now, or when I'm trying to find work or something, but then, bam, I'm right back in it again. I OD'd three times in the last two years. Almost didn't come back from the last one, but I made it because I knew I had this little guy to look after. You and me against the world, right, pal?

Then we found out he's sick, and I mean, here's the thing. This skinny little guy is all I have. Didn't used to be skinny, used to be big as a bowling ball, but his heart's still the same size, you know? I got no family that wants anything to do with me, friends bailed a long time ago, so now it's just me and him. He's the only thing that keeps me coming back when I OD.

But sooner or later I'll screw up and I won't make it back even with him waiting for me. I know that as sure as I know I'm standing here, so who's gonna take care of him if I'm dead on the floor? He'll starve to death. Not that he's eating much now, but still, he'd starve or die of thirst and I can't let him die all alone in the dark, you know?

The other side is, if he dies first and I keep going, when I OD again without having him waiting for me, giving me a reason to wake up, I'll never find my way back, and then I'll be the one dead on the floor all alone. It's completely fucking inevitable, especially given how things went down the last time, when I almost died. Sometimes it feels like parts of me didn't make it all the way back, and they're in a hurry to hook back up with the rest of me.

I've gone as far as I can, Mark, we both have, so when we go, we go together. He's a good guy and he's my friend and we look after each other, right to the end, don't we, Soldier?

Anyway, like I said, he doesn't eat or drink much anymore, so he doesn't poop a lot either. Sleeps most of the time. He won't be any trouble. We'll just hang and look out at the world and be with each other until it starts to get dark, you know? Is that okay?

MARK ANTONELLI: Yeah. No, that's okay, Zeke. We're cool. Thanks for telling me.

ZEKE: Okay. So can we get breakfast now? Soldier used to like waffles, so I'm thinking maybe I can get him to eat something.

MARK ANTONELLI: Yeah. Sure thing. Let's go.

ZEKE: All right, come on, pal. Waffles!

END RECORDING

Karen_Ortiz

This journal entry will be longer than the others because something important happened today and I want to get every word down right.

After breakfast at a Denny's in Omaha, Nebraska—which may be the saddest sentence ever written, no offense, Omaha, but seriously—Lisa said she had an idea. I think we all groaned inside given how well her last idea worked out, but she surprised everyone by saying she'd Googled the area and found out there was a botanical garden a few minutes away that was supposed to be pretty this time of year. Mark wasn't into the idea because obviously, but I thought it would be fun and said so.

Lisa appreciated my support. We still have our ups and downs, but overall it's been easier with us since we had that big talk. Besides, she's been kind of down the last couple of days, so I thought this could cheer her up a little.

Mark kept trying to find some reason not to do it, but the place wasn't far, and we're not exactly on a schedule.

"Everyone always says stop and smell the flowers," I said, "so why not? I've always wanted to visit a botanical garden, so this is another item I can cross off the bucket list."

When Vaughn and Theo said they'd be open to checking the place out, Mark grumped about it but finally agreed to make a quick stop. "May as well," he said, "because from here on out, the only thing worth seeing in Nebraska is the Colorado border."

See, Nebraska? It's not just me. You really need to work on this place.

Ten minutes later we pulled into the Lauritzen Gardens. The parking lot was almost empty, which we thought might be a bad sign but then we remembered that it was two o'clock on a weekday, and the kind of people who would go to a botanical garden are also the kind of people who have real jobs at real offices and can't go until the weekend.

Theresa said she was staying behind. "I didn't get much sleep last night, so I'm going to try and get some rest. These so-called bunks are really uncomfortable."

"Yeah," I said, "this place is gonna be the death of us yet." Okay, a little bitchy, but there's a time and a place, and this was both.

She didn't even look at me, being really pissy about it. I bet she never travels anything less than business or first class. Her boyfriend said he'd stay with her because of course he would.

Lauritzen turned out to be bigger and nicer than I expected. (Full props, Omaha.) Lots of walking paths covering a hundred acres, rare flower conservatories, and a bird sanctuary. When Tyler saw on a map that the place had a railroad garden with seven functioning G-Scale (whatever that means) model trains, he took off down the path, huffing and puffing like I imagine the trains do. Then the rest of us split up and went our own way.

I made it halfway down the main walk before the Spider said, *That's far enough*, and we went into an old wooden gazebo to get out of the sun. Sometimes meditation helps with the pain, so I closed my eyes and sat for a bit, breathing slow. Then a shadow fell over me and I looked up to see Dylan with two ice cream cones.

"Vanilla or chocolate?"

"Chocolate," I said firmly.

"Crap," he said, and handed me the cone. "I knew I should've gotten two of them."

He sat next to me in the shade and we looked out at the garden for a while without saying anything. The gazebo was big and brown and airy, surrounded by deep green trees and flower beds that were all kinds of colors. I recognized a few of them, like hydrangea, but the rest were a mystery and I wasn't about to get up to look at the teeny-tiny signs.

I pointed at one of the flowers. "I wonder what that one is?" I asked, more rhetorically than anything else. (I've always wanted to use the word "rhetorically" in a sentence without trying to force it but never had the chance. Another bucket item fulfilled!)

Dylan squinted against the light. "Lenten Rose."

I sat up, surprised. "Seriously."

"Yep," he said, and pointed to another flower bed. "Hydrangea."

"Okay, that one I know."

He kept going. "Viburnum. Astilbe. The long white one, that's meadowsweet. Those other two are Jacob's Ladder and Jack-in-the-Pulpit."

"Bullshit, those aren't even flower names. You're making that up."

He went outside, picked up one of the teeny-tiny signs, and handed it to me. Jack-in-the-Pulpit. Shit.

"How do you know all that?" I asked.

He put the sign back and brushed off his hands. He's a big man so he has large hands, but they aren't thick like most guys. His fingers are long and tapered thin, like a pianist. I hadn't noticed that before.

He leaned against one of the railings. "When I was a kid, my folks sent me off to stay with my aunt every summer so they could have some them-time. She was a florist, so she'd put me to work pulling flower stock from the cold-room. Whenever I got one wrong, she'd twist my ear and send me back in again, so I learned the name of every flower in her shop and a bunch more in self-defense."

"If you know so much about this stuff, why didn't you want to see the gardens?"

"I mentioned the part about her twisting my ear, right?"

"Got it."

Then he looked back at the garden and held up one of those long, elegant fingers. "Just a second."

He stepped out and came back with some of the white flowers he'd identified as meadowsweet, pausing to wash them off with a hose. "I don't think you're supposed to pick those," I said.

He shrugged as he sat next to me. "They'll grow back, and I don't see any cameras," he said, then handed one of them to me. "They're edible. Try one."

"Now you *are* making stuff up."

"My aunt used to make tea out of them. Said it helped with heartburn, arthritis, bronchitis . . . worked as good as aspirin but didn't upset the stomach."

"You seriously want me to put this in my mouth," I said, and grinned. *I just pitched you an easy one, go ahead and hit it back, I double-dare you.*

"That would be the general idea," he said. "Here, I'll go first."

I'll admit I screamed a little as he chomped down on the flower.

"Try it," he said.

I hesitated, but since he didn't spit it out or turn green, I sniffed it, touched it, then took a little nibble off the edge of a cluster of white flowers. It was surprisingly sweet. Then I remembered it was called meadow*sweet*, so Miss Obvious, right? The more I chewed, the sweeter it got.

"This is actually pretty good," I said.

"Told you. Also, yours had some ants on it, so there's added protein."

I moved to elbow him but stopped at the last second. I didn't want to give the Spider a reason to ruin the moment.

"You okay?" Dylan asked when he saw me pull back. I'd told him all about the Spider the night we spent talking in the parking lot of the strip club. The way he stood there with his arms around me but not touching me, without moving or trying to take advantage, just warming me by his closeness, meant a lot to me.

"I'm good," I said, though he could tell I wasn't being one hundred percent honest. "Can I ask you a question?"

"No, I don't know why they call the other one Jack-in-the-Pulpit."

"Not about that," I said, and for a second I hesitated, not sure how to bring the subject up, then decided to just go for it. "I was wondering about the night when you took on that asshole outside the motel who was hitting his girlfriend, and later at the festival when you tackled that guy who was on top of Lisa—"

"Yeah, Mark and I had a talk about that," he said, looking down at his shoes. "I lost my temper. It won't happen again."

"No, it's okay, I was just asking because you didn't have to jump into either of those, and you could've been hurt, so, you know . . ." I left it there, not sure what else to say.

He nodded silently long enough that I was just about to say *I didn't mean to pry* when he looked up again.

"My sister, Carrie, is four years older than me," he said. "There was a brother in between, but he got sick when he was six months old and passed away. Carrie and I grew up in this broken-down old house at the far end of a small town in Wyoming. We didn't have a lot of money for food or clothes, but we got by, you know? Behind where we lived there was just woods and gullies. You could walk for almost two miles before hitting another house. Lots of people wanted to build there, but it'd cost too much to level the area, so it stayed undeveloped. We used to go in there a lot. We'd walk and walk until we got tired, then we'd walk and walk back home again. That's what Carrie used to say when my mom asked where we were going. 'For a walk-and-a-walk.' After a while she started saying it like Fozzie Bear, so it came out 'For a *wakka-wakka!*'

"Anyway, one day we went for a walk while we were waiting for Dad to come home so we could go out for pizza. I was eleven, she was fifteen. We got about half a mile in and were about to turn back when we heard voices. We knew that some of the other kids used to hang out in the woods, it wasn't like it was our personal forest, but any time we saw them we'd hide in the shadows until they left so nobody would bother us.

"But this time, they saw us first. Eight of them, all guys, seniors at the same high school where Carrie was going. They came down the side of the hill toward us, asking what we were doing there and giving us shit for how we were dressed. I was scared, but the thing about my sister is, she's fucking fearless. Sometimes I think the more scared I got, the braver she got to make up the difference. So she told them to fuck off, grabbed my hand hard, and started up the hill.

"They dragged us back and surrounded us like a pack of fucking wolves. I thought they were gonna beat us up, but then I saw Carrie's eyes and they were big and wide and for the first time scared because she knew where this was going. 'Run!' she said.

"I wasn't gonna leave her, but it didn't matter because two of them grabbed me before I could move and pinned me to the ground. I fought back but these were big guys, football players, they had six years and a hundred pounds on me.

"One of them grabbed Carrie and she hit him as hard as she could and then they were all over her, trying to bring her down. She fought so hard. I've never seen anyone fight that hard before. But there were too many of them, and they slammed her to the ground and started ripping her clothes off. I was kicking and screaming, trying to get out from under the other guys, but they held me down and—"

Dylan stopped and looked off, and I could see that his eyes were wet. "They raped her. Right in front of me. Even switched places with the guys holding me down so they could get their turn. When they were done, they said if we told anybody what happened nobody would believe us and they'd kill us. When they let me go I started screaming and hitting them and I guess one of them knocked me out because that's all I remember until I looked up to see my sister standing over me, her face bruised, bleeding between her legs.

"Well, she *did* tell our parents, and we *did* tell the cops, and the jury *did* believe us, and every goddamn one of those assholes *did* go to jail because they didn't understand that my sister was fucking fearless. Once it was all over, my folks sent her to live with my other aunt, and that fall she enrolled in a school in the area, far away from where it all happened and all the kids who were friends with the guys who raped her, who said she was a slut and a whore and she had it coming.

"A year later she transferred to a college out of state. I didn't see her much after that, and when we did meet up it was hard, you know? She wasn't the same, my parents were never the same, nothing was. There was a distance between us that hadn't been there before, partly because I could never forgive myself for not stopping them."

"Dylan, you were eleven, there was nothing you could've done."

"Logically I know that, but emotionally that doesn't change a goddamn thing. I will never, *ever* stop thinking that I could've done *something* to save her. So yeah, when I see some asshole hurting a woman, the part of me that wasn't able to help my sister goes out of its fucking mind and there's nothing I can do about it and nothing I *want* to do about it except beat the guy's head in until there's nothing left but bits of bone and blood and . . ."

He pushed down the anger until his voice leveled off. "Sorry to drop all that on you, but you asked."

"It's okay," I said, and noticed that I was resting my hand on his arm. I didn't remember having put it there, but I let it stay anyway. "Do you think that's why you joined the army? So you'd have a way to hit back at the bad guys?"

"I don't know," he said. "Never really thought about it."

"And your sister? How's she doing?"

He managed to serve up a grin. "She got her Master's in Social Work, then signed on as a counselor with a battered women's shelter in Boston. Every day she has to hear stories like what she went through, face all that emotion and turn it into something good so she can help people. I couldn't save her, but goddamn if she didn't save herself and everybody she meets in that place. Sometimes, when one of the residents needs to go back for her property, Carrie goes with her, just daring the guy to try something so she can put him away. Like I said: totally fucking fearless."

"Hey, you two!" Mark called over from the path. "We're heading back to the bus. Five minutes or we leave without you."

"Okay," Dylan said, then turned back to me. "Guess we should head back."

As we started walking, I wondered what it must be like to live life totally fucking fearless. I also realized to my surprise that the Spider was being fairly quiet. The meadowsweet had helped a little, which Dylan almost certainly knew would happen when he got it for me in the first place.

He's always trying to save someone, I thought.

TylerW1998

I've never been much of a plants-and-flowers guy . . . the pollen messes up my lungs and I have enough trouble breathing as it is . . . but I've never seen model trains up close, so that was fun. Then I went for a walk until I started to get dizzy, and sat on a bench to catch my breath. The sun was warm on my skin and made me feel better. Anything to get the blood flowing.

Then I heard someone say, "I made something for you."

I turned to see Theo holding a wreath of leaves freshly rescued from the ground. "Let me see how this looks on you."

"I can't . . . I have a problem with pollen."

"I can fix that. Did you see a water fountain around here any-where?"

"Yeah, back that way."

Theo ran to the fountain, washed off the wreath, and ran back. "Pollen sticks when it's dry. Washing should get rid of most of it. Give it a shot."

I put the laurel on top of my head, which summoned laughter. I can't remember the last time I saw someone with so much easy joy.

"You look like a Roman emperor! All bow before His Royal Magnificence Tyler Maximus Caesar, the emperor historians always forget to mention!"

"Bastards!" I said.

"Bastards, indeed! Any pollen awfulness?"

"None."

"Then my work here is done. Enjoy the sun!"

Then Theo bowed and ran off like a kid who just got out of school on the first day of summer vacation.

So much life. So much laughter.

I sat there, grinning like an idiot, water running down my temples from the laurel, bathing in the warm sunlight until Mark called everybody back to the bus. It was one of those moments of perfect beauty Karen talked about, and I tucked it into the back of my mind like a bird hiding something shiny in its nest so I can look at it whenever I want.

LIsa

Welcome to HomepageAds.com, America's premier choice for personal ads. Please enter the text of your free advertisement in the space below.

Email address (this will not be displayed): **lisarousseau@ccop.edu**
Subject: **Easy Money, Easy Job**
Pay or No Pay: **$200**
Description: **Real simple. I'll pay $200 to anyone who will go to 2725 Ambassador Road, in Durham, North Carolina on a weekday night after 9 p.m. Please make sure the man who lives there is home. Knock on the door and tell him, "Lisa wanted you to know that the Bitch burned your daughter's suicide note and blocked her number on your phone so you wouldn't find out about it." Then leave. After receiving video proof, will send payment via your preferred method (Bitcoin, PayPal, etc.). Willing**

to add another fifty dollars if you can actually pronounce the capital B in Bitch. All contact through this site.

Save Advertisement? Y

Thank you for using HomepageAds.com! Your advertisement will be published within 24 hours.

Have a great day!

AdminMark

It's been a long day, so I told Dylan to stop at a motel so we could get a good night's rest, maybe even take tomorrow to just chill since we don't have a pickup for two days. Our penultimate stop in Nebraska is Bellevue University, where we're supposed to meet the next rider at a dorm party on Betz Road. Rather than send Dylan or go alone, I said that anyone who wanted to come along was welcome since it's a university and we'll all blend in (well, except for Vaughn). Might be a good chance to blow off some steam.

Honestly, I could use a break as much as anyone else. Don't know why but I'm feeling a little down, like I got sideswiped by a bug, or maybe the road is starting to get to me.

As I read back that sentence, it occurs to me that anyone else might look at it and think, *You're on a bus with a bunch of people planning to commit suicide. Why would you look anywhere else for a reason to be depressed?*

Because that's honestly not a factor. Let me explain.

During my freshman year in college, a guy in my History of English Literature class committed suicide one night by jumping off the campus bell tower. Unfortunately he bounced off a ledge into a garden thick with trees and bushes and nobody found his body until that weekend, when the gardeners came in to do cleanup.

The staff and instructors were worried about how we'd take the news, so that Monday, after the dean told everyone what happened, I walked into EngLit to find a grief counselor waiting for us. She talked about how upset and confused we must be, and wanted us to know that we were in a safe place, free to express our feelings. She expected us to react the way she'd been trained to expect: with tears, sobbing, and incomprehension.

She got none of those things. I mean, yeah, the guy who jumped wasn't a jerk, so we were sad that he was gone, and for sure some of us missed him more than others, but on the tears/sobbing/incomprehension scale of one to ten, we were hovering at about two, tops.

I guess she thought we hadn't understood her when she said it was okay to let it all out, so she tried broadening the discussion to ask how many of us knew someone who had committed suicide or attempted it. I think she expected maybe one or two hands to go up.

We all raised our hands.

We tried to explain that suicide had become so common in our demo that it just doesn't have the same shock value anymore. It's like, *Shit, I got hacked* and *I failed my midterm* and *Bobby from PE class blew his brains out.* I won't say it's an everyday occurrence because that's overstating the case, but it's not too far from the truth either. Five thousand millennials commit suicide every year. It's our second biggest cause of death, and the way things are going by next year it'll probably be number one. Or, like radio DJs used to say back in the day, number one with a bullet, right?

That's half the reason we weren't drowning in tears.

Here's the other half.

My grandfather used to talk about how he had to do these Duck and Cover drills when he was in the second grade. They'd be studying math or history and suddenly the teacher would shout "Bomb!" and everyone would dive under their desks and cover their heads because of *course* that would save them from a thermonuclear fucking weapon. And there he is, sixty years old, and he's still not over it. *A thing like that changes you forever,* he'd say.

But here's the thing: nobody ever nuked the second grade. Yeah, I'm sure it was scary as shit to prepare for that, but it never actually happened.

By contrast, everybody I know grew up with school shootings. We're the first bunch who came up knowing for an absolute, stone-certain fact that at any moment, somebody could walk into the cafeteria and execute us. It wasn't a vague, formless idea or an abstract possibility, it was real. Every time we saw another school get hit, it was like, *Well, I guess I'm next.*

No disrespect to my grandfather, who was actually a pretty nice guy, but seeing news reports about kids your own age getting their faces blown off on a monthly, sometimes *weekly* basis changes you and how you look at death. It's there with us every day. As terrible as this is going to sound, we're *used* to it, and we try not to be scared by it.

People grieve over someone getting killed when it comes as a surprise, when it's rare, when it's not supposed to happen. If you wanted us to grieve, then you should have made it rare in the first place, fixed things so *you'd* stop killing us and we wouldn't have to be killing *ourselves.* But you didn't, and we *know* you didn't, so yeah, when one of us goes down we don't grieve about it the way you did, the way you *want* us to.

And don't you dare fucking judge us for it.

_____

VaughnR

I've never been much of a drinker, usually just a beer or a glass of wine with dinner, but the motel where we stopped for the night was across from a bar and it was still early and there was nothing else to do, so I decided to go for a quick drink, then head back and get some sleep.

It was one of those little taverns you see a lot in Nebraska that's probably been there as long as the town, with lots of old wood and leather booths, a dart board that hasn't been used in a long time, and a pool table that's missing a few balls. But at my age, I should talk, right?

I was about to take a seat at the bar when I saw Theresa and Jim in one of the booths. Wasn't sure what I should do about it, but Carolyn would say it's bad form to ignore someone you know, and so far they hadn't done anything to offend me, so when Jim waved to join them, I headed for the booth.

"What can we get you?" he asked. I told him a beer and he repeated it to the waitress.

We talked for a while about nothing in particular, that kind of conversation you get at a party where nobody knows anybody else and you're probably never going to see them again, so it's okay to be dull or stupid or both. But while both of them were a little dull, neither of them were stupid, and they seemed happy for the diversion.

"Sometimes the bus feels a little like high school," Theresa said. "Cliques, right? 'Don't talk to those guys, they have cooties.'"

I told her I hadn't heard anyone say cooties in a long time, and she said it was her mother's favorite expression and it stuck. It didn't take much prodding to get her to talk about her family some more. Apparently her father was a real piece of work. Racist. Violent. A drunk. Even though he'd inherited all his money instead of working for it, he turned around and said she wouldn't get a penny of it if she married an African-American.

"I told him I'd rather be dead than live in that house with him a second longer," she said. "That's when he told me he was 'connected' to some really bad people, that he had Jim's license plate number, and if I went with Jim he'd hire someone to find us and Jim would get hurt, or worse."

"Maybe he was bluffing," Jim said, "but just to be safe I ditched the car after picking up Theresa and we looked for a way out that wouldn't leave a trail for anyone to find later. We thought about getting bus or train tickets, because you can buy those for cash, but then Theresa showed me Mark's ad and I thought, well, why not?"

"Sounds like you're running away more than looking to kill yourselves."

"We just want to find the right place to do it, that's all," Theresa said, "because it needs to be done in a way that's beautiful." I could tell she was getting her back up about it. "You don't think we're serious, do you? You think this is just a game to us, same as Lisa and the others?"

"Not my place to say," I told her, but that only pissed her off more.

"Show him," she told Jim.

He started to say "We don't have to prove any—" but she cut him off.

"*Show* him."

He reached into his backpack, pulled out an unmarked bottle of pills, and opened the top so I could look inside. The pills were blue and pink, with the number 45 printed on them.

"Medical-grade arsenic," she said. "Jim was going to med school when we met and he was able to go back and get them from the university lab. We could do this today, right here, but what Mark described, driving over a cliff in San Francisco at sunset . . . like I said, it's beautiful and if I have to pick a way to go, I'd rather do it that way. But if anything goes wrong, or my dad finds us before we can make it to San Francisco, this is our way out."

Jim was getting uncomfortable with the conversation, and changed the subject to happier topics, like the day they met and how much they were in love with each other. Then Theresa excused herself to go to the bathroom.

Once she was gone, I leaned in to Jim so we could talk quietly. "She doesn't know, does she?" I said.

"Know what?"

"Jim, when you're twenty, trying to get sleeping pills or Vicodin takes an act of Congress, but when you're sixty-five they back up the truck and give you pretty much anything you want. They throw it at you like candy because at that age, why not? So I've seen pretty much every kind of pill there is, and while I was looking after my wife during her decline I learned to recognize every pill by sight to make sure she didn't get the wrong one.

"And I know amoxicillin when I see it. Blue and pink, with 45 stamped on the pink side."

His face fell when he saw I had him dead to rights. "Please don't tell her," he said. "Saying I had poison was the only way I could stop her from doing something stupid on her own."

"So Lisa got it right, you *don't* want to kill yourself."

"Me? Fuck no."

"Then why pretend otherwise?"

"Because she's got a temper like you wouldn't believe, Vaughn. If I try and talk her out of killing herself while she's this mad at her father, she'll just turn around and do it. So I'm trying to keep the situation from escalating until she calms down enough for us to figure out how to deal with her dad."

"So why get on the bus?"

"I thought if she could see a bunch of people who really *are* serious about taking their own lives, she might decide she's not one of them. Meanwhile, it'll show her that I'm listening to her, which buys me time to try and change her mind.

"So don't tell the others, okay? Because like I said, she's got a temper and if one of them says something about it . . . trust me, you don't want to be on the other side of what happens next."

"I promise," I said, just in time to see Theresa coming out of the bathroom. As she sat back down, Jim changed the subject to their relationship and how great it was. I smiled and nodded until I finished my beer, then thanked Jim for picking up the tab and headed to my room.

I came back with a lot more respect for Jim. He's trying to save her, preserve their relationship, *and* find some way to reconcile with a man who clearly hates his guts and can't be trusted. That's a lot of weight for anyone to carry, but he's doing the best he can with it.

I hope things work out with them better than they did with me. God knows they couldn't do any worse.

IamTheo

After being blocked the last few days due to the excitement of signing on for this expedition, I was finally able to get some writing done tonight on the stories, filling up most of my last notebook before deciding to get some sleep. Unfortunately, when my brain is in writing mode, it's incapable of shutting down on command—it just takes all that energy and turns it inward, projecting random thoughts and bits of dialogue on the inside of my eyelids until I surrender to the inevitable and get back up again. So with the sun starting to peek through the curtains I decided to put some of that free-floating energy to work and write a bit about why I'm here.

At risk of overthinking everything—and as someone who got a BA in Gender Studies and made it halfway through the Master's program for Political Theory, that's apparently something I do all the time—I think there are two ways that people commit suicide.

The first way people kill themselves is a kind of spontaneous combustion. It comes out of rage or shock or sudden deep depression and catches you by surprise, and before you even realize you're doing it, you're reaching for the gun or the knife or the pills. It's as if something inside you gets too sad or too angry to survive anymore and it explodes, taking you with it. I think it happens most often to the very people who don't think they could ever kill themselves, because they're not paying attention when their switch gets flipped in the middle of something awful.

The second is more like a time-delay fuse. It comes when you've been wounded for days or weeks or years and you finally reach a point when your heart gets very quiet and very still and you realize that you simply cannot live in the world anymore, when you say, *I have no purpose here, no place, no function, no reason to keep going.* Why stick around when you're not free to be yourself, you're not wanted, your future isn't what you thought it was going to be and every day you're being elbowed a little further off the planet? It's not that you *can't* take it anymore, it's that you *refuse* to take it anymore. The decision doesn't come like a lightning bolt out of anger, despair, or self-pity; it's more like standing up on your hind legs and announcing to the world, *You're all a bunch of assholes and I never asked to be invited to this stupid party in the first place so I'm outta here.*

Last year, a friend of mine decided she'd had enough of the bullshit and wanted out. Rather than go the spontaneous combustion route, she spent weeks hand-writing letters to everyone who mattered, telling them what she was going to do, and why, and how it wasn't their fault. She could've just written emails and timed them to go out when appropriate, but she wanted a more personal touch. When she was done, she packed up a picnic lunch, dropped the letters in the mail, and went to her favorite park to sit by the lake. As the sun went down, she sorted the trash into the appropriate bins, strolled over to a walking path where she knew her body would be found the next morning, sat with her back against a tree to minimize the mess, put the business end of a gun in her mouth, and pulled the trigger.

I don't belong in this world. I could go into a million reasons why I've come to that conclusion, starting with all the bullying earlier in my life, to my screwed-up family and the fact that I'll never have the kind of job or life that would make sticking around worthwhile, but it all adds up to the same thing. I don't belong here. Could I have an easier time if I embraced a more conventional approach to my life and my gender? Sure, but then I wouldn't be me. If I have to choose between being allowed to live in this world by being false to everything I believe in, or going to a world I've created in my own head, even if it's not real, where I can be myself, I'll pick the latter every time.

That's what I've done, and what I'm doing, and with all due respect for the process and the (not exactly enforceable) agreement I signed when I got on the bus, I don't feel the need to describe the proverbial final straw that broke the equally proverbial camel's back. It would just give people the ammunition they need to say *Aha! That's why it happened, that one very specific thing* and dismiss everything else, letting themselves off the hook for whatever role they played in this process.

I read once about a man who was getting dressed one morning, and as he bent to tie his shoes, one of the laces snapped. He looked at the shoes for a moment, then got up, walked to the window, and jumped twelve stories to his death. Clearly he wasn't distraught about the shoelace, that's ridiculous. It was all the things that the shoelace *represented*, everything that led up to that one singular moment when the shoelaces became the One More Thing he couldn't handle and he dove out the window.

I don't want people thinking I did this because of a shoelace. My reasons are my own, and I don't have to justify them to anyone.

Last year I found an old book on manners at a used bookstore, and one of the chapters said that when someone invites you to dinner or a party and you don't want to go, you don't have to respond with a bunch of excuses, explanations, or justifications that will just end up sounding exactly like what they are. It's your choice, your life, and you don't have to explain yourself. The proper response is simply, *I appreciate the invitation, but alas I cannot attend the party. Please give my regards to everyone who can make it.*

I appreciate the invitation, but alas I cannot attend the rest of my life.

Please give my regards to everyone else who can hack it.

I'd always heard the phrase "Live every day as if it were your last," but I never really understood what it meant until now. Everything I do is potentially the last time I'll ever do it, so I go as deep as I can, savoring every moment, looking at all the details that I missed before because I didn't *have* to pay attention, as if I was immortal, and tomorrow was guaranteed. Now everything is luminous. Everything is joyful. There's no more worry about the future, about getting a job, or making plans or being judged or hitting the right grades or who I should be or where I should be or when I should be there. No more hesitations, second thoughts, recriminations, or doubt.

I am the arrow loosed from the bow. I go where the air and my velocity take me.

My life is my own, it belongs to no one else, and I will do with it as I wish.

So exciting.

TylerW1998

Woke up in the middle of the night and couldn't breathe. I could feel my lungs moving, but nothing was happening, like I was drowning. Fighting panic, I grabbed the sports O2 canister I keep in my bag and sucked down oxygen until it passed. When the room stopped spinning, I licked my finger and the spit was pinkish and frothy. Pulmonary edema. Not the first time, but it may be getting close to the last time.

I spent the rest of the night sitting up in bed, trying not to use the O2 unless I really needed it. I wanted to text someone, just to distract myself, but it was four in the morning and I didn't want to bother anybody.

And I just started crying.

Whenever something really terrible happens, I think there's a part of our brain that says, *This isn't real, it's just a nightmare, and any minute now I'll wake up and it'll all be the way it's supposed to be,* except you don't and it isn't and it's as awful as it ever was. Your leg is stuck in a bear trap and you can't open it and you can't get out and there's nobody around to help you, there's just this searing pain that gets bigger and bigger until you black out, and when you finally wake up again there's this split second when you think, *Thank God that wasn't real,* then the pain comes back and it *is* real and your brain keeps looking for a reset button that's not there, going crazier every day because there's no way out.

That's how I've felt ever since my condition started taking a turn for the worse two years ago. I suppose I should be grateful because the doctor didn't think I'd even make it this far, and yeah, it's great that I did, but the thing is *two years isn't enough.*

It takes just two years to get an AA degree, two years for a baby to grow molars, two years of dating before anyone in your family takes the relationship seriously, two years for Mormon missionaries to do whatever the hell Mormon missionaries do when they're in Africa or China . . . two years is a thirty-second time-lapse video of a freeway under construction, *two years is a heartbeat!*

And I'm nearly out of those.

And it's not fair, because I've never hurt anyone or done anything to deserve this. I don't want to die. But I also don't want to spend my last days in a hospital room, hooked up to IV drips and monitors with a breathing tube stuck down my throat, drowning in pink froth until my lungs fill up and my heart explodes. This is better. I'm just afraid that my illness might not let me get all the way to San Francisco, that my road may be a lot shorter than the one Karen and Lisa and Mark and the rest are on.

But at least I'm not alone on that road, and though I can't do a lot physically right now, being here for them in other ways helps me feel like I'm doing something good on my way out.

If I have to die, then let it be with people I care about, doing something to help them. Let me die for a *reason.* That's not so much to ask, is it?

Hi, I'm Audio Recorder!
Tap the icon to start recording.

MARK ANTONELLI: Test one two three . . .
ZEKE: Hey.
MARK ANTONELLI: Hey.

ZEKE: D said you're going to a party.

MARK ANTONELLI: Sort of. I'm supposed to meet the new guy so he can scope me out, make sure I'm legit before signing on while I'm doing the same to him. All the frats are having parties tonight, so it'll probably take a while to find the right place. Shanelle, Theo, and Lisa are coming along.

ZEKE: Oh, good because Lisa's been a real—

MARK ANTONELLI: Yeah, I know. It'll be good to give her a break from Theresa. You saw what happened this morning?

ZEKE: Yeah, I didn't hear what they were arguing about, but for sure Lisa was pissed. I keep waiting for shit to go down with them.

MARK ANTONELLI: You want to come to the party?

ZEKE: No, man, too much noise, not Soldier's scene.

MARK ANTONELLI: How's he doing?

ZEKE: He's pretty tired. He slept most of the day, but he's awake now, so I thought I'd take him for a walk. I carry him to different trees and flowers so he can sniff at everything. For a cat, that's like going on vacation, right?

MARK ANTONELLI: Sure. Just don't go too far from the bus in case we have to bug out.

ZEKE: Okeydokey.

MARK ANTONELLI: Hey, Zeke—

ZEKE: Yeah?

MARK ANTONELLI: If you have time to write up a journal entry, it would be great.

ZEKE: I haven't had a chance.

MARK ANTONELLI: I know, but everyone else is doing it, so . . .

ZEKE: No, it's okay, you're right. I'll try to get something down after the sniff tour.

END RECORDING

SunnyShanelle

After graduating high school, I went to a community college for about a year before giving up. I used to dream about getting a degree in psychology so I could be a counselor to kids who were as screwed up as me (fun fact: most people in asylums want to be psychologists when they get out, so what does that say about crazy people, psychologists, and me?), but even if I got an AA my folks couldn't afford to send me on to a four-year college and I wasn't earning enough to go on my own, so what was the point? And I couldn't focus on anything. I was depressed all the time. All I wanted to do was sleep and eat. Mainly eat. Then sleep when I couldn't eat. Mama tried cutting back on dinner to help me lose weight, but I'd just sneak money out of my dad's wallet to buy junk food and hide it under the bed. The more I ate, the more depressed I got, and the more depressed I got, the more I ate. I was sleeping twelve hours a day, going to bed at dawn, then getting up when it was dark. Sometimes I didn't see the sun for days. Which of course just made me even more depressed.

When my dad realized I was dipping in his wallet, he said that if I wanted money I had to earn it or get it as a reward for losing weight. Since the back half of that wasn't going to work, I tried getting a job at the mall, but nobody wants a fat girl selling clothes. They like finger-thin bulimia cases that would snap in half if you touched them the wrong way. And nobody wants to hire someone my size for a job that takes a lot of heavy lifting because they're afraid I'll have a heart attack and fall over dead and their insurance won't cover it.

I finally found a job working for a phone solicitation company that helped people consolidate debt when they were behind on their credit cards. I actually kind of enjoyed it because I felt like

I was helping people and nobody knew what I looked like on the phone, they just heard my voice, and my sunny disposition won them over! I even had guys flirting with me during the calls, and that was a first for sure!

One of these was Phil, and once we realized he was only about ten miles away he kept asking me for a date. I told him he wouldn't want to go out with me because I was a "big girl." When he asked how big, I texted him a photo. He texted back "no problem" and asked me to meet him at a restaurant downtown for dinner. He was twelve years older than me, but that was okay. I figured we could meet in the middle of him being too old and me being too big.

I spent hours getting ready. I wanted to look all sparkly for the big night, so I picked up some Laura Mercier Baroque eye shadow which looks good with my complexion. It cost twenty-three dollars, but it was worth the investment. I was so excited that I got to the restaurant twenty minutes early.

He showed up right on time, but when I walked over to him, I saw The Look in his eyes. The *I didn't know you were* this *big* look. He tried to hide it, but it was all over him. "Hey, I sent you a photo," I said, and laughed, trying to make it not a big deal.

"Yeah, I know, you did, it's just . . . cameras always put on twenty pounds, so I assumed . . ." He ran out of words as the hostess took us to our table.

He didn't talk as we went over the menu, but I could feel him getting upset. Not just upset, *angry*, like I deliberately got fat that day just to piss him off. I asked him what was good here to eat. "It's all good," he said without looking up from the menu. Then the waiter came over and I asked if we could have some sparkling water. When he brought it over, Phil said he had to go to the restroom.

He never came back. He gave the waiter twenty bucks for the water and a tip, then slipped out the back.

It was the Valentine's Day card all over again. He hadn't set out to do it deliberately, but that didn't change how it hit me, and I started crying. When the hostess came over to see what was going on, I told her what happened and she said that if I wanted anything to eat, it was on the house.

But for a change, I wasn't hungry. Just angry. I mean *really* angry, at him, at me, at the world, at everything.

And I drank every drop of that fucking bottle of sparkling water, because he owed me at least that much.

The next day I decided he owed me a lot more than that, so I canceled all his cards, tanked his credit rating, and gave his address to a collection agency he'd been ducking.

My boss fired me when he found out what I'd done. I was mad about it, but the other girls working the phone bank said I should just be glad he didn't sue me, but I knew that if he did, it would open up a big can of worms about how well he was running things if one person could do all this, so he did what he could to fix the damage, then booted me out the door. And I was right back where I started.

That's when I started cutting myself.

I was home alone, angry at what happened, at Phil and my boss and myself and my folks, and I could feel a pressure in my veins getting worse every second, like somebody pumping too much air into a balloon, until my whole body was shaking and I felt like if I didn't let the pressure out I'd explode, so I picked up a steak knife and dragged it across my arm, not too deep, just enough to draw blood. And just like that, I got all quiet inside, like I let the rage out of my veins, and the pressure dropped and I actually felt better. I looked at the blood like, *Oh, hello, friend, nice to meet you.*

After that, any time I found myself getting upset I'd go into a bathroom if I was out, or my bedroom if I was home, and make a little cut, usually high up on my thigh, where nobody could see it, and let a little blood out. I always felt better afterward. Even my folks said I seemed happier and calmer. Then Mama saw bloodstains on the wrong part of my pants when some of the scabs came off, and all hell broke loose.

More later. Going to a party!

Hi, I'm Audio Recorder!
Tap the icon to start recording.

MARK ANTONELLI: If I record this?

VOICE 16: Shit, yeah, record away, I got nothing to hide. Is that just voice or voice to text?

MARK ANTONELLI: Voice to text. Just a second, let me edit this. Music's pretty loud, but it should be okay with the microphone.

EDIT VOICE? Y/N   Y

ENTER VOICE 16 NAME: PETER

MARK ANTONELLI: Okay, that should do it.

PETER: Test, test. So how come I'm just Peter and you're Mark Antonelli? Shouldn't I be Peter Routh?

MARK ANTONELLI: Fine, hang on, one second.

EDIT VOICE? Y/N   Y

ENTER NAME: PETER ROUTH

PETER ROUTH: Can we also put in my middle initial?

MARK ANTONELLI: Fuck off. And stop staring at the screen.

SHANELLE: Mark! I brought you a beer!

MARK ANTONELLI: Thanks, Shanelle. This is Peter, he wants to join up.

PETER ROUTH: Once I know you're serious.

MARK ANTONELLI: Once we know you're serious.

SHANELLE: I'll let you two fight it out. I gotta go keep an eye on Lisa.

PETER ROUTH: Did you know he only has you on here by your first name?

MARK ANTONELLI: Will you stop with that shit?

PETER ROUTH: Let's go over there so nobody can hear us. How many people you got so far?

MARK ANTONELLI: Counting me and the driver, eleven. I figure we'll max out at about fifteen. So what're you studying?

PETER ROUTH: Double major, philosophy and psychology. Which means I win most arguments I get into, and if I do lose, I can make you feel bad about it afterward.

MARK ANTONELLI: So why do you want to come on the bus?

PETER ROUTH: Because of my fashion sense. Why the fuck do you think?

MARK ANTONELLI: I'm asking because everyone who's signed up so far has a reason.

PETER ROUTH: And you don't think I do?

MARK ANTONELLI: I'm just saying, you're a good-looking guy, you seem to have your shit together, you don't seem sick or depressed or . . .

PETER ROUTH: You want the whole thing?

MARK ANTONELLI: I got no other plans for tonight. Why do you want to kill yourself?

PETER ROUTH: That is totally the wrong question. People don't decide one day to kill themselves. Never happens.

MARK ANTONELLI: I've got nine other people on the bus who would disagree with that.

PETER ROUTH: I'm just saying that the suicidal impulse is always there. It's like when your car pulls to the left, and you have to keep both hands on the wheel to keep going straight because if you take your hands off, the car veers into oncoming traffic. Same with suicide. The pull is always there, but because we have things to do, because we have reasons not to kill ourselves, we keep both hands on the wheel. So it's not so much that people decide to kill themselves, it's that one day they run out of reasons not to kill themselves. They take their hands off the wheel, surrender to the pull of the suicidal impulse, and next thing you know, bam.

MARK ANTONELLI: So what made you decide to take your hands off the wheel?

PETER ROUTH: It's been a long process, but if there's one thing, last summer my girlfriend, Jessie, was hit by a car. She spent months in a coma with no brain activity, just gone, nothing there, but her folks kept her plugged in because they could afford it, because they didn't believe the doctors. If Jessie could have seen what they were doing to her, she would've done anything to stop it. Same thing happened to my father, they kept him around long after he would've wanted because he was in no condition to say let me go. I'm not going to let that happen to me. I'm taking hold of my destiny.

MARK ANTONELLI: Yeah, but you're, what, twenty-four? You've got years ahead of you.

PETER ROUTH: So did Jessie, and look what happened. Don't you get it? Maybe it happens tomorrow crossing the street, or a year from now, or twenty years from now. It doesn't change the fact that all of us are going to decay and endure horrific shit that nobody should ever have to endure and I'm not doing it. No fucking way. I'm gonna go out loud and powerful and raging while I still can.

MARK ANTONELLI: But there's a lot you could do.

PETER ROUTH: As what? A cog in a machine? For a corporation? For a boss? For some faceless master on a distant mountaintop? Just so I can end up in a cheap apartment because I can't afford a house, sick all the time because I can't afford a doctor, overeducated and underemployed, and the planet's completely fucked because of corporate greed and plastic and too many people clawing at every last drop of whatever's left? Who wants that shit? Me? Hell, no.

MARK ANTONELLI: So for you, suicide is a rational choice.

PETER ROUTH: Given everything I just described, suicide is the only rational choice.

MARK ANTONELLI: If that's true, then why is society so against it?

PETER ROUTH: Because it breaks their control over us, because doctors are afraid of getting sued for missing the warning signs, because credit card companies want to get paid and families don't want the guilt. In primitive societies, when somebody wanted to walk out into the snow or give it up to the wolves, they let him. If he wanted to go back to creation or another birth, they said fine, do what you gotta do. You've heard of seppuku, right?

MARK ANTONELLI: Sure, everyone has.

PETER ROUTH: It's suicide, no different from chugging pills, but calling it seppuku somehow makes it brave, makes it the honorable thing to do. In early Greece and Rome, people killed themselves all the time. It was just an accepted part of life. In Rome, if you wanted to kill yourself, you went to the Senate, walked them through your reasons, and most of the time they said great, no problem, here's some hemlock.

MARK ANTONELLI: Bullshit.

PETER ROUTH: Totally true, it was just that casual. They called it a virtuous death. The only people in Rome who weren't allowed to kill themselves were soldiers because their asses belonged to the Empire, slaves because it wasn't good business, and people accused of crimes because if they died before a judgment could be made, the state couldn't confiscate their money. It's always been about money and power and control and who has it and who doesn't. Shit, the Church didn't say boo about suicide until Augustine came along in the sixth century to say that only God had the right to decide when we die. Well, I say fuck that. Killing yourself may be the only decision you can ever make that is truly, honestly, and one hundred percent your own.

MARK ANTONELLI: Do you ever breathe? I mean seriously.

PETER ROUTH: It's the ultimate fuck-you to the system. That's why the courts made it illegal, and the medical world made it a sign of mental illness, even though the assumption that all suicide is the result of mental illness has never been proven and never will be.

Back in the nineteen fifties in London, if you tried to kill yourself and the court decided that you were crazy when you did it, that was fine because it gave the system the authority to put you in a box with no control over your body, your property, or your money. What scared them was the possibility that the court could go the other way and decide that you were sane when you tried to kill yourself, which acknowledges that suicide can be a rational decision, and that's the last thing the politicians wanted. They said they were worried that it would send the wrong signal to others who were thinking about doing the same thing, but the truth is they didn't want to lose the control that a verdict of insanity gave them over people.

So they passed laws that made trying to kill yourself straight-up illegal, regardless of whether or not you were sane when you did it. They put it in the same category as murder, or trying to break into someone's house. They called it felo-de-se, which means a felony against yourself, if you can believe that shit. You want to know what else they called suicide?

MARK ANTONELLI: You've spent a lot of time on Wikipedia, haven't you?

PETER ROUTH: I studied this shit for two years, motherfucker, and they called suicide, quote, the crime of depriving the King of a subject, unquote. As far as they were concerned, you belonged to the Crown. So if you killed yourself and the court declared that you were sane when you did it, they took your family's land, property, and money as penalty for trying to steal from the Crown. Since the government can't take your stuff away anymore for trying to kill yourself, they've gone back to saying it's crazy.

But that's just not true. Suicide is the tenth leading cause of death in the United States, fifty thousand last year, twice as many suicides as homicides, but doctors could only point to psychological issues in less than half of them. That means the rest of them weren't crazy, they knew exactly what they were doing. That's why I had this tattooed on my chest. See right here? What does it say?

MARK ANTONELLI: Do not resuscitate.

PETER ROUTH: You think I'm not serious? You think I'm just dicking around and I don't really mean any of this? That's why I picked this up the other day—here, let me drag out my backpack.

MARK ANTONELLI: Whoa. What's that, a katana?

PETER ROUTH: Wakizashi, the smaller version. I didn't know if you guys would show up, if you were real, if I'd agree to go with you, or how you guys planned to finish it up, so if this didn't work out, I figured tonight's party would be my goodbye. Go out old-school, you know? I'm as serious as anybody else on that bus, Mark, maybe more so because for me this isn't an emotional decision, it's not some kind of impulse, I'm not doing it because my mom didn't love me or I have a tumor or my girlfriend just broke up with me or I'm super depressed, well, maybe a little, but Jesus fuck, these days, who isn't? I'm doing it because it's the only choice that makes any kind of goddamned sense. So if I get on the bus with the rest of you, great, we'll do it together later, but I'm also cool with doing this right here, right now. I can go either way.

MARK ANTONELLI: Then come on the bus. Totally signing off on you.

PETER ROUTH: Great, as soon as I sign off on you. Want another beer?

MARK ANTONELLI: Fucking A.

END RECORDING

LIsa

Tonight was very strange.

Ever since I got that email from the Bitch, I've been sleeping more than usual. Just didn't want to deal with it. I think my fellow passengers are happy when I conk out, and I can't blame them. So yeah, I've been pretty down, though I had to smile when the guy who delivered my message called to say that when my dad found out she'd burned my note, the whole thing turned into a big blowup. So Dad, if you're reading this in the Aftermath: please don't invite her to my funeral, because if she shows up, I swear I'll crawl out of my casket or my urn (depending on how much is left to work with) and kick the shit out of her.

Anyway, when Mark said we were going to a party, I got excited for the first time in days, and the hyper part of my brain (not the Crazy Lisa part, we're past that now) went into overdrive. I couldn't keep still, so I was popping Molly and Bluetoothing Caravan Palace through the bus speakers and dancing in the aisle with a crowd that wasn't there, and TheresaAndJim were being all pissy about it and nobody else joined in, but I didn't give a shit if it was just me dancing because Just Me was Just Lisa and for once I was totally down with that. Everybody else just rolled their eyes like "Well, there she goes," except Shanelle, the new girl. She thought it was funny and said she was going to keep an eye on me when we got to the party so I didn't get in trouble "because girl, I have heard some stories." That was a surprise, and kind of nice.

The whole time we were walking across campus trying to find the dorm, I'm jumping up and down like some kind of goddamned jackrabbit. I was happy to be out of the bus and going to a party and Molly was being so *exceptionally* sweet to me that I offered to introduce her to Shanelle, since they had not previously met, but she only took a quarter and Theo passed, so that left me to be the Fun Machine for the evening.

And I tried, I really did. The place was shaking, the music was great, there was a lot of really good booze and everybody was into it . . . but I couldn't kick loose, like something was holding me back and I thought, *Molly, you bitch, you straight-up ghosted me just when I needed you,* so I dug around in my goody bag until I found some shrooms. Washed them down with beer and waited for the hit.

Usually with shrooms, I can feel myself shaking off my body and letting go pretty fast. But this time I got stuck inside, like I was looking at everything through a periscope in the top of my head, me watching me watching them watching me. I was inside, outside, and above but not quite *there*, if that makes sense. Then the music and the voices went away and everything got really quiet.

When I was in high school, I went through this phase where I was fascinated by YouTube videos of Ye Olden Days. Around the turn of the century (the last one, not this one), somebody would rent a truck or a horse-drawn wagon, load up a hand-cranked camera, and go down one street after another, shooting silent film of cities like New York or Chicago or San Francisco. Grainy little movies of people just living life, driving around, crossing the street or selling newspapers. I couldn't get enough of them. I'd get real close to the screen, trying to see past their faces to what they were thinking, where they'd been and where they were going and what they'd do when they got there, and I'd think, *All those people are dead, and all those buildings are gone . . . that place, those people, and the world they knew doesn't exist anymore,* like I was looking at them through the window of a time machine.

That's how I felt tonight. Like I was a time traveler peeking in at the party from another time and place. No sound, no voices, no music. Except they're not the ones that are going away.

I am.

In a few days or weeks, they'll still be having parties, there will be booze and Molly and music and dancing. But I won't be here to see it. The world I know won't exist anymore.

Somebody turned the camera around, and now I'm the one looking out from a piece of film, long gone.

I am no longer a part of this world. I am a picture in somebody's yearbook. A face on a security video somewhere, adrift in time.

I am a memory.

––––––––––––––––

Username: Zeke

Hey, Mark, it's Zeke! Just leaving this here to follow up on what you said about writing a journal entry. So here it is. But wait! Should I have said Hey, Mark or Hey, Somebody Else? If all this gets beamed up to the Starship Enterprise when the bus goes over that cliff in San Francisco and you never get to read it, maybe I should start this with Hey, Whoever! Or To Whom This May Concern! Or Hey You! Ha-ha! I like that one.

Hey, you!

Well shit, now I have to actually write something.

But see, here's the thing. I don't think any of the stuff I'm supposed to write about actually means anything. If I tell you I was born here, I went to school over there, my folks were good or bad or not there most of the time, it doesn't tell you who I am right now. Past's dead. If we let something that happened years ago decide who we are right now, well, that's pretty stupid, right?

The only thing I remember from my half year of math in junior college is that time doesn't actually exist. Everything is happening at the same time, there are no straight lines from here to there. It's only perception and the way our minds work that make us think that *this* thing happened today, *that* thing happened yesterday, and *something else* is going to happen tomorrow. It's quantum mechanics, and I'd love to explain that to you more, but I never made it past the intro class! Only reason I remember the part about time is that I thought it was really cool. It means that right now I'm being born, right now I'm graduating high school, right now I'm shooting up for the first time, right now I'm getting on the bus, and right now I'm dying. That's crazy! But there's math behind it, so I guess it's true.

If there's no such thing as the past, if there's only right now, then why dwell on it, right? Move on. (Yeah, I know, there's no such thing as "moving on" if the future is also bogus, but you know what I mean.)

So yeah: What to write? I don't think I have a lot to say that's worth much of anything. My folks would agree with that, for sure. Always did.

One thing I guess I should say is: thank you for letting me on the bus so I could get to know everybody here, even Lisa, and have some company to go along with me and Soldier on our last big adventure! It really means a lot to both of us.

Thinking about it a little more, maybe there is one thing I can say. Something I only figured out the other day.

Like I said, Soldier and me are close, but in a funny way. I mean, he's never been ultra-affectionate. He'd let me pet him and pick him up and carry him around without trying to wriggle away, but he's not one of those cats you see rubbing up against people, or booping heads, that sort of thing. Never came up and licked my face. I just figured he was shy, you know?

Any time I had some money, I'd buy food for Soldier first, then get whatever I needed with what was left. I looked after him. Protected him. Because he loved me. You could see it in his eyes. Love, man. Crazy stupid cat love that was five times bigger than he was.

But he never came over. Weird, huh?

So while we were looking out the window on the bus today, I remembered something. Don't know why, it just came up at me, like when you're sitting at a stoplight with your brain in neutral waiting for the green and something you hadn't thought about since forever swims up at you out of nowhere and you think, where the hell did that come from and why now?

I remembered the day I went out to score some party favors and left the door open by accident. We were squatting in this abandoned apartment, no water or heat but it had a roof and walls and that was all we needed. I hadn't had Soldier very long and he was always looking out the window like he wanted to go for a walk. It was a pretty rough area, so I kept the door closed so he wouldn't wander out and get grabbed or lost or hurt, but this one time I was withdrawing pretty hard so I was kind of spaced and not paying attention so I forgot to close the door when I went out.

When I came back and saw the door open, my heart just sank. I ran inside, figuring by now he was long gone, but there he was, sitting in his favorite spot, right where I left him, front legs tucked under his chest, really calm, just looking at me like, *Of course I wouldn't leave*, as if I could've gone away for five years, and he'd still be sitting there when I came back, waiting for me. And I realized how any time I left the room, wherever he was when I left was where he was when I came back. Whenever we went for a walk, he always stayed beside me, never getting too far behind or ahead, so I'd always know he was right there.

And I finally got the message.

Soldier didn't need to show me all the time that he loved me. He knew it and I knew it and that's that. What he was doing was giving me a safe place to put my own love.

It's like he was saying, *I'm never going to leave you. I'll wait for you. I want you to know that I'll always wait for you, that it's safe to love me, that you have a place to put all the feelings you can't give to anybody else because it's too dangerous, because you're worried they won't understand, and they won't wait for you. I'm here. I love you. And I will wait for you. I'm not going anywhere.*

And I just started crying.

That's why I can't let him die alone. I can't let him go too far ahead of me, or fall too far behind me. We walk together. When he gets to the other side, he'll wait for me until I come to pick him up and hold him. And I don't want him to wait a minute longer than he has to.

It's love that put us on the road, Mark, or whoever's reading this. Love is what put us on the bus, and love is what's going to carry me and Soldier across to someplace where we can play forever.

Crazy, huh?

TylerW1998

The only drawback to explaining the Blueness of Me to newcomers is that by now everybody else already knows the story and they've started to develop a sense of humor about the whole thing. So when Peter, the latest member of our merry band of misfits, got on the bus and saw me, before I could launch into my explanation, Shanelle grabbed him, pointed at me, and said "Ohmygod, he just turned this color, what should we do, oh shit, call 9-1-1!" and Peter's grabbing for his cell phone and I'm trying to explain the situation while she's laughing her ass off.

"It's Chronic Smurfitis," she says, and hugs me. "We need to get him back to his village, fast. Sleazy Smurf will know what to do."

Humor is so subjective.

VaughnR

Carolyn and I tried for years to have children, but it never seemed to work out. There was one miscarriage about a year after we got married, and after that, nothing. For a while we thought it was me, but the doctor said everything looked normal. It took a lot more tests, but finally the doc said that Carolyn had this thing called Primary Ovarian Insufficiency that stops the ovaries from functioning properly. We tried different treatments, but none of them worked so finally we gave up. We talked about adoption but never followed through, and settled into being just the two of us together. What with both of us being our folks' only children, I guess we were used to the idea of being on our own.

When Carolyn's dad retired, he and his wife moved to Alexandria, Ohio, because the world was getting too big and busy for them and nothing much ever happened in Alexandria. Before leaving, he asked if I'd run the company in his absence. I'd never seen myself as a boss, sitting in an office moving around pieces of paper all day, but that's where I ended up. Every morning I'd get up at seven, make coffee, two scrambled eggs and toast, moving real quiet because Carolyn liked to sleep in, read the paper (yes, some of us still do that), then walk the two blocks to work, which mainly consisted of requisitioning supplies, walking the floor, and approving purchase orders for the same sixteen kinds of false-faced fiberwood boards that we'd been producing for the last twenty years. At seven p.m., half an hour after everyone else left for the day, I'd finish the day's paperwork, close up the office and walk the two blocks back home. Most days I'd spend the walk thinking about whether we'd done better or worse than the day before, or trying to guess what Carolyn was going to make for dinner that night.

Other days, though, I used to think about sneaking into the car when I got home, driving to the airport, and taking the first plane out to anywhere: Bali, Rome, Berlin, Hawaii, or any of the other places I'd never been. I began to wonder if I was living my life or my life was living me. But I always tucked the thought away before walking past the car in the driveway and through the front door.

There was only one time when things kind of got away from me a bit. I was working late one evening after everyone else had gone home, approving a bunch of purchase orders, when I realized I'd grabbed the wrong file from the cabinet. This one was from five years earlier. I got them confused because both sets of orders were from the same construction company in Ohio, for the same things, in the same style, in the same amounts they'd been ordering since Carolyn's dad opened the company. Looking at those purchase orders side by side was like looking at five years of my life doing the same thing, over and over and over.

The only way I can describe what happened next is that everything went all upside down in my head. One minute I'm staring at those two identical sets of paper, heart racing, hands shaking harder and harder, and for a second I think I'm having a heart attack but I guess it wasn't because the next thing I remember is sitting on the floor in the middle of my office, the filing cabinets tipped over and papers scattered all over the floor, the desk and the window blinds half torn off, and all the framed pictures on my desk are broken and there's glass everywhere.

I didn't move for a long time, just sat there, breathing hard, in case whatever happened might happen again, but it didn't, so I called Carolyn to say I had to work late and spent the next couple of hours putting it back the way it was. I picked up the cabinets, pulled the blinds all the way up so you couldn't tell they were torn, threw the broken glass into the recycling bin, then walked the two blocks home and tried really hard never to think about it again.

My folks passed away just after I turned fifty. My mother went first of complications from pneumonia—she was always fragile that way—and my father passed a year later of a stroke. Not long after that, Carolyn's folks also started doing poorly. Sunsetting, the doctors call it. So we sold the company, cashed out a pretty decent retirement fund, and moved to Alexandria to look after them. Back when Carolyn and I got married, we used to talk about growing old together and facing the end side by side with love and courage. When our conversations got too serious, she'd sing, to the tune of that old nursery rhyme "A-Hunting We Will Go": "Together we will go, together we will go, heigh-ho the derry-o, together we will go." It made her laugh every time. And sure enough, here we were, together on a road that was a lot shorter in front of us than it was behind us.

Carolyn's dad died about a year after we moved to Alexandria, and her mom two years later. Once they were gone, I thought we might travel a bit. We had the money, we could have afforded it, and neither of us had been much farther than Chicago. I talked to her about Bali and Hawaii and Rome and Berlin, but, see, Carolyn had allergies and bronchial problems that never quite cleared up after a bout of pneumonia a few years earlier, and she thought it was too risky to go messing around with airplanes and recycled hotel air, and I couldn't leave her to go traipsing around the world by myself, so—

Okay. Stop it.

I need to stop dancing around this, quit trying to justify why I did what I did like I'm in a courtroom. That's all I've been doing since it happened, running the reasons through my head over and over as if they'd make a difference.

Just get to the point. Say the words. You can do it.

Okay. Here it is.

I killed my wife.

I killed Carolyn.

Seeing it written out like that somehow makes it seem smaller than it is. I thought it'd feel more like an explosion. But it's a relief to finally admit it.

The turn started when Carolyn got real sick two years ago. I won't go into what it was and how she got diagnosed and how we reacted to the news because once you hit sixty, there's really only two kinds of illness: ones where you get better and ones where you don't. This was the latter. She declined pretty fast, and by the end of the year she couldn't get out of bed anymore. I put in a respirator beside the bed to help her breathe, and paid a nurse to come in twice a day to keep track of her condition and help out with feeding, bathing, and other necessities.

After a while, Carolyn stopped talking. She'd just lie there and sleep. Sometimes her eyes would flutter open for a few seconds, but they were always focused somewhere past the wall, not on me or the nurse. Most days I don't think she even knew we were there. When animals know they're going to die, they go somewhere quiet where they can be alone. Carolyn couldn't go somewhere quiet, so I think she found that alone-place somewhere inside her head.

The night it happened, I'd finished turning her and tucking her back in for the night. When someone's bedridden, you have to turn them twice a day so they don't get bedsores, because the sores can form underneath, where you might not see them, and when they break they can get infected and you won't know there's a problem until they get septic. I was going to head to my room and get some sleep, but instead I stood by the bed for a while. Her eyes were closed, cheeks pale, and the only sounds in the room were the beep of the respirator and her forced breathing.

"We probably should've traveled after all," I said, though I knew she couldn't hear me, "before all this happened. Yeah, you might've gotten sick from the travel, but it wouldn't have made much difference since this started pretty soon afterward."

And the more I thought about that, the more I got mad.

We *could* have traveled, *could* have gone places and done things, but she always said no, it was too risky.

I could've gone to college out of state to study architecture, or pursued a job as commercial designer for that big firm in Los Angeles, but she said no, it was too risky.

Everything I ever wanted to do, she was right there to say no, be sensible, take the safe route, stay here, don't put yourself on the line, don't take a chance because you might fail.

And if you're wondering why no always trumps yes, it's because when you're married it takes two to say yes but only one to say no. Besides, there's no risk in saying no. No means everything stays the same, you're in control, and you don't feel like you've lost out on anything. No is safe, no is *always* safe, but saying yes is dangerous because anything can happen.

For coming onto fifty years, my life had been one great big pile of no. Anything I wanted to do or try, any place I wanted to go, anything that meant anything to me, it was all no, no, no, no, no, no, and no.

And for the first time since that day at the office, I felt my blood pounding in my veins and my hands were shaking and suddenly all those years of lost opportunities rose up inside me with a fury I can't even describe. I'd wasted my life in a job I never wanted in the first place. If I'd been the one who was afraid to take chances, that'd be one thing, but I wasn't. *She* was the one who was always afraid! Her parents, *they* were afraid! And I listened to them and went along with it even when I knew in my heart that I was making a mistake, because I was trying to do the right thing, so yes, I have to take my share of blame for that, but it's not fair! It's not right to be in your sixties and realize that everything in your life that could have taken you to new places, everything that mattered, everything that could have made *you* matter, has passed you by and now it's too late and your life is one big catalog of missed opportunities and there's no going back. You're done and it's over and there's just the not-very-long wait until the game is called on account of darkness and they shovel dirt over you.

I never even had the courage to confront her because I didn't want to hurt her *and she knew it.* She knew I would always let *no* trump *yes* because it was easiest and safest for *her*. So I smiled and shrugged and said *I'm totally fine with that* and *It's not important* and day after day denied the anger that was eating me alive instead of telling her what this was doing to me or saying, *Fine, then I'll go without you.*

And as I stood beside the bed, my breath coming fast and shallow, hands shaking with decades of unspoken anger, I realized that there was a way for me to show her *exactly* how I felt about a lifetime of no, and before I had a chance to think about it, I reached for the respirator valve and turned off the air.

For a moment, nothing happened. The life signs monitor was the only sound in the room, beeping every ten seconds.

Then she gasped and arched her back, fingers stretched out and clawing the air, eyes wide, mouth open, trying to suck air with lungs that refused to obey. She couldn't scream, so the monitors did it for her, shrieking in the rack behind me.

Her terrified eyes found mine, saying, *What are you doing, turn the valve back on, there's still time, don't do this, save me!*

I reflexively reached for the valve to turn the air back on, but then everything inside me got real quiet. I lowered my hand and looked down at her. "No," I said.

It was the first time I'd ever said it to her.

"How do *you* like it for a change? No! You hear me?! *No! NO!*"

Her eyes clouded over as she arched again, body trembling, gasping for air, hands clenched into tight fists, opening and closing over and over, faster and faster and then—

And then she just stopped. She was still looking at me, but after a bit I realized she wasn't blinking. It felt less like she'd died and more that she just kind of forgot to keep living, the way a thought gets away from you. The monitors screamed that there was a problem, but I waited another five minutes before opening the respirator valve and dialing 9-1-1, just to be sure.

When the ambulance came out, they checked to confirm she was dead, then ran back the data from the monitors to figure out what happened. That's when I began to get scared and I looked at Carolyn, her eyes still open. *Thought you'd get away with it, didn't you? Told you it was too risky.*

But when they finished reading back the charts, they said it looked like she'd died of cardiorespiratory failure. They said they could do a full autopsy if I wanted more information, but I said no for obvious reasons. Most folks don't know this, but once you're past a certain age, coroners only perform autopsies if somebody in the family asks for one. When you're old and wired up to a machine that breathes for you and keeps you alive second by second, nobody's especially mystified if you fall over dead one day. *PARSON THOMAS, 83, DIED IN HIS BED TODAY, FOUL PLAY SUSPECTED* is a headline no one has ever published and never will.

Her funeral a week later was a small affair because neither of us had any relatives closer than second cousins. After we put her in the ground I walked from the cemetery to the house, about two miles in all. Not really thinking about anything. Just numb, I guess. When I finally got home, I sat on the bed, hands folded, and looked at myself in the vanity mirror where Carolyn used to sit and do her makeup.

Well, now *what do I do?* I thought.

And I didn't have an answer.

When the life insurance check came a month later, I walked it down to the bank. I must've been preoccupied thinking back to what happened that night because I didn't hear the teller when she said "Checking or savings?"

"Checking or savings?" she asked again when I glanced up. "God knows you don't want to take it in cash," she joked. "Way too risky!"

An hour later, after being referred to the head teller, the assistant bank manager, then finally his boss, I walked out the door with eighty-two thousand dollars in cash just to spite her.

I already had enough in my savings account to get by for whatever time was left to me, so I decided to treat the cash as mad money. I stacked it on the kitchen counter and just looked at it for a few days while I tried to figure out what to do next. I wanted to use the money for something good, and thought about donating it to the church Carolyn and I joined after moving to Alexandria, but they'd never gone out of their way to make us feel at home. The minister even forgot Carolyn's name twice during the funeral. So I made some charitable donations to a food kitchen, a homeless shelter outside town, and a few other places, but that barely touched the total.

I could travel, I thought, *finally see some of those places I always wanted to visit.* But there's not much fun in going alone, so that option kind of dried up on the frying pan. I took a couple of classes in self-defense, mainly to tone the old muscles up a bit because when you live alone it never hurts to know you can take care of things if there's a problem, like with what happened at the concert. Even thought about going back to school for that architecture degree, but there wasn't much point since I'm too old for anybody to hire me as a first-time designer. Buying a fancy car didn't make sense because there was no place for a hundred miles in any direction worth driving to in a Ferrari or a Porsche, and it'd probably get stolen anyway.

Then the guilt started showing up in force, creeping in during the night when I was trying to sleep, then coming back the next day when I thought I could distract myself with TV or movies or reading. Her eyes were all I could see.

Ending Carolyn's life had not begun my own, it just removed the routine of years without providing anything new in its place.

I'd been trained not to do what I wanted; now that I had the time, the money, and the opportunity, I couldn't think of one god-damned thing I wanted to do.

When I was a kid, there was a pony ride in a vacant lot downtown. For a dime a shot, you could ride the pony five times around a circular track bordered inside and out by guard rails. It was a pretty good deal at the time, but I always felt bad for the pony, penned up all day every day, just going round and round in circles.

One afternoon, I was coming home late from school and saw the owner unlock the guard rails and walk the pony to a holding area at the back of the lot. I ran over to the fence, all excited. At last the pony would be free, and he could do anything he wanted.

So what'd he do?

He walked round and round in circles. Because that's all he knew.

Saddest goddamn thing I ever saw.

And I decided that if that's going to be my life, a pony going around in circles until I fall over dead, then I might as well end it now and be done with it.

I'd just started going on the internet, researching ways to kill myself that wouldn't hurt or be too messy, when I saw Mark's ad. I figured if I'm gonna go, I may as well do it with a bunch of like-minded folks. As I fired off the email, I could hear Carolyn's voice in my head saying that this was probably some kind of scam, that once I got to the rendezvous whoever was behind this ad would show up to kill me or steal the life insurance money I'd decided to bring along as an emergency fund.

It's dangerous, I thought. *It means taking a risk.*

Good, and long overdue. Let's do it. Finally. Let's take a risk.

Live dangerous, die young.

Well, one out of two, anyway.

———————————

AdminMark

Karen_Ortiz

We stopped for the night at this cute little hotel called the Cozy Up 2 Us Inn. Since by now there was a lot of personal stuff on board, Mark said that some of us should always sleep on the bus, so Dylan, Theo, Zeke, and Mark took the bunks while the rest of us went inside. We were all pretty tired, and the mattress pad on my bed was so thick and soft that even the Spider was happy to call it a night.

After breakfast (noon again . . . do suicidal people like to sleep late even when they're not depressed?), Mark said he had a surprise for us. We drove twenty minutes to the River Wild Shopping Mall, which had closed down a few months earlier and was going to be demolished so the state could build a high-tech prison. That feels a little redundant, but maybe that's just me.

I'd never been inside a shopping mall that was completely empty. Even in the early mornings when there usually aren't a lot of shoppers, there were still salesclerks getting ready for the day and food-court employees and music coming from the PA system. Now there was just us and Peter's security guard friend who was the only one on duty because the owners didn't want to spend money for more than that since the place was going to be torn down soon anyway.

The strangest part was that there were still Christmas decorations up and signs announcing sales, and the stores hadn't been completely emptied. The guard said that the big, expensive stuff like TVs and furniture had been taken out, but there was no point in moving the rest because by the time it got counted, boxed, and shipped to other stores, the perishable stuff would have expired and the extra moves would've damaged the rest too much to sell. It was cheaper to bulldoze it along with the mall and write off the loss. I found that really annoying. I mean, they could've donated it to charity or a homeless shelter that would've picked it up for free, but I suppose that's against the rules of capitalism. Easier to throw up the fences and pay a guard to keep people out.

"Here's the deal," Mark said, "and just so everyone's clear, this was Peter's idea, so if it sucks, blame him. It's half performance art, half psychodrama, and half letting off steam."

"That's one hundred and fifty percent," Tyler said, because nerd.

"My degree is in Creative Writing, not Math, so as long as it works in a sentence, I'm fine." I was glad to see Mark was having fun with this. He'd seemed kind of down the last few days, and this was a nice break in routine. Besides, it's good for him to let someone else have an idea once in a while.

"It's all about closure," Peter said, walking toward us with a baseball bat he'd liberated from one of the stores. "In counseling sessions, when the patient needs to take out their anger at somebody they can't hit or who's dead, the therapist will substitute a pillow, a punching bag, or one of those weighted inflatable balloons that look like clowns, the kind you can hit all you want and they keep coming up—"

"Weebles!" Zeke said, cradling his cat inside his army jacket. "I found one in my uncle's basement under a bunch of magazines from the seventies. That's what was written on the box. 'Weebles wobble, but they don't fall down!'"

"That works," Peter said. "Your boss being a dick? Hit the Weeble. Mad at your sister? Hit the Weeble. Got a bunch of repressed rage at your dead father? Beat the shit out of that Weeble. We've all got Weebles, and some of them put us on the road to where we are today. So why not vent some of that anger on our way out?"

He went on from there. Like, a lot, because Peter really loves the sound of his own voice. Running it through the *Can we please just get to the point* filter, he said this was less about expressing our anger against individual people and more about striking out at the symbols of all the things that had hurt us or let us down. So yeah: performance art. Therapy. Acting out.

Vengeance.

Vaughn thought it was a stupid idea and said so. Thank you, Vaughn! "I'm not going to beat up a shopping mall," he said.

"Then don't. Anybody who wants to pass, not a problem. For those who want to come and play"—and here he hefted the baseball bat—"there's a sporting goods store with baseball bats and hockey sticks, and some leftover two-by-fours, pipes, and rebar in the maintenance office."

"Whether you take part or not, if you could journal about this, it would be a really cool addition to the story," Mark said. Like I wasn't already pulling my weight. I'm starting to feel like the Dr. Watson of our group. *The game's afoot!*

"Let's go!" Peter yelled and ran off, his voice echoing through the mall. "Last one to strike out at our imperialist oppressors is a Trotskyite stooge!"

Some people stay in college way too long.

TylerW1998

Baseball bat in hand, I sit on a bench beside a dry, empty fountain, and decide I don't want to do this. I don't want to break anything, and I'm not mad at anyone.

Lisa, on the other hand, is having the best day of her life.

Crash! and a mall directory goes to the floor in a spray of glass as she runs past me into a Sephora, busting up cosmetics counters and displays, then racing back the other way to take out her next target, laughing and whooping like the Road Runner in those old Warner Bros. cartoons. *Meep-Meep-WHAM!*

"Come ON!" she says, dragging me off the bench and up the escalator to the next floor. "Batter up! Bottom of the ninth! Battah battah battah, go go go go GO!"

Swear to god, she's a UFO in human form.

So now I'm feeling even more like a stick in the mud with a baseball bat (which I guess makes it *two* sticks in the mud) as I walk around looking for something to hit even though I don't much feel like hitting anything. I feel stupid. Worse than stupid. I feel like one of those zombies from George Romero's *Dawn of the Dead*, wandering a shopping mall looking for something from my earlier life that I can't quite remember, just walking back and forth until the rotting flesh slides down my legs and puddles around my ankles like old socks.

Then I see it, beside the entrance to a clothing store.

A full-length mirror.

A *blue* full-length mirror, with me right in the middle, blue on blue.

I don't attack it. I don't break it. I don't raise the baseball bat and smash my reflection into a million pieces because I'm not that much of a cliché, okay?

Instead of me hitting the mirror, everything I see in the mirror hits *me*.

The shopping mall is blue in the reflection.

The stores are blue, the baseball bat is blue, Lisa beating the shit out of Ronald McDonald is blue. Both of them are blue. *All* of it is blue.

And I realize that I've been looking at the world through this blue filter ever since I got diagnosed. When I meet someone for the first time, I explain why I look this way before even saying my name. My illness actually walks into the room before me. It's bad enough that I let it take center stage, defining and literally coloring every relationship and conversation. What's worse is that I've been using it as an excuse to hold back, so I don't have to engage with other people, so I can stay stuck inside my own self-limiting self-pity . . . *the illness won't let me do this, the illness won't let me do that, the illness might not let me get all the way to San Francisco* . . . hiding so far inside the blue that my whole world looks like this mirror, and yeah, okay, on reflection (ha!) maybe that *is* an obvious metaphor, maybe I *am* a cliché, and maybe all of that has been obvious to everybody else, but *I* never had that thought before because there are some things you never really understand until it's five seconds to midnight.

I've been doing it all backwards, like I'm the disease that's living in this body instead of a body that has to live with a disease. I've been quiet when I should have roared, even if that meant coughing up blood; I've sat silently while others walked or danced instead of running flat-out even if it meant falling over dead because at least I would have *done* something instead of letting the disease define me.

That stops now. Maybe I *won't* make it to San Francisco, maybe I *will* fall over dead tomorrow or the next day, but that doesn't matter anymore. What matters is making sure that however many minutes I have left *count* for something. So I'm not going to hold back anymore, and I'm not going to be blue. Not anymore.

And I know just how to start.

I walk away from the mirror and leave the baseball bat leaning up against the glass. I don't need it. I don't need to hit anything or be angry at anybody.

I need to dance.

Let's go.

SunnyShanelle

The mannequins in the clothing store window still have their clothes on: skinny dresses on skinny plastic bodies, just like the skinny silicone bodies that used to come in here and buy them because only a body that somebody built in a factory or liposuctioned down to the bone could fit. These aren't clothes for real women. Real women have curves, and like my mama said, I got more curves than a mountain road.

Shit, I *am* the mountain.

And this store is the enemy. Has always *been* the enemy.

I laid the hockey stick upside my shoulder and smiled at the nearest plastic face. "Hi, sweetie," I said. "You look like you need something. Trying to figure out what. It's right at the tip of my tongue, you know? What could it be, what could it be? Wait, I know!

"Girl, you need a ham sandwich," I said, and swung hard at the window, BAM!

Goddamn window didn't break. What do they make these things out of, anyway?

I was about to try again when I saw Vaughn staring in the window of a travel service. Not moving, not hitting anything, just staring. I called over to ask if he was okay. When he didn't answer, I figured he didn't hear me, so I walked toward him. "You okay?" I asked again.

"Yeah, I'm all right," he said.

I'm good at knowing when somebody's lying, but you never tell that person *You're lying* because that just makes them lie more. People are funny that way. And though we haven't had much chance to talk since I got on the bus, I can tell that Vaughn's the kind of person who keeps his wounds to himself, same as me, because we don't want to bleed all over other people. So I just stood there beside him for a minute, both of us looking at pictures of places to go around the world. VISIT THE GREEK ISLANDS. EXPLORE THE ROMANCE OF ITALY. THE MYSTERIES OF THE SPHINX AWAIT.

"You ever been to any of them?" I asked.

He shook his head. "No."

"Yeah, me neither. Always wanted to, though."

He nodded. "Yeah, me too."

Then I saw the crowbar in his hand. "Can I borrow that for a second?"

"Sure," he said.

I swapped him for the lame-ass hockey stick. The crowbar weighed a ton and felt solid in my hands. Just what I needed to do some serious damage. But just to be sure, I hauled back and smashed the shit out of the travel agency window before heading back to the clothing store.

"I *said* you need a ham *sandwich*, girl!" And I hit that window so hard that not only did the glass come down like sheets of ice, the swing caught the mannequin and sent her ass over teakettle, wig going one way, necklace going the other, dress hiked up over her silvery head.

Vaughn came up next to me, shaking his head and smiling, and that was good because he hadn't been smiling a minute before. "Well, *that* dummy will never threaten us again," he said.

"Yeah, I didn't like the way she was looking at me."

"So does this make us looters?" he asked.

"You planning to take any of this with you?"

"No."

"Then we're not looters *or* vandals. We're redecorators."

He smiled bigger, like there was some private joke behind his eyes. "Interior designers?"

"Interior *and* exterior," I said, smashing away more of the glass. Then I handed him the crowbar and pointed to another manne-quin. "Your serve."

"We're supposed to hit what we're mad at. I'm not mad at her."

"She's giving me the skunk-eye."

"She is?"

WHAM. Knocked her head clean off, one shot.

"You're a gentleman," I said.

He bowed just a bit. "Thank you, madam."

We laughed. It felt good, then Vaughn's eyes went all soft, like he was trying to figure out how to say something. But before he could get there we heard a loud screech from the speakers and we froze, like: What's that? Are the cops here?

We were about to start running when the screech went away

and the mall got quiet for a second. Then a voice came through the PA system. "This is your DJ speaking!"

It was Tyler!

"It's too fucking quiet in here. Let's fix that."

Then we heard music. Twenty One Pilots. "Goner." I wondered how he knew it was one of my favorites, but I guess it's the favorite for anybody on the way out.

I turned back to Vaughn. "Want to dance?"

"I can't."

"Your leg broke?"

"No, I just . . . I don't know how to dance the way *you* dance."

"Black girls dance same as any other girl, with our feet on the floor and our hearts in our heads."

"I wasn't talking about that," he said, and he looked kind of hurt. "I mean I dance like an old fart dances, not like the way everybody your age dances."

"Then dance like that," I said. "You do you, I'll do me, and we'll meet in the middle."

"We'll look silly."

"Yeah, I know. It'll be great."

Took me about two minutes of dancing around him before the smile finally came back a little, and he danced with me.

Nobody says no to a sunny disposition . . . *and lives!* LOL

Username: PeterWilliamRouth

This is Peter Routh, trying (for the third time) to create this account because every time I try to save it, the program keeps glitching. The last time it switched the font to Comic Sans, and if that sticks I'm killing myself right here, right now.

Okay, file saved, everything looks okay. Will mention the problem to Tyler since he's apparently the resident tech guy and DJ.

I've chosen as my targets of opportunity every ATM and cash register in the mall! If anybody reading this after I'm gone doesn't understand the choice or the metaphor, it won't do any good for me to try and explain. Everybody else, you get it. Meanwhile: two down already!

For number three I smashed the shit out of a Macy's, then started across the mall to a Forever 21 because under the circumstances that name really pissed me off. Then I saw Theo sitting on a bench, writing in a journal.

"What's up?" I said.

"This is my favorite brand of journal: heavy paper so the ink doesn't come through, college ruled so I get the most words per page, faux leather binding because I love the feel of it. I order them online because they're hard to find, but I didn't have a chance to stock up before I left to get on the bus. This is the last one I have and I'm almost at the end. Then I looked in the office supply store on the second floor, and they had a ton of them."

"So why'd you grab just one?"

"It's one hundred and twenty-eight pages. Usually takes me about a month to fill up one of these. Mark says we should be in San Francisco in a week, maybe ten days, so one should be more than enough."

"Okay," I said, "but meanwhile I thought we were supposed to be destroying things."

"I am."

"So what are you destroying?"

Big grin. "The world."

"Fair enough," I said, and continued toward Forever 21. Less talk, more action!

To the barricades!

_____

Karen_Ortiz

I thought this whole thing was a stupid idea downstairs and now that I'm upstairs, I think it's even stupider. I don't have a Weeble, I have a Spider, and it's inside me, not outside, so the only way to hit the thing I'm mad at is to bash myself in the head and that seems counterproductive. The only good part was passing Zeke and his cat in the food court. He was sitting on the counter of a Subway kiosk, opening up a small can of food.

"There wasn't much left inside, but I found some tuna fish," he said, as happy as I've seen him. "It's Soldier's favorite! He hasn't been eating much lately, but this should get him going."

He popped off the top, pinched out a small bit of tuna, and gently put it to his cat's lips. "C'mon, pal," he said, "here you go." His voice was so soft and gentle it almost made me cry.

I kept walking to give him some privacy, and wound up in front of a store selling exercise equipment. The door was already open, so I went inside. Any time I've ever tried to exercise, the pain was so great that I couldn't go more than a few minutes before I had to stop, so the store was as alien to me as the surface of Mars.

I walked down a long row of exercise bikes with gaps where the more expensive machines had been pulled out, leaving the cheap ones behind. By now I was looking for a place to rest for a bit, so I straddled the last bike in the row. It had a video screen and fans that could cool you down and simulate the feel of air blowing past.

I turned on the bike and toggled the fans. They had that smell you get from electronics that haven't been used before, but the breeze felt good. Out of curiosity, I slipped my feet into the pedals, and when I moved them the screen came to life, showing a bike path between two rows of cherry blossom trees. I thought it was an odd choice until I realized that the bike was made in Japan and this was the default screen. I let the image stay. It was pretty.

I turned the pedals some more, and the image moved forward, just a little. I turned them again, moving slowly, careful not to tempt the fire beneath my skin as I glided toward an infinite horizon of cherry blossoms. The pain wasn't too bad, so I risked pedaling faster, pretending that if I pedaled long enough and fast enough I could outrun the Spider and go right through the screen to that peaceful place, and I wouldn't have to die or be in agony, just riding a bike, that one simple thing that everybody else could do. Then the familiar pain started to arc up my legs, searing through my spine, then flashing out into the rest of me. *The Spider's trying to slow me down, to stop me from reaching the cherry blossoms because it knows I'll be safe there.*

I felt tears on my face. *I can make it,* I thought, pushing down the despair. *Just a little farther and I'll leave the Spider behind.*

But no matter how fast I pedaled, the horizon never got any closer, the cherry blossoms always just a little too far to reach. Then the Spider sank its teeth deep into my legs and I could feel myself passing out from the pain. Breathing hard, I grabbed the handlebars and held on tight, stars flashing behind my eyes.

"Wherever you were going, it looks like you almost got there."

I turned to see Dylan behind me, and his face fell when he saw the tears. "Are you all right?"

"Yes . . . no . . . it doesn't matter. It is what it is." I hadn't outrun the Spider at all. Not even close. It was still right there.

I started to get off the bike, but there wasn't any strength left in my legs. I started to tip over, but Dylan grabbed me before I could hit the ground. "Go easy," he said.

He held on as I climbed off the bike, making sure my legs were screwed back on properly. "Sorry," I said, "this must look pretty stupid."

"No, not at all." Then I noticed he was still holding on to me. He must have noticed it about the same time because he started to back off.

"You don't have to let go," I said. "Besides, I'm still a little wobbly."

"You and Bambi, right?"

Before I could answer, Tyler's voice echoed across the mall, followed by Twenty One Pilots' "Goner," and it took everything that had been so awful a minute earlier and made it beautiful. We stood there for a moment listening to the music with his arms around me, the same as he'd done in the parking lot outside the strip club, except now his skin was touching mine.

Don't be an idiot, I thought. *Don't ruin the moment. Don't make it awkward by saying something that'll make him try to find polite ways to say what you both know he'll say.*

But I said it anyway. "Listen, Dylan, I know you're not one of the group, this is just a job, and you have to be respectful, and I know from what you told me about your sister that you'd never do anything inappropriate or wrong, but . . . I just want you to know it's okay to kiss me . . . I mean, if you want."

I didn't look up at him after saying it. Didn't want to see the rejection in his eyes.

Then he reached down and, very gently, raised my chin up so I could see his face. And he kissed me.

It hurt like a sonofabitch.

But I treasured every second of it.

Then we heard a crash as big as the end of the world, followed by Lisa's trademark whoop and Mark's voice booming out.

"We struck the mother lode!" he yelled. "Avengers, assemble!"

LIsa

Ohmygod I haven't had this much fun since forever! If I'd known breaking stuff could be this entertaining I would've turned to vandalism a long time ago! As soon as Peter put the baseball bat in my hands I was like, *Yes! Let's go fuck some shit up!*

I totally lost whatever was left of my mind, and it was great!

I smashed my way into a Cinnabon, the glass door bowing and cracking and splintering like ice, and I kept swinging, boxes of frosting and sugar and powdered cinnamon crashing into the walls and it smelled great and *I* smelled great and I was laughing and falling and getting up covered in sugar and I didn't care, swinging for the bleachers, piles of lemonade cups and straws and stirrers exploding like fireworks and no I don't have a grudge against Cinnabon they were just the first store I saw and I regret nothing and I ran out with the baseball bat over my head, yelling as loud as I could as I smashed into clothing stores and an Apple Store and I totally fucking obliterated Sephora and at those prices don't tell me they didn't have it coming and I hauled back and hit the window of a jewelry store as hard as I could and I guess they use reinforced glass because the bat bounced back hard and clocked me on the side of the head and I just laughed because it was completely fucking hysterical and I kept going, smashing everything that was smashable and it was amazing and I was amazing and then I heard Mark call my name.

"Help me with this!" he said and I think I yelled louder than I've ever yelled before when I saw what he was pushing out the door of a stationery store: a wheeled counter with row after row of greeting cards.

God, I've always hated those fucking things.

I ran up beside him and we were pushing and laughing and tripping and we got to the third-floor railing and Mark yelled "Fire in the hole!" and it crashed through the railing and bounced down two floors BAM-BAM-BAM and when it hit the bottom it EXPLODED in a cloud of colored paper, all red and blue and puppies and rabbits and glitter-glued red lips, WHAM!

"Avengers, assemble!" he yelled and we raced down the escalator, leftover cards snowstorming down from the upper floors as we attacked the mothership. Fuck you, *Get well soon!* Fuck you, *Condolences on your loss!* Fuck you, *Deepest Sympathies* and *Life Goes On* and *Forgive and Forget* and *Life Is Too Short to Be Unhappy*, even though technically I agree with you and fuck you, *Smile When You're Sad*, and fuck you twice, *Serenity Prayer* and *Congratulations Graduate the Future Is Yours!*

Mark jumped on the counter like a caveman bringing down a bear and Karen joined in, and Tyler and Shanelle and Peter and even Vaughn, which surprised the shit out of me, and we were fucking warriors, man, shredding *Hope you're having a great day* and *Just a thought* into confetti, no, a *cardfetti* of hearts and flowers and bees and mountains and rainbows and fragments of *One Day at a Time* and *Let God Do It* and *Surrender to Gratitude* and *Be Awesome*, which I personally tore up because I hate that lie the most out of all the lies they feed us to make us feel we're special for doing nothing so they can keep us quiet and controlled and guilty and stupid! We were paying them all back, and the music was rocking and it was beautiful and everybody was laughing and snowball fighting with envelopes and ribbons and bows and throwing torn paper in the air.

And of course Theresa had to ruin the whole thing.

And I finally fucking lost it.

Hi, I'm Audio Recorder!
Tap the icon to start recording.

TYLER: Okay, recording because shit's going down.

THERESA: I'm just saying—

LISA: Yes, you are, and nobody gives a fuck.

THERESA: We could get in trouble.

LISA: Who cares, we're here to kill ourselves and you're talking about getting in trouble for littering.

THERESA: We could be arrested before we get a chance to—

LISA: Not a problem, bitch. Cops show up, as a personal favor I will totally beat your ass to death with this.

JIM: That's an ugly thing to say.

LISA: Like gets like, babe.

THERESA: When I signed on for this trip, I thought it would be something beautiful.

LISA: And it was right up until you opened your mouth because everything you say is all about you and just about you and you don't even belong here! You're just pissed off at your daddy and acting out and I'm sorry, Miss Fucking Entitlement, but we're here for the real deal, not because we need a time-out.

THERESA: You don't know me.

LISA: I know a fake and a liar when I see one and you need to get the fuck out of my face and off the bus.

ZEKE: I don't mean to jump in but—

LISA: You're a pretender same as you've probably been your whole life, and you and your fuck-buddy here should—

ZEKE: If I can just, I'm sorry—

MARK: Zeke, what is it, man, what's wrong?

ZEKE: I've been trying to feed Soldier, but he's not eating and he hasn't eaten in days and now he's giving me the look, I mean that look, you know, and I think he's gonna go soon, like fast, and I just, I just, ah, shit—

THEO: Oh, Zeke, I'm sorry.

ZEKE: Can we go somewhere, I don't know, somewhere pretty? Maybe by the water? So we can say goodbye. I don't want him to, you know, not in a shopping mall, someplace quiet with tree smells and . . .

MARK: Yeah, we can do that, let me check the map.

PETER ROUTH: It's okay, I know a place.

MARK: All right then, everybody back in the—

END RECORDING

AdminMark

With Peter giving directions, D drove north to the Platte River and looked for a spot to pull over where we wouldn't be too exposed. About two miles from the nearest house we found a road that led down past a bunch of cottonwood trees to a cutout beside the river. I was nervous about getting stuck in the mud, but we pushed on a little farther and parked under a train bridge. There was no way we could be seen from the road, and the other side of the river was just empty land thick with weeds. D said they were bluestem and switchgrass, but they looked like weeds to me, and honestly who gives a shit what they're called, the important thing was that we could park there for a week without being seen, and from the collection of torn blankets, fast-food containers, and beer cans under the bridge, we weren't the first people to figure that out. There was also an old, low-slung rowboat that had been dragged up the incline and tucked under some concrete pilings to keep it safe from the elements until whoever owned it came back to do some fishing.

The Platte drained south to the Mississippi, and where we'd parked it was about half a mile across. It was one of those slow, shallow rivers that sneak up on the land by inches; you could walk five feet into it before hitting any real depth. The sun was getting low, red light ribboning up the water until it faded out where we were standing. Not a bad place for last looks.

While the rest of us stretched our legs, Tyler dug a pit for a fire (I offered to help, but he insisted on doing it himself) and Zeke walked down to the edge of the river and sat on the ground, Soldier cradled in his arms, wrapped in one of his shirts. He nuzzled Soldier's face up alongside his own so they could look out at the water together and started talking to him, real low and soft. From where I was I could make out a few words—*pal* said several times, *I love you*, and *It's okay, you can let go, I'll be right here to catch you*—then I moved off. Some conversations aren't meant for other people to hear.

While everyone else was taking in the view or walking along the river, I took advantage of the momentary quiet to pull D aside so we could go over the next few stops. Driving this far north had pulled us way off course, and this was our second unplanned stop. We'd already been in Nebraska too long (and I bet all kinds of people have said *that* before), and I was worried that we might have to reschedule the rest of the appointments. But D said we could make up the time by taking the 30 nonstop until we hit the I-80. We could then stop for the night in Kearney and be back on schedule for the next pickup at eight in Lexington, our last stop before crossing into Colorado.

We'd just finished working this out when I saw Jim standing behind me. "Can I talk to you for a sec?"

"You already are," I said. "What's up?"

"What happened back at the mall, that wasn't right, man."

"I agree. We can't have that kind of infighting going on."

He nodded for a moment, then glanced over his shoulder to where Theresa was standing by the river. *She put him up to this. Doesn't want to do her own dirty work.*

"Yeah," he said, "and that's why we think you need to choose whether you want Lisa to stay on the bus or us."

Even Dylan looked surprised. "You're kidding, right?"

"No, look, there's just one of her and two of us, so we kind of outvote her, and we bring a lot to the table. Theresa's got tons of credit cards if we get in trouble, I'm good with repairs . . . from what we can see, all Lisa does is yell and make trouble."

"She was here first."

"Yes, she was," Jim said like it shouldn't matter. "Meanwhile, Theresa's tired and upset, so we're gonna wait in the bus while the rest of you do whatever you're gonna do because it's best to keep Lisa and us apart at this point."

"Okay," I said, "let me think it over and get back to you when we're not in the middle of things."

"I appreciate that, because it's real important to keep Theresa on the bus because—"

Whatever he said after that got lost because at that moment all I could hear was Zeke.

I've never heard any man cry out like that. Not even my grandfather when his brother died. There was just this awful sound coming from way down deep inside him, loss and pain and anguish and sadness, and he was rocking back and forth, his face pressed into Soldier's fur. Ever since he'd gotten on the bus, he'd always been smiling, just goofy Zeke and his secret cat, and now he was broken right down the middle and no one knew what to do about it. Then Karen knelt down next to him and put an arm around his shoulders. Theo was next, then Lisa and me and the rest. Zeke was quiet-crying now, but once in a while a sharp *Ah!* slipped out, like his soul was trying to catch its breath.

Everyone was crying. It didn't make any sense. We came on this trip to die, we're *okay* with dying. But there we were, crying with a guy we barely knew, because something he loved more than anything else in the world had just died, leaving him alone in ways all of us could understand.

VaughnR

When Soldier passed, I suggested we give Zeke some space to get himself together, and he seemed to appreciate that. After a few minutes he stood and came over to us, carrying Soldier wrapped in one of his shirts. "Thanks for getting us here," he said, and his breath kept catching in his throat. "You can go on now. We'll be all right."

Mark started to say okay, like he was ready to go, when Tyler asked, "So what're you going to do?" All of us knew what he was really asking. *How are you gonna do it, and do you need any help doing it?*

"Speedball," he said. "I'll get my stuff."

As he headed for the bus, Shanelle must've seen my expression and realized that I had no idea what a speedball was because she said, "Heroin plus coke equals goodbye."

"But what about—" I couldn't bring myself to say *his body.*

"Not our problem," Mark said. "We should get back on the bus and head out so he can do what he needs to do."

"Seriously?" Tyler said. "We're just gonna leave him like this?"

"Everyone agreed when they signed on that if one of us decided to check out early, it's their business and nobody else's."

"We can't just drive off and let him kill himself and lie under the bridge like a dead animal," Theo said. "That's not right."

"I agree," Peter said. Then he glanced over at the pilings under the bridge and I saw an idea come to him. "Give me a hand, Vaughn?"

I knew immediately what he had in mind. "Sure thing."

Before Mark could object, we went up the slope to the rowboat that had been tucked up under the bridge and dragged it down to the waterline. It was pretty old and not in the best shape, but there wasn't much leakage.

It'd do.

"Viking funeral," Theo said, and nodded approval.

When Zeke came back with his bag, we explained what we had in mind. He nodded for a minute, then said "Yeah, cool, I get it," and started pulling out his kit.

"You don't have to rush," Lisa said, and her voice was softer than I'd ever heard from her. "How about we walk you to the door? We won't go through, but we can at least see you out."

"You sure?"

"Yeah," Karen said, "we're sure."

Now it was Lisa's turn to retrieve her bag. When she came back, she walked over to each of us, handing out pills like it was Holy Communion.

She stopped in front of me, held out the bag, and gave it a shake. "Your turn."

Inside were what looked like dried mushrooms and a pharmacy's worth of pills in little plastic bags tied with rubber bands. I picked up one that was filled with pink, blue, orange, and green pills, round with stars or words etched on them. "Don't know what I'm looking at," I said. "I don't think the pharmacy in Alexandria carried anything like this. Pretty colors, though."

"Molly," she said, and handed me one of them. "MDMA. Ecstasy. The lady and I go way back. Good choice."

I started to ask *Is it safe?* and flinched inwardly at the old-man thought behind it. I could imagine Carolyn saying, *You shouldn't take pills from someone else if you don't know what it is or what it does, it's much too dangerous.*

Is it safe? Look at where you are, why you're here, and what you're doing. Does safe really matter?

No, it doesn't, I decided, and dry-swallowed the pill.

We hadn't heard any traffic from the road in a while, so Dylan figured it was okay to run some music from the bus. As the last of the sun disappeared, Karen and Lisa sat on either side of Zeke, their faces cradled against his chest, with the rest in a tight circle around them. Nobody spoke. There was just the music and the moment.

And me, feeling stupid.

I wasn't part of their tribe. It wasn't my "scene," my demographic, or my music. Not by a long shot. Seeing them clustered together, I felt a million miles away and a thousand years old, once more on the outside looking in.

Then just as suddenly, I wasn't.

I don't know if it was the Molly or the Moment, but it felt like I was seeing their faces for the first time. Their voices were warmer, their looks in my direction an invitation. *Why are you sitting so far away?*

I felt a sting of tears at the joy of being connected to these strange but beautiful people who had accepted me as one of their own. And I could feel every thought behind Zeke's decision to go out tonight, his profound loss but also the love that looked back at him from the other side of the infinite. *I'm waiting for you, I'm here, I'll always be here.*

We'll walk you to the door.

Now I understood what that actually meant.

As if watching myself from somewhere outside, I leaned in and wrapped myself into the cluster. Someone took my hand and I didn't know who it was and it didn't matter because we were all the same person, joined by the music and stars that were peeking out overhead. I'd never felt that close to anyone before. They were me and I was them and we were *us*.

And we were beautiful.

We held on for a long time, not speaking, until I felt Zeke say *It's time* before he actually spoke the words. We sat back to give him room as he pulled out a small plastic bag containing a yellow-white ball the consistency of chalk. Being new to these things, I didn't know what constituted a fatal dose, but when Lisa saw it, her eyes went soft and wide. "Yeah, that'll do it," she said.

He cooked the speedball over a small fire, mixing it with water and lemon juice until it became liquid, then drew it into a syringe that glittered with the moonlight.

Then he found a vein and pushed.

"Boat's ready," Dylan said. I hadn't noticed he was gone until he came back. "I took a road flare from the bus and put it in the boat along with the sheets. When you start to feel the fall, light up the flare and hold it up as long as you can. When it goes down, we'll know you're gone."

Zeke nodded and Dylan hugged him. They *all* hugged him, and he let them pet Soldier to say goodbye. I stood back a bit to let them have their moment, but then Zeke came over and stood in front of me. In the dim light his tired eyes looked like black basketballs, but his face was luminous as he stared past me to his intent. Then he pulled me close.

"Be good, man," he said, his voice lower than before and distant, like a part of him was already gone. "They need you more than you know. And thanks. Wish I could've known you better. Next time, right?"

"Yeah, next time."

"Say goodbye, pal," he said, and I petted Soldier's sleeping face.

"Okay," Zeke said, forcing his voice back up, loud and strong and defiant. The deep breath before the plunge. "Where's my ride? Who's got my wheels?"

Dylan and Tyler pushed the boat forward until it touched the water and bobbed slightly. "Right here, Zeke."

He started toward them, then wobbled somewhat and stumbled. Theo and Peter moved to help him, but he waved them off, determined to make it on his own.

Hands shaking from the speedball, Zeke settled into the boat and tried to figure out where the oars went and which end to use. "Don't worry about it," Tyler said. "The current's slow but strong. Once you're in the middle of the river, it'll take you where you want to go."

"All the way down the Mississippi," Peter said.

"Beauty," Zeke said, and they helped him push off. He didn't look or call back to us. He'd said everything that needed to be said in this life.

We watched in silence as the current caught the boat and it began drifting slowly downstream, barely visible in the moonlight. The only sound was the slow lapping of the river and our breathing as we strained to see into the night.

Just as the boat was about to pass from view, a bright red flash lit up the night and I could see Zeke holding the flare high, Soldier cradled in his arms, the sight brave and noble and sad and glorious.

Then the flare guttered low for a second and we thought that might be it, but he raised it high again. *Like you told Soldier, it's okay, just let go.*

Then the flare dropped out of sight and the river was dark.

"He's gone," Karen said, her voice a hoarse whisper.

Then with a sudden WHOMPH! the gas-soaked sheets in the boat ignited. Flames rose into the sky, red light reflecting in the water like a second sunset.

The boat receded into the darkness until the fire dimmed and disappeared from sight, taking with it everything Zeke had ever said or done, and everything he might've said or done in all the years he might have had left. And that's when this whole thing finally hit me.

I think it hit everyone else, too. Because there's a world of difference between hearing about someone dying and watching it happen right in front of you.

Now it was real, for all of us, and the feeling of connection that had been so strong a moment earlier was replaced by the sense that we were looking at each other from different ends of a telescope. I was at the end of all the choices I'd made in life. I'd had my run and now I was done. But they were still at the beginning of their choices, and someone had to say something about it. It wasn't my place, and I didn't know if they wanted to hear it, or if they'd think I was being patronizing, but it needed saying and it needed saying now.

"Is everybody still good with where all this is going?" I asked. "Seeing what we just saw, feeling what this does, what it means and what it costs, is everybody still okay with giving up all your tomorrows? Because if any of you has any doubt whatsoever, now's the time to mention it."

They looked at each other, and I could see that they understood why I'd asked the question, and why I *had* to ask it now. The answer was already in their eyes as Karen said it for them. "Yeah, we're good."

Just like that. So much meaning crammed into three words.

I nodded. "Then I guess we're doing this."

"We should go," Mark said. "Just in case anybody saw the fire." He seemed irritated by something, but at that moment I didn't much care what had crawled up his ass and died.

As we started toward the bus, I glanced back at the river and imagined Zeke running through a green field with Soldier chasing close behind, laughing and playing. Free at last.

"Godspeed," I said, and to my surprise the others repeated it. Godspeed.

AdminMark

That didn't go the way it should've, the way everybody agreed it was *supposed* to go. I liked Zeke as much as anybody else, but now we're *all* screwed because of what happened. When I said we should give him the privacy to do what he was gonna do, I was sure they'd respect that and get back on the bus. Who would've thought Tyler would lead the insurrection? The only good thing is that, as far as I can tell, nobody saw what we did—and that's the operative term, what *we* did, not just what Zeke did—and I don't think any of us are inclined to talk about it to outsiders, so we should be able to ride this out quietly, but still: not good. At all.

PeterWilliamRouth

From: Peter Routh GrailHunterZero@gmail.com
To: Tammy Routh TamlynRouth2728@ucla.edu
Subject: Re: Worried

Hey, Tammy

"Tammy, allow me to introduce you to the Center of the Universe. I think you two will have much in common."

Just kidding but not really. When have you ever known me to be influenced by someone else's opinion? Remember how you looked up the word "stubborn" in the dictionary and said it had my picture next to it? Whatever I do or don't do, it's because I choose to do it and for no other reason. Nobody else is to blame and nobody else gets to take the credit.

So don't worry about me. Everything will be clear soon enough, and if it isn't, I sent a letter winging your way yesterday that should explain everything in more detail. Given the USPS, I'm sure it'll arrive sometime between now and the heat death of the universe.

You are my sister and I love you, and you have nothing to apologize for or feel responsible about.

If you really want to do something for me: be happy. That's all I've ever wanted.

Love, P.

Tammy Routh TamlynRouth2728@ucla.edu wrote:

> I tried to call you yesterday, but all my calls went to VM so I tried the dorm but they said nobody's seen you since some big party. Please let me know you're okay and you're not going to do anything you shouldn't. I know I got mad and said some stupid things the last time we talked and THAT whole subject came up, but it was only because I love you and I'm scared you might actually follow through. The worst thing in the world for me would be to think my anger pushed you over the edge into doing something stupid just to prove to me that you could do it when I said you couldn't. I didn't mean you were a coward or

afraid to do it, just that I think you're too smart to do anything like that.

I haven't told Mom and Dad you're off the grid yet, I don't want to worry them if it's nothing. Again, I'm not mad or upset, I'm just worried.

SunnyShanelle

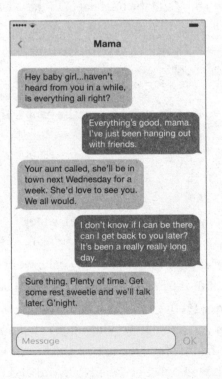

AdminMark

To: (Almost) Everyone
From: Mark Antonelli MDAntonelli@gmail.com
Subject: Moving On

I know we're all exhausted, but we need to keep going until we hit Kearney if we're going to make the next pickup on time. Besides, there aren't any decent motels between here and there, and with everything that happened tonight I think we could all do with a good night's sleep.

I'm sending this as an email rather than just telling everyone because I'm leaving TheresaAndJim out of the chain. We had a good vibe going before they showed up, and since then it's been really tense and it's obvious that some of you want them gone (hi, Lisa). I'd be more inclined to give them time to sync up with everyone else if they were contributing or journaling the trip, but they haven't made a single entry and that's the price of admission, so I'm making the executive decision to boot them off.

But I don't want a scene, so when we get to Kearney, I'll suggest that we all sleep in the next morning and get back on the bus at noon. While they're asleep, the rest of us will load up at ten and take off. Yeah, they'll be pissed, but by this point I think inertia is the only thing still keeping them here and they'll be just as happy as us to get away from the tension.

Ping me back to let me know you got this so we don't end up leaving without you.

————————————

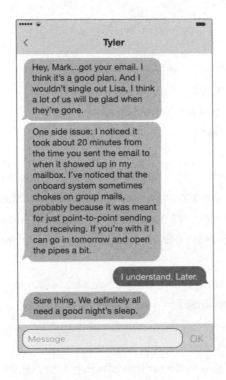

Tyler

Hey, Mark...got your email. I think it's a good plan. And I wouldn't single out Lisa, I think a lot of us will be glad when they're gone.

One side issue: I noticed it took about 20 minutes from the time you sent the email to when it showed up in my mailbox. I've noticed that the onboard system sometimes chokes on group mails, probably because it was meant for just point-to-point sending and receiving. If you're with it I can go in tomorrow and open the pipes a bit.

I understand. Later.

Sure thing. We definitely all need a good night's sleep.

Message   OK

Karen_Ortiz

When I finally got into my room—had to get the key recharged twice when it wouldn't work—I was exhausted but still couldn't sleep. Everything that happened with Zeke kept running through my head. It was beautiful, but also tragic and devastating and even after I got into bed I still couldn't stop crying. Sometimes I didn't even know the tears were there until I felt something wet rolling down my cheek.

And I didn't want to be alone with that.

So I called Dylan, which was silly because he was literally across the hall but it would've been weird to show up at his door in the middle of the night, but I really needed to talk to someone who would care. We spoke for nearly half an hour, then he said this is silly and I should just come over. So I went across the hall and we kept talking. By now it was almost two a.m., and we were both tired and I knew I should go back to my room, but we were on the couch together and I didn't want to leave, so I asked if I could stay with him.

At first he said no, concerned that after everything that happened earlier I wasn't thinking clearly or making good decisions. And maybe that's true, but I think there's a time and a place for bad decisions, and if this was one of them, I was fine with that. So I talked him into it, but he said that nothing could happen between us that night because he wouldn't feel right about it. The trouble with gentlemen is that they can be a real pain in the ass, but I pinky-swore I'd be good and we climbed into bed and passed out.

When I opened my eyes again, I was spooned behind Dylan, my left arm under his head. Careful not to wake him, I peeked past him to the bedside clock: 7:45 a.m. He'd set the alarm for eight. So I had fifteen minutes to make this happen.

I reached around and lightly stroked his chest. I guess army guys learn how to shut out the world when they sleep because he didn't even move. Okay, challenge accepted. I let my hand drift south until it slipped beneath his shorts. I'd never touched a penis before, and I was surprised by how soft it felt. They were always so rock hard in porn that it never occurred to me it could be this soft and velvety. I felt a thrill go through me, like an explorer who had just discovered a whole new country.

Then it twitched, and I knew Dylan was awake.

"What are you doing?" he asked without turning around, his voice low.

"What does it feel like I'm doing?"

"We had an agreement."

"Yes, we did," I said, but didn't remove my hand. "We agreed nothing could happen last night. It's not night anymore."

"Still, we probably shouldn't do this."

Aha! He said probably! His dick finally got his brain on the line.

I tightened my hand. "There's someone down here who disagrees with you."

He rolled over to face me. "I don't want to take advantage—"

"You're not," I said. "That's why I made the first move, so technically, *I'm* taking advantage of *you.*"

"That's a first," he said, and smiled.

"I like you," I said, "and I'm going to be gone soon, and I don't want to be by myself for whatever's left. Don't send me back to my room alone."

He studied my eyes until he could see the truth in what I was saying, then nodded.

The clock chimed eight o'clock.

He turned it off, rolled back, and kissed me.

As he moved down my body, I didn't tell him that this was technically my first time. I didn't want to put that kind of pressure on him. I'd seen enough porn to know what to do and how to do it. His touch was so gentle, knowing how sensitive I am to pain, and his eyes kept meeting mine to make sure I was okay.

I braced myself as he started to enter me. I'd already been opened by toys, but I was always in control of the motion so I could back off whenever it started to hurt. Now he was in charge, and I tightened, anticipating the pain, but he was so careful as he entered that there was no pain at all, and he held himself up off my body so we only joined at the soft places. It felt amazing, so different from the toys, and so *warm* . . . I'd never considered that part.

There's another person inside me, I thought, *and he's keeping the Spider at bay.*

I came quickly, probably because I wasn't expecting to. It just kind of slipped through when I wasn't looking, and when I glanced up, Dylan had a big grin on his face. "You're very proud of yourself, aren't you?" I asked.

"I have no idea what you're talking about," he said, and started moving faster now that I'd come, like I'd given him permission to enjoy himself.

When he got super hard, I could tell he was about to finish, and he started to pull out. "No," I said, though I could barely talk by now. "Inside."

"You sure?"

"I want to know what it feels like."

"What do you—" he started to ask, but I wrapped my legs behind him and pulled him in hard, my arms tight around him as he came.

Once he could breathe again, he finished the sentence. "What did you mean, what this feels like?"

When I told him the truth, he had the most stricken look on his face. "Oh God, I'm sorry, you should've told me, I would've . . . I don't know . . . made it special, or—"

I told him I didn't want that. I wanted to feel it like every other woman does, almost casually. I didn't want to make a thing about that part; I wanted it to be about us, right then, and nothing else.

He said he understood, and I think he actually did, just a little.

Then he glanced past me at the clock. "Shit! Nine fifteen! We gotta go, but—"

I could see that he didn't want to cut the moment short, still concerned about making it Special.

"You're right," I said. "You should stay in bed for a bit longer."

"Okay—"

"That way I have first dibs on the shower!"

Then I kissed him, flicked his nose, and ran into the bathroom, laughing and slamming the door behind me.

IamTheo

I awoke a little before dawn and couldn't get back to sleep. With four hours to kill before the Great Escape at ten a.m., I decided to work on one of my stories for a while. When I hit a good stopping point, I popped into a group chat that some friends from college started about a year ago. Others joined later, friends-of-friends, many of them deep into the anime/cosplay community. Since everyone's spread out over half a dozen time zones, there's almost always someone hanging out online to text with, but I don't talk as much as I used to; mainly I just lurk and watch the dynamics of the conversation. I like to think of it as my own personal human terrarium.

It's funny how rarely people in my "demographic" ever actually see each other in person. Instead of getting together to party, hang out at a bar, or get in a car and go out to dinner, most of us just text each other. So for us, watching old movies like *Diner* or *American Graffiti*, where everyone sits around a table in big groups, having long talks late into the night, is like visiting a foreign culture for anthropology class. We work, watch TV, or study, mostly alone unless there's a roommate, and at the same time we're texting back and forth to each other. Sometimes we text to the person in the next room because it's easier than getting up and making actual human contact.

It occurred to me recently—did I mention I overthink everything?— that most of what society considers "normal social interaction" is the by-product of the sex urge. Twenty years ago, going out on dates, getting dinners, and hitting parties was essential to getting laid. Sex workers aside, you couldn't just order in orgasms with a side of pizza. Sexual frustration leads to personal frustration leads to blue balls, which leads to *Let's get out of here and go to a club and pick up some chicks or something.* Cars, bars, dinners, and late-night clubbing equaled sex, and sex equals *Thank god, now I can finally get back to whatever the hell I was doing before my hormones kicked the shit out of me.*

Hookup apps and a lack of disposable income swept away most of those mating rituals. Swipe left, swipe right, open the door, fuck, and go back to your life. If even *that's* too much work, there's the latest hands-on sex-tech. Used to be that women had tons of fancy dildos and guys just had blow-up dolls and pocket pussies, which even they couldn't take seriously. Now if a guy gets horny, he fires up porn, pulls out a Fleshlight or one of the other ten zillion high-tech masturbators that can vibrate faster than any human being and don't need to be fed or entertained and gets off, after which he can spend the rest of the day playing video games. And yes, as just noted, women also use toys to get off, but they have a greater inclination toward conversation and community, so the post-orgasm door isn't shut as tightly as it is for men who just need a dick break, a beer, and a first-person shooter to be happy.

Wouldn't First-Person Shooter be a great name for a male sex toy?

The need for sex, particularly among men, fed the socialization machine. But once they could get what they needed through simpler, alternative, and less time-consuming methods, there was less incentive to actually go out and spend money they didn't have or face the dick-shrinking embarrassment of going dutch. Socialization has decreased so much that nearly everyone I know feels shy, like they don't know how to hold a conversation or go on a date or function in a group. They're not sure they have anything interesting to say, and no one tells them otherwise because no one's talking, just texting. I have friends who are "dating," but they only hook up every other week when one of them texts to come over for sex, then they go their separate ways until the next time the Fleshlight breaks down.

And *that's* why there are no cell phones, smartphones, iPads, or laptops in the Silver City of my stories.

Okay, it's coming up on nine thirty and I've killed enough time. My co-conspirators should be slinking onto the bus any time now. On with the Great Escape!

VaughnR

The morning was unusually cool, with a low haze that hovered over the parking lot. Everyone except Tyler was already on board, and while we waited for him, I walked over to where Mark was standing by the door, checking his watch for the tenth time.

"You sure we're doing the right thing?" I said. I'd promised Jim that I wouldn't tell anyone else what he told me at the bar, but now that we were about to dump him and Theresa, I was having second thoughts. "Maybe we should give them another chance."

"No way," Mark said. "We were doing fine until they showed up, then everything turned toxic. Best to ditch their sorry asses and move on."

I was about to press the point when Tyler came out of the motel and waved to us. "Sorry, sorry," he said. "Overslept."

"It's okay," Mark said in a voice that said the opposite, and let him go up the steps ahead of us.

"All right," Mark said as Dylan closed the door behind us, "onward."

Dylan nodded and aimed the bus toward the exit.

It'll be all right, I told myself. *Jim didn't like the tense atmosphere on the bus any more than we did. Maybe the shock of being dumped and having to deal with this on their own will make Theresa more open to reconsidering their path.*

It was a comforting thought. But there was a part of me that didn't believe it for a second.

SunnyShanelle

Mama once said, "You know what the definition of a bore is? Somebody who brings nothing to a conversation but his presence." That was Theresa and her man. They never brought anything good to the group dynamic. We'd be laughing and talking and then they'd show up and chase the fun right out of the room. So nobody minded much when we left the motel without them.

Once we were out of Kearney, we stopped at a diner for breakfast. Vaughn had a coffee and some bread, then said he was going outside to get some air. After a bit I looked out the window and saw him sitting all alone on a bus bench like somebody just broke up with him, so I finished my eggs and left the rest behind because it's not like I'm gonna suffer from a lack of pancakes, though they were pretty good, and walked outside to join him.

"What're you doing out here all by yourself?" I said.

He squinted up at me and shook his head. "Just thinking."

"Those thoughts taking up the whole bench or is there room for me?"

He scooted over and I sat next to him, watching the traffic. I wanted to give him time to say whatever was on his mind. Except he didn't, so I asked what he was thinking about.

"I don't know," he said. "I think I worry too much."

"Worry about what?"

"Nothing . . . everything."

"Think you can narrow that down a little? Maybe pick a spot somewhere between Genesis and Revelations?"

He frowned like he didn't appreciate being pushed, then crossed his arms and leaned back on the bench like *If she's gonna sit here, I may as well talk about it.*

"I'm just thinking about Zeke and TheresaAndJim and what's down the road, and hoping that we *did* the right thing and that we're *doing* the right thing and what's going to happen when we're *done* doing what we're doing. Worrying is what old farts like me do when we feel like the world's getting away from us."

"You're not that old," I said. "Age is just a number."

"And there are some days when I'd agree with that," he said. "Other days, not so much. I'm older than I ever thought I'd be. At least that's how it feels. There's one age where, when you die, people say, *Oh, how sad, he left much too soon.* And another age when they say, *Well, you know, he had a good run.* That's where I am, the stage where all I have to look forward to is mental decrepitude, adult diapers, and trying not to drool when they pull the plug."

"Way too much information on the diapers, but I get it. So what else are you worried about?"

He chewed at the inside of his cheek for a second, then said, "Look, Shanelle, I don't want to bring up the same question I asked everyone back at the river, but you're still young. You're smart, funny, attractive—"

"Pretty would've been better than attractive."

"Okay, pretty," he said, and smiled. "You're the only woman who ever asked me to dance like she meant it, not like it was something she was expected to do. All the more reason to say maybe you shouldn't be doing this. You've got your whole life ahead of you."

"Vaughn, you have no idea how many times someone's said to me, *You've got your whole life ahead of you,* and honestly, it's a curse. It's like somebody sends you to prison for life without parole and when you get there the guard says, *You should be happy, at your age you could be stuck in this little bitty cage for fifty or sixty years! You've got your whole life ahead of you!* Thanks, but no thanks."

I could see he still didn't get it, so I explained. It was the first time I ever talked about it with anyone who didn't have me sitting on a couch under a bunch of diplomas.

I told him about getting dumped by Phil, and how I got tired of being dissed, ditched, and depressed, and went into what my therapist called my "wild-girl stage." I started going to clubs late at night because when it gets near closing time and there's men who still haven't hooked up with anyone, it doesn't matter if you're too skinny or too fat or too ugly or too anything, there's gonna be at least one guy there who wants to fuck you. So I went from no sex to getting fucked almost every night. It was hardly ever the same guy twice, but I didn't care. Every fuck was like a punch in the face to everybody who ever treated me bad or stood me up.

I thought it'd make me feel better to get laid regular, but none of it ever made a difference. I'd come home even more depressed than before. But I kept doing it anyway because what else was I gonna do?

Then one night I went with this one guy to his apartment and I was really drunk and once we were alone he said, "Hit me." And I was like, what? He said it again. I thought it was weird and kind of silly, but I went ahead and hit him, just kind of easy. "No, harder," he said.

So I hit him. "Again," he said. So I did. And then I don't know what happened, but next thing I know I pulled back and just really hit him hard, like all the anger I had at everybody else who hurt me over the years was coming out all at once, and I just kept going at him and hitting him and now he's yelling stop but I don't, I kept hitting him and he's covering his face and I'm crying and finally I ran out and left him behind.

I spent days being scared that he was going to come after me, or tell the police, or sue me, or blackmail me, or do something to hurt me back. I didn't go out because I was afraid of running into him, didn't sleep, I was constantly in the bathroom because my stomach hurt from fear about what he might do or what would happen if my folks found out what I'd been doing.

The more I kept worrying about it and thinking about how I ended up in that situation in the first place and everything I'd been doing, the more disgusted I got and the more I went into a spiral. I hated my life, hated men, hated everybody. I went full-on rage and there was no place to put those feelings and it was tearing me apart and this time nothing helped, not the cutting or the anti-depressants or the drinking, so I was just gonna drive out of this world once and for all, except I didn't have a car but my folks had two, so after they left for church I went in the garage, closed the door, and turned on the engine. Would've worked, too, except they came home early, and when they opened the garage, they found me and pulled me out. I spent the next 72 hours in the hospital under suicide watch, and though I knew by now what to say to get out when the window expired, I was just as firm as ever in my decision that there was nothing left for me in this life, which is why I'm here now. It's not like I don't have choices, it's just that all my choices suck and I'm tired of fighting about it. I want out, that's all.

It was a lot to process, and he spent a long time looking down at his hands. "We all make mistakes, Shanelle," he said, like he was talking about me but at the same time more than me, like there was something else behind his words. "We get angry, we lose control, it's not something we plan and it doesn't make us bad people, it . . ."

He ran out of words for a second. Then he looked back up at me. "This man, the one you met, did he ever come after you?"

"No. But a couple of days after I replied to Mark's ad, I was downtown getting a few things for the trip and I turned around and there he was. I totally froze. He seemed as surprised to see me as I was to see him.

"'I've been looking for you!' he said, and I started to try and defend myself because I was sure he was going to dial 9-1-1, but he just kept on going.

"'What happened that night,' he said, his eyes all wide and excited, 'what you *did* to me . . . could you do it again? Please?'

"He was a complete freak," I said, and just laughed.

Even Vaughn smiled. "And that didn't change your mind about all this?"

"No. What happened was the last step on a road I'd already been on for a long time. I'm done. Besides, there's a part of me that believes in reincarnation, which makes death the ultimate makeover, so I'm putting in a request to come back as a skinny little Asian girl with a fat bank account and a tiny ass."

"I understand, maybe more than you think, and I'm sorry you had to endure all that, Shanelle. You're a beautiful woman and you deserve so much better."

"Beautiful's even better than pretty!" I said, and smiled, making the moment small again. I put my hand on his. "You're a good person, Vaughn. I'm glad we met."

"Thanks, same here," he said, and started to take his hand back, but I locked fingers before he could get free. "Mine!" I said, like the seagulls in *Finding Nemo*. "Mine-mine-mine-mine-mine!"

Got a big old laugh out of him on that one.

And there we sat, holding hands while everyone else finished breakfast, waiting to get back on the road and our journey to the inevitable.

Gonna be the biggest, baddest makeover ever.

———————————

Karen_Ortiz

After lunch I stood outside the diner, eyes closed, face tilted up, taking in the sun, when I felt someone come up behind me. I thought it might be Dylan, but it was Tyler, who asked if he could talk to me.

"I've got kind of a problem," he said, glancing around to make sure nobody could hear us, "and you're the most sensible person here, so I wanted to get your opinion. The other day I noticed we were having some issues with the onboard server that were slowing down the system and I told Mark I could fix it for him. He texted back, *I understand, later,* which I thought meant, *Okay, just not now,* but looking back I think he was saying let's *talk* about it later. Anyway, going off what I thought he said, I started poking around the server, clearing caches and dealing with some latency problems when I saw something I wasn't supposed to see."

"You didn't go poking around in our journals, did you?"

"No," he said, real fast, "no, no, no, no. I could see the file names when I admin'd into the system, but I didn't go near them. No, this was a folder buried deep inside the cache. I found it when I tried clearing the folders automatically and this one wouldn't delete. I thought maybe it was corrupted and would have to be deleted manually, so I opened the folder."

"Okay. So what did you find?"

"Best if you read it yourself, if you're okay with that, so I can get your opinion about what to do. My gut says I should confront Mark about it, but since I found it while I was doing something I probably shouldn't have been doing in the first place, I don't exactly have the high ground, you know?"

"I'm not sure if I'm comfortable looking at something that Mark intended to be private," I said. "I mean, if the situation was reversed and I found out that Mark had read any of my uploads, I'd feel betrayed."

"Totally a different situation, and for what it's worth, he hasn't done that. There would be an admin record showing time and date of access, but they're all clean. So he's been honest about that part. It's the rest that I need your advice about."

I told him I'd think about it and let him know later.

I swear, any time you put more than two people together in a small space, there's always drama.

LIsa

Given the stolen glances around the table at breakfast, my Spidey sense tells me that Dylan and Karen got together the other night. It even looks like Vaughn and Shanelle are becoming a thing, and who would've seen *that* one coming? Meanwhile, I'm so horny I'm masturbating three times a day, even on the bus when no one's looking. I know it's the whole bipolar thing, but godDAMN it's a bitch some days. And why are there no cool names for masturbation when women do it, but a ton of them for men? Rubbing one out, jerking off, beating the bishop, burping the worm, choking the chicken, wanking, fapping, jacking, knob job . . . and what do women get? *I masturbate three times a day.* Cold. Clinical. Oh, sure, there's Jilling Off, but that's just a riff on what the guys say, Jack and Jill, but it's only Jacking Off because that's the motion, right? Like a jackhammer. The only thing Jill's known for is falling down a hill, and why the hell am I even going down this rabbit hole in the first place?

Point is, we need a marketing campaign to come up with better terms for when women masturbate. How about finger-dipping, polishing the pearl, riding the pillow, slishing, sloshing, or in my case, *I had a typical Saturday night* three times today?

When Mark's ad promised a party, I figured it'd be a nonstop fuckfest between pickup and Delivery Unto Death. And while some parts have been good, and I really like (most of) the people, it's just not what I thought it would be. But what is, right?

Still, it's a long way to San Francisco, so we'll see who comes on next. Better be someone hot, because if this keeps up I'm gonna fracture my wrist.

AdminMark

Having left early and with almost no traffic on the road, we made it to our next pickup two hours ahead of schedule: Lexington, Nebraska (not Kentucky—why are so many names recycled?), our last stop before the Colorado border. Feels like we've been in Nebraska forever, but it's a big state and a lot's happened since we crossed in.

With a population of just over 10,000 and an area of less than five miles, Lexington is one of those places tucked way out in the middle of nowhere that used to be about a lot of things that aren't there anymore. Used to be an old trading post until it burned down. Used to be on the Pony Express line until it went obsolete. Biggest employer used to be a beef-packing company before it got sold to Tyson. But the Museum of Military Vehicles is still there, so that's good news for the *How Many Kinds of Jeeps Can You Name?* crowd.

Since there probably aren't a lot of tour buses going through town, I told D to look for a spot where we could hang without being seen. He found an alley between two auto repair places that had closed for the day. High concrete walls, no sidewalk, no direct line-of-sight from the street . . . you'd have to know we were there to know we were there.

We were getting low on supplies, so D and Tyler volunteered to check out the local stores to see what they could dredge up. I told the others that they could stretch their legs and walk around as long as they didn't draw attention, but so far nobody's taken me up on that. I think everyone's just tired and looking forward to a change of scenery. Besides, from the town website, the only events going on today are meetings of the Town Council, the City Development Committee, and storyteller time at the library.

Colorado, here we come!

VaughnR

"So what are you writing?" Lisa asked Theo out of the blue. I think she does it to test people, surprising them with a question that might seem natural if there had been a few sentences lined up in front of it to pave the way, but which come across as in-your-face when dumped into the middle of a perfectly good silence.

"Nothing important," Theo said, and continued writing.

"Back at the mall you said you were writing about destroying the world," Peter said. "Isn't that important?"

I could see Theo's eyes clicking through a dozen different replies before landing on *Okay, fine, we were going to get into this sooner or later and there's nothing else entertaining going on, so let's do this.*

"Rather than *destroying* the world, maybe a better way of describing it would be *replacing* this world with another. For as long as I can remember I've daydreamed about a world that I belonged to more than this one. So I started writing stories about it, filling one notebook after another with histories and people and fashion, down to the smallest details, so it would feel as real as this one. I like to pretend that when the story's done, the lie of this world will fade away, and I can slide into the other one and live there forever."

"When do you think you'll be finished?" Shanelle asked.

"At the end of our trip," Theo said, and we all knew what was meant by that. "I'll write one last page, close my eyes, and when I open them again, I'll be in a high tower overlooking the silver city and the most beautiful sunrise in history."

"Can you read us a little of it?" Karen asked.

"I don't know," Theo said, frowning. "It's pretty rough."

"Totally fine with that," Peter said. "Besides, there's not much else to do until Dylan and Tyler get back."

Theo hesitated, then flipped pages, looking for one part in particular. "Okay. I'm pretty happy with this section. You're *sure* you want to hear it?"

"Of course we are," Lisa said, "stop stalling."

Theo smiled, then sat back, took a slow breath, and started reading.

I wish I could repeat it. I'd give my left nut to recapture what that moment felt like, but I don't have the words, only Theo knows which ones to use and what order to put them in. If I even tried, whatever came out the other side wouldn't be worth a fraction of what was in those pages: a city in a far-off land where people were polite and friendly, leaders were wise and just and fair, and there was beauty everywhere, tall towers of stained glass that stretched high into a deep blue sky, great domed buildings covered in gold and marble, libraries that held an infinity of books, and, outside the city walls, deep green forests with trees so old that they just kind of dozed through the centuries. It was all so clear, so *real*, that I felt I could reach out and it would be there.

As I closed my eyes to better see the place in my mind, a phrase I heard when I was a boy came back to me. *The kind of place where a man can live his life full measure.*

It took me a moment to realize that Theo had stopped speaking. When I opened my eyes, I saw everyone else had done the same thing. We blinked in the fading daylight as if we were coming back into this place, this moment, these bodies.

At first nobody spoke, still processing it, then Lisa said, "That was—"

And Karen finished it. "—beautiful."

"Oh, fuck you," Mark said, and I got my back up until I saw he was grinning as he said it. "I have a *degree* in writing, I've *studied* writing, I've worked to be a writer since I was *sixteen*, but I've never written anything like that. I could sit here for two years and not come up with something that amazing."

Theo smiled and nodded appreciation for the compliment. "I'm not a writer. I don't think I could tell proper stories or write books. I just started writing my way out of this world because I couldn't see any other way to do it."

Then Mark's phone pinged with a notification and all hell broke loose.

AdminMark

Hi, I'm Audio Recorder!
Tap the icon to start recording.

MARK ANTONELLI: Here they come, get the door!

KAREN: You okay?

TYLER: Yeah, just let me catch my breath.

DYLAN: There are cops all over the place, Mark. We saw cars taking up position and cutting off traffic south of here.

PETER ROUTH: How do you know this has anything to do with us?

TYLER: As we walked past one of the police cars, we heard the dispatcher confirming the description of the bus, how many people were inside.

SHANELLE: How did they even know we were coming?

LISA: Theresa. Shit, that fucking bitch, she told them.

VAUGHN: You don't know that.

MARK ANTONELLI: No, she might be right. When I was talking to Dylan about the next stop here at eight, I turned around and Jim was standing right behind me. I didn't think too much about it, but he must have heard us and she got him to tell her.

PETER ROUTH: Fuck!

SHANELLE: I didn't see any police cars when we came in.

DYLAN: Maybe they just got the call, or if Theresa told them we were coming at eight, they might have decided to wait before deploying, and we got in just under the wire.

MARK ANTONELLI: Doesn't matter, screw the pickup, we're out of here.

DYLAN: We can't leave, that's what I'm trying to tell you. This whole town is one big cul-de-sac in the middle of nowhere. There's nothing to the north, west, and east of here, just a couple of access roads way on the other side of town and the police would nail us before we even got close. Every other road north dead-ends except the 21, and from what we heard they've just blocked off the on-ramps. The only other way out is the Lincoln Freeway going south and they've got roadblocks there too.

SHANELLE: How do they have that many cops in a town this small?

DYLAN: County courthouse and county jail are right up the street. Places like that always have lots of cops who don't have much to do, and besides, the way this town is built there aren't a lot of roads they need to cover. This is probably the most exciting thing that's happened here all year.

LISA: Why come after us like we're terrorists? We didn't do anything wrong.

MARK ANTONELLI: In Nebraska, assisted suicide is a felony, no different from murder. Add in conspiracy and illegal disposal of a body and we're talking three or four felonies each times eight of us, that's a huge haul.

LISA: So what do we do?

MARK ANTONELLI: I don't know.

SHANELLE: Mark, I got on here to take care of business, not spend the next two years of my life in jail.

LISA: Or a psych ward, those fuckers.

MARK ANTONELLI: No one's going to jail, we just need to figure a way out of this.

VAUGHN: What about a distraction? Something that'll get the police to pull some of their cars off the blockade long enough for us to slip out?

PETER ROUTH: Like what?

VAUGHN: I don't know.

MARK ANTONELLI: I saw a dumpster down the street, we could set it on fire.

DYLAN: Not big enough, it'd just take one car to escort the fire trucks.

LISA: This whole situation is a dumpster fire.

TYLER: How about me?

PETER: We just need to figure out our options, there has to be—

TYLER: Guys, listen, I can do this, let me—

KAREN: Tyler, no.

TYLER: I don't think we have much choice. Dylan, you saw what they're doing, same as me. The way they're spread out, is there any way out of here? At all? Do we have even a chance to get out?

DYLAN: No. Like I said, it's south or nothing, and south's buttoned up tight.

THEO: What if we just wait them out?

TYLER: Sooner or later they'll figure out we got here early and start looking for us, block by block, security camera by security camera, and they'll find us. Even if we ditch the bus and split up, there's no place to hide.

PETER: Okay. So what's your idea for a distraction?

TYLER: I go out and make a scene, get them to focus on me.

THEO: Tyler, you can barely stand up, nobody's going to see you as a threat.

TYLER: They will if I borrow the katana Peter showed us the other day.

PETER ROUTH: Wakizashi.

LISA: Seriously, now?

TYLER: It's light enough for me to hold, but enough of a threat that they'll send squad cars in to swarm me. They won't stay on the blockades waiting around for a possible threat when they've got a real one right in front of them. With luck that'll open a door for you to get away.

LISA: And then what? What about you?

TYLER: I don't know, Lisa. I'm making this up as I go.

KAREN: You'll go to prison.

TYLER: Karen, the way I've been feeling lately, I won't even make it to trial. I didn't want to say anything before, but even without all this I'm honestly not even sure I can last long enough to reach California. If I can't save me, I can at least save the rest of you. Let me do this. Let me do something with my life that I can feel good about.

PETER ROUTH: I hate to say it, but he's right. We don't have a lot of options. A diversion is the only thing that might work.

MARK ANTONELLI: Okay. I don't like it, but we need to get out of town and this is the only play I can see. Tyler, I want you to FaceTime us every step of the way so we know where you are and what's going on.

DYLAN: I'll jump online and download a police scanner app—that way we'll know when the cops call in their cars, which ones and where. As soon as I see a clear road out, we go.

SHANELLE: And if we do get out, then what?

VAUGHN: We get the hell out of Nebraska as fast as we can. We're less than an hour from the state border. As long as the police aren't in direct pursuit, they'll have to turn this over to the Colorado state police and that'll take time.

DYLAN: We should figure out a way to let Tyler know we're clear so he can surrender to the police.

THEO: Dylan, Tyler, please, don't do this, there has to be another way.

TYLER: It's okay, Theo. I'm okay. It's—

END RECORDING

Karen_Ortiz

I can't stop crying.

This wasn't how he wanted to go. It's not how any of us would want to go. But he was brave and gentle, and even though he was afraid, at the end he did it anyway, and the best way to honor what he did is to tell all of it. So I'm going to try and calm down so I can remember every detail.

After he left the bus, Tyler turned on FaceTime so we could see what he was seeing. It wasn't much of a downtown, just a few blocks that hadn't changed much since the town was built, so they still had that frontier look. Low red brick buildings with an old Chinese restaurant, a bookstore, an appliance store, a furniture store, and a Western Union office. For some reason, they had three different drugstores all on the same block. There weren't a lot of people around and most of the shops had closed for the night. The rest were empty or looked like they'd been shut down a long time ago. How do you make a scene when there's no one there to see you do it?

He kept walking until he found a jewelry store that was still open. It was so smart, and so Tyler, to pick a place that would have a direct line to the police.

He put his phone on the back of a parked car and angled the camera toward the store. The plan was that as soon as we had a way out, we'd put a sheet of paper over the camera at our end. That would make Tyler's screen turn white and he'd know that we were making a run for it and he could go ahead and surrender.

Once he went inside the store, we couldn't see what was happening, but suddenly we heard the alarm go off and the salesclerks ran out into the street.

When Tyler came out again, the cover of the katana or whatever Peter called it was gone. He held up the blade, yelling, *I'll kill you! I'll kill all of you!*

He was trying so hard to look dangerous, but even through the FaceTime and the darkness, you could see he wasn't a threat to anyone. He was alone and scared and my heart broke watching him trying to be something he wasn't.

Nothing happened for what felt like forever. He'd raise the blade, wave it around, and pace back and forth, yelling at people who weren't there, then go back to the doorway of the store and lean against the wall, breathing hard.

"Cars coming in from the north," Dylan said, listening to the police scanner.

"Shit," Mark said. "North won't help us. Even if the road's clear, it's too far, we'll be seen and stopped."

I heard police sirens racing down the street and looked back at the screen. The cars were outside camera range, but through the speaker I could hear them screech to a stop, doors opening and slamming shut. *Put the weapon down!* one of them yelled. *Drop it! Now!*

Tyler didn't. *Stay back!* he yelled, and stepped inside the doorway to make it harder for them to come after him. *I'll kill you!*

He was trying so hard. But in his condition, it was like watching a mouse trying to intimidate six pit bulls.

"They're calling for backup," Dylan said, listening to the police scanner.

"Who's responding?"

"Not sure," Dylan said, "dispatch is putting the word out . . . I'm getting vehicle numbers but not locations."

I glanced back at the screen. Tyler must have felt the same urgency as us because he wasn't seeing nearly enough police cars, so he used the blade handle to break one of the store windows.

"He just upped the ante," Dylan said. "Code 56, property damage. That should—"

Then he straightened, focusing on the chatter. I don't think any of us breathed. Then he looked up. "Four more cars coming in."

"Where?" Peter asked.

"From the south."

"*Where* from the south?"

"*I don't know, goddammit!*"

We could hear more sirens approaching. *If they grab him before the blockade clears, then he's suffering all this for nothing.*

"Grant Street!" Dylan yelled. "Blockade unit moving north from Grant!"

"Is that an on-ramp street? Can we get there?"

Dylan checked the GPS. "Four blocks east, then two down, yeah, there's an on-ramp to the 80, we can—"

Then he paused, listening to the scanner again. "Shit, they're sending a unit from the north end to cover Grant."

"Then we need to go right now," Mark said, "before they slam the door."

Dylan was already behind the wheel. The engine turned and he hit the gas. "Hang on!"

We sped out of the alley and turned right down a big wide street with no place to hide if even a single cop car swung by.

I held on to the seat and craned my neck to watch the screen as bright lights from the arriving cars hit Tyler and whited out the windows. He covered his face, blinking hard against the glare.

"Will he be able to see the phone when we give the all-clear?" I asked.

"I don't know," Dylan said, never taking his eyes off the road.

"How far are the replacement cars?"

"Close," Dylan said, the pedal jammed all the way down. "Come on, you piece of shit, move!"

When we hit Grant, he turned right so hard the wheels on that side came up off the ground and the bus almost flipped. Then they slammed down and he white-lined it down the street. We could see the freeway entrance just a few blocks away.

Tyler stepped out of the store, shielding his eyes so he could check the phone.

"We're close enough," Peter said. "Give him the go-ahead."

Vaughn put a sheet of paper in front of the phone camera, whiting out the image on Tyler's side, then pulled it away again, going back and forth to make sure the contrast would be noticeable.

Dylan hit the on-ramp and swung the bus onto the freeway.

Shielding his eyes, Tyler checked the phone at his end, and when he saw the white screen, he nodded in acknowledgment and the stress seemed to go out of his face.

Okay, Tyler, I thought, *now just put down the blade and surrender.*

Instead he rested against the doorway and closed his eyes, like he was gearing up for something.

Don't do it, I thought. *No no no. Please don't do it. Not like this.*

Then he opened his eyes and, with whatever strength he had left, pushed away from the door, holding the blade out in front of him. Breathing hard. Scared. But ready. Resigned.

Already gone.

He raised the blade above his head and, with a yell, charged the police.

I looked away.

The others cried out as the sound of gunfire came over the speaker. I don't know how many times they fired, but it seemed to go on forever. When I looked back, Tyler had fallen out of camera range. Several police came forward, guns raised in the ridiculous precaution that he could still be alive after taking that many bullets.

Everybody was crying. Peter leaned against the seat in front of him, arms folded in front of his face while Theo sat facing the window, away from everyone else. Beneath the tears Dylan was angrier than I'd ever seen him, and I got the sense that if he didn't have to be responsible for getting us away he'd go back there and tear the whole town apart with his bare hands. Nobody spoke until Mark cleared his throat.

"Um . . . okay, it'll . . . it *should* take them a while to figure out we're gone, so we have half an hour, maybe more before they radio for support, and they won't know which way we went so—"

"Not now," Vaughn said, his voice hard. "Not goddamn now, okay?"

Mark nodded and looked down at the floor.

The Nebraska police wanted us because we'd helped a friend check out early, because that was what he wanted. Because that's a crime.

But for the police to shoot someone who was clearly incapable of hurting anyone rather than tasing him, that was okay, that was legal.

Suicide by friend? Wrong.

Suicide by cop? Perfectly fine.

In what universe can that possibly make sense?

After we turned onto the 76 and crossed into Colorado, Vaughn suggested we find someplace to sleep for the night where nobody'd notice the bus.

Dylan said we couldn't risk a hotel until we knew how bad our situation was, so he pulled off the freeway south of Julesburg and found an empty fireroad that led to a tree-lined cutout well off the main road. We'd sleep in the bus and figure out what to do in the morning.

Lisa, Shanelle, and I took the bunks. Dylan was going to sleep on one of the front benches, but Theo insisted he take the fourth bunk, and he was too exhausted to argue.

As I cleared a space to lie down, I noticed my phone had an unread notification. I almost ignored it but decided to take a look anyway.

And I found this.

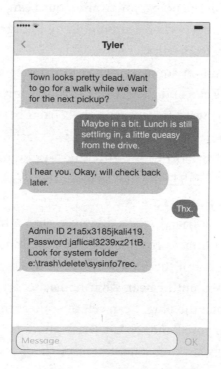

I realized Tyler must have sent it after leaving the bus but before switching on the camera so no one would see him doing it. Because he trusted me.

And as I thought about that, I started crying all over again.

Tomorrow. I'll look at the folder tomorrow.

Sleep first.

Goodbye, Tyler.

See you soon.

―――――――――

AdminMark

I keep looking out the bus window, waiting for the splash of blue and red lights. We're deep in the woods and far enough off the main road that there's no passing traffic, but I can still hear cars in the distance, and every time a siren goes by I hold my breath until it Dopplers away from us.

Brain wired up on adrenaline, I keep running everything that happened with Zeke and then Tyler through my mind over and over, looking for ways to protect myself from being arrested and having the material confiscated before we reach our destination. Even if we have to abort before reaching San Francisco, with luck there might be enough in the files to make this work, *if* I can get out of here with my skin intact.

D said he has a friend who's a lawyer with a big firm in New York, so I asked him to fire off an email to find out how much trouble we're in and if there's a way out of it. I'll hold off making any final decisions until I hear what he has to say, but right now my gut says to pull the plug. I can tell the others that it's too risky, that we're too exposed and we can't risk going forward, which by the way is totally fucking true. Some of them probably can't afford plane or train tickets out of here, but Vaughn apparently has a chunk of cash stashed away, and I think he'd be open to chipping in to help everyone get clear.

Best to quit while we're ahead, if "ahead" is even still an option.

Update: Two a.m. D just forwarded me the lawyer's reply.

And yeah, it's about as bad as I thought.

———————————

To: Dylan Mack DylanMack@dylanmackservices.com
From: Jamie Delarossa j.delarossa@tldslegal.com
Subject: Re: Inquiry

Hey, Dylan!

I was going to drop you a note this weekend, so good timing (at least in that respect). The Lieutenant is putting together another reunion for the weekend of September 23rd and he wants everybody there but he doesn't have your new email. Wanted to make sure you were cool with me forwarding your info given the circumstances of our last gathering. He says the theme this year is Drink Until You Puke, Puke Until You're Sober, Then Start Drinking Again, which I'm pretty sure was the theme of the last two reunions, but I'm not going to be the one to tell him that.

Okay, on to business.

I listened to your voicemail a couple of times (sorry I missed the call, I was prepping for a deposition), and did a little digging to try and answer your questions. I need to emphasize at this point that because

I haven't been engaged as your attorney, and technically can't since we're friends, anything I say can be produced in discovery should any legal issues arise out of your situation. So this email is intended as strictly informational and not advisory in any way. I am speaking as your friend, not your attorney.

I'll start with the second incident first, since in some ways it's the most clear-cut. As I understand it, other than your friend, none of you were directly involved in the altercation with the police. This removes any immediate consequences for the rest of you. Could there be some elements of conspiracy if, say, anyone encouraged him to take these actions? In theory, yes, but that would be difficult to prove. In previous cases where Defendant A did something criminal after being wound up by Associate B, prosecutors have found it almost impossible to prevail against Associate B in court, especially if the others with you can testify that Defendant A acted on his own. Absent any clear-cut evidence of conspiracy, I suspect that a judge or grand jury would be reluctant to pursue the case, so unless an overzealous DA sticks his nose into this, you *may* be okay on that count.

When it comes to the first incident, things are unfortunately a lot more complicated. The couple who were traveling with you were witnesses to the incident but not directly involved, which saves them from criminal liability. This removes the defense of "they're only pointing the finger at us in return for immunity." It also gives them a measure of credibility that's hard to beat in court if your chosen defense is he-said/she-said.

In the state of Nebraska, assisted suicide is a Class IV felony, which carries a maximum penalty of two years imprisonment, a ten-thousand-dollar fine, and another year of probation. In the case of first offenders, the penalty can be adjusted downward to probation without prison time and a moderate fine. However, given the Justice Department's latest "throw the book at them" sentencing guidelines, I wouldn't count on the reduction.

Complicating matters further, your boss is correct that once you add in conspiracy to assist with suicide, fleeing the scene of a crime, inappropriate disposal of a body (which confirms knowledge of guilt), *and* interstate flight, things can get really nasty, really fast. Depending on prosecutorial guidance, anyone convicted of those charges would be subject to five to fifteen years in prison.

The good news, at least for the moment, is that you are now in Colorado, which is one of a handful of states where assisted suicide is not considered a crime. This raises a number of sidebar issues that are beyond my area of expertise, so I emailed one of my associates who was formerly a state prosecutor to get his thoughts, strictly as a theoretical matter. His reply follows:

<<What an interesting question! If the Nebraska AG wants to pursue this, and given his history on this subject I have every reason to believe he will, the next step will be to criminally charge the participants in Nebraska and ask Colorado to extradite them to Nebraska for trial. Prevailing laws require cooperation between state law enforcement agencies, so under normal circumstances Colorado would have to honor this request, but I question whether they would extradite someone for an offense that is not illegal in Colorado, especially since we're talking about assisted suicide, which is a politically charged issue that could bring the Colorado AG and other elected officials under fire from local pressure groups.

If the underlying Nebraska "crime" isn't considered a Colorado "crime," then that also mitigates against the related charges, i.e., if assisted suicide is legal, then a group of people consenting to work together in that cause would not be considered conspiracy because what they're doing is not illegal. There is no underlying crime.

If I were sitting in the AG's office in Denver and this warrant came across my desk, the politically smart thing would be to keep my head down and not get involved, especially since those involved are just passing through. From his perspective, the sooner they get out of his jurisdiction, the better. However, if they commit any acts considered illegal in Colorado that lead to them being arrested, all bets are off. Not only would they be facing charges in Colorado, but once in custody it becomes politically easier to extradite them to face charges in Nebraska. So as long as they keep moving and don't break any local laws, they should be reasonably safe for a while.

But all that changes the moment they leave Colorado. There's still a Nebraska warrant out for them, so they risk being arrested if they travel to a state where assisted suicide is against the law, which is basically every state surrounding Colorado. They're caught in a ring of fire, fair game for any red-state AG or DA with something to prove or a point to make.>>

You remember that phrase Sergeant Abrams used to describe you-know-who? "Like a monkey with his fist around a nut in a jar, he can't pull it out and he won't let go"? That's where your friends are right now. As a group, they can't stay in Colorado indefinitely (though I suppose they could try) and they can't drive into any of the neighboring states because they'll face immediate arrest. If, as you suggest, the woman who tipped off the Nebraska PD didn't interact much with the other passengers and thus may not have a lot of personal information that could be used to identify them, the safest solution for everyone would be to abandon the road trip, split up, and grab the first planes back to their home states. While they remain together, they're at risk, but individually they might be able to slip away, after which they may be too much trouble to identify and track down on an interstate basis.

This is particularly true in your case. The form signed by your employer confirms that you are only driving the bus, and that none of this is taking place under your authority. As long as you did not directly participate in the assisted suicide, you should be able to get away clean, especially if the others will confirm the points above should this ever end up in a courtroom.

If they *do* choose to keep moving forward, my biggest worry would be the Utah State Attorney General. He made his reputation as a hardass on everything from abortion rights to assisted suicide, and this is just the kind of red-meat, heavy-press situation that he loves to dig into. To get a better sense of what he might or might not do, I reached out to a colleague of mine who works in the Assistant District Attorney's office in Provo on a strictly unofficial basis in case he has any insight. If I hear anything back, I'll let you know ASAP.

Once again, I am not advising you as your attorney. I am speaking only as your friend, and as such, my advice would be this: Get the fuck off that bus right now and grab the first plane home before anything else goes wrong.

Hope this helps.

Sincerely,
Jamie Delarossa

————————————————

VaughnR

Every time I closed my eyes last night, all I could see were Tyler's final moments. Ever since the concert, he was beating himself up for not being strong enough, or fast enough, or brave enough, or whatever enough. But what he did last night was the bravest thing I've ever seen. I hope he knows how bright he shined there at the end, and that it lets him pass over with pride.

As the sun started to come up, Shanelle slid into the bucket seat next to me. "You should at least *try* to get some sleep," she said.

"You didn't," I said.

"Difference is, I'm young. I can get by without sleep. You're really old, and you need it."

I frowned at her. She smiled back. I glowered. She smiled even bigger.

"You're not very good at looking like a serial killer," she said. "Now come on, turn your back to me."

"Why?"

"So I can help you sleep."

I didn't want to argue, so I did as she asked and leaned my head against the window.

"There you go," she said, and began rubbing my neck and shoulders. "My dad had insomnia for years. My mama used to do this to help him sleep, and showed me how to do it too."

"It's not going to work," I said.

"Not if you keep yammering."

I hmmphed and closed my eyes.

Then suddenly it was three hours later and Dylan was standing at the front of the bus saying he'd gotten a reply from his attorney friend.

I turned and blinked at Shanelle, who had this great big cat-who-ate-the-canary look on her face. "Told you," she said, then Dylan started reading the email.

When he was done, everybody got real quiet. It was a lot to digest. Stay together or break up? Keep going or call it a night?

"Either way," Mark said, "the important thing is that it looks like we're safe for a while now that we're in Colorado, so I think we should check into a motel, take some time to recover from everything that happened, then meet for breakfast to decide our next move."

I raised my hand and suggested we find someplace a little more comfortable than the usual cheap places we'd been staying in so far. I'd seen a billboard for a Sheraton down the road a ways and that sounded just about right by me. Some of the others were concerned because they were running low on funds, so I volunteered to make up the difference. If we were going to decide whether to keep going, turn back, or split up, we should make that decision clear-eyed and rested.

Not that I actually needed that time to decide; I'd made up my mind in the time it took for Dylan to read the email. But my bones are cold and I want a proper night's sleep in a proper bed with a proper shower and proper room service because goddammit those things matter when you're sixty-five years old.

That's the thing about getting old: it reshapes your perspective and you start seeing the world differently than you did before. I'm not talking about feeling on the inside like you're still a man of thirty and then you see your reflection and you're not sure who that old guy is or how the hell he snuck into your mirror, or the part where your body starts to betray you. That's obvious. The real stuff, the *important* stuff, is more subtle and it sneaks up on you slowly.

When people turn fifty, they're pretty confident they'll be around to hit sixty. When you're sixty, seventy is still pretty reachable, but it's not as much of a given as sixty because more things can go wrong. And if you reach seventy, every day after that is a crapshoot.

Nobody on either side of my family made it past their early seventies, so when someone from NASA talks on the news about having colonies on Mars in fifteen or twenty years, a part of my brain adds up the numbers and says, *You know you won't be here to see that, right?* It's not like a big sad moment or anything, it's just the math, and after a while you get used to it. *Man, it'd be great to watch folks walking around on Mars, but by then I'll be in the ground, so let's see what's on TV tonight.*

I chose to help Zeke cross over early because I believe we should be able to end our lives when we see fit instead of dragging things out. In return, society wants to punish me with a prison sentence longer than I have to live.

And that's not an acceptable option.

So I think we should keep going. If the others decide to shut this down and go their separate ways, well, that'll be hard because I've come to like them more than I expected when we started this, but I'm not going back. I'll probably head over to Denver, eat and drink my way through the last of the Carolyn Death Fund, and when that's done, order in my favorite breakfast, steak and eggs with hash browns cooked crisp, then take a nosedive off the tallest building in the city.

So I guess we'll see what tomorrow brings.

LIsa

After spending all night on the bus, I thought about taking a nap once I got to my room but instead dropped off my bag and went for a walk to try to shake off the last couple of days.

It feels weird to say it that way, "to shake off the last couple of days," like I lost my laundry or had to spend time at the DMV or something. Zeke's gone. Tyler's gone. The normal reaction, the *expected* reaction, is to be broken by the loss, and yes, I'm going to miss them, especially Tyler. We started this together, got on the bus together, he was fun and gentle and I liked him and I'm going to miss him a lot.

But *dying is what we came here to do.* So as much as a part of me misses those guys, another part of me is like, *You made it! You said you were going to walk off the Earth and you did it! My turn next! Hold a seat for me, I'll be there as fast as I can!* Nobody in a World War Two kamikaze squad waved to the guys leaving on a suicide mission and thought, *Gee, I hope they make it back okay!*

Dying is the point, you know?

So there's a big difference between what we're doing and, say, Dylan getting hit and killed by a car. That would be an utter, complete fucking tragedy, something to weep over, to feel awful about and mourn, because Dylan *wants* to be here. The rest of us don't. Dylan wants in. We want *out.*

If it would've been me stepping out in front of the police to buy the others time to get away and do what they came here to do, I wouldn't want tears. I'd want a complete fucking balls-to-the-walls celebration because I finally made it out. And Tyler would feel the same way about it. No more coughing, no more fainting, no more pink froth on his lips when he thought nobody noticed. He's finally free, and he went out doing something impossibly brave and beautiful.

Doesn't mean it wasn't hard to watch, because it was.

Doesn't mean I didn't care, because I did.

Doesn't mean I won't miss both of them terribly, because I already do.

But it also means that *we're doing what we came here to do,* and if all of us aren't good with that idea, then we shouldn't be here.

So yeah: I wanted to go for a walk and shake off the last few days because it was hard on every level and I needed space to heal up. I was heading toward some woods behind the hotel that I thought might have some good walking trails when I saw Dylan sitting on a bench all by his lonesome.

"Hey!" I called.

He shaded his eyes from the sun and I got the usual eye-roll when he saw it was me, but I'm used to it by now. "Thought you'd be sleeping," he said.

"Yeah, me too." I plopped down next to him and noticed a small plastic bag. "Did some shopping?"

"Went to a weed dispensary down the street. Need to put my brain into neutral for a while."

"Love of my life!" I said. By now I'd gone through most of the weed in my bag of wonders, and the rest was getting dry. "What'd you get?" I asked, digging through the bag. "Gummies? Fruity snacks? Brownies?"

"Pre-rolls."

"Wow, going old-school."

"It's all we had when I was in the army, so I got used to it. Don't trust edibles unless I make 'em myself so I know how much is there."

The bag had three pre-rolls each of Blue Dream, Bubba Kush, Trainwreck, and Lemon Haze. "Lightweight," I said. "I'm surprised they didn't give you some training wheels and a booster seat to go with these."

"Can't go hardcore if I'm gonna drive the bus tomorrow."

"Yeah, well, the way things are going, that's a pretty big if." I grabbed one of the blunts and lit up.

"You could've asked," he said.

I exhaled smoke. "Can I have one?"

"Sure."

"So what's the point of asking?"

He sighed, pulled out a Blue Dream, and lit up.

As we sat and smoked, it occurred to me that while I know where *I* stand on all of us dying, I had no idea what Dylan felt.

"So what do you think of all this?" I asked, because why not?

He shrugged. "It's not my decision. Whether you keep going or break up the band, that's your call. I'm just the driver."

"Not that . . . I mean the reason we're on the bus in the first place?"

I could see him stiffen a little. "You mean the suicide thing?"

"Yeah, that."

He took another hit off the blunt. "Not my place. Like I said, I'm just the driver. My job is to get you from Point A to Point B, not to make judgments about who's doing what, why, and whether or not you're right to do it. That's all down to you."

"So you don't have an opinion about death?"

"Wasn't in the job description."

"Bullshit. You saying you never had anyone close to you die?"

His face darkened a little. "I was deployed to a free-fire zone in Afghanistan. Of course people died. Any time we were deployed to the field we knew there was a chance of being killed by the enemy, and some of us were, but when the order comes you go anyway, because that's the job, and what happens next, happens next."

"Not really the point," I said, "so let's try this: If you're on patrol, and the enemy throws a grenade at you, and one of your guys jumps on the grenade to save his unit, everybody says he's a hero, right?"

"Well, sure."

"But if he knew he'd never survive jumping on a grenade, then technically, he committed suicide, right?"

He shifted uncomfortably. "Yeah, I suppose."

"So why is one suicide right and the other wrong? Why does one guy get a medal while somebody else gets posthumously shamed? How is what that soldier did any different from what Tyler did to save us?"

He struggled with the question for a bit, then shook his head. "Questions like that are way above my pay grade, Lisa. Things happen in combat that are just different. You can't equate the two."

"Okay, so did you know anybody in the army who committed suicide *outside* of following orders or being in combat?"

"A few, yeah."

"Like?"

He didn't want to talk about it, but one of the benefits of weed is that even when you *think* you don't want to do something, there's a part of you that really *does*. So as long as you don't get couch-locked behind a bag of Fritos, it peeks out whether you like it or not.

"An Air Cav pilot at our base was flying recon one day when he spotted a pickup carrying shoulder-mounted surface-to-air missiles driving through a village that had been evacuated the week before, so the pilot got a quick go-order to engage. He fired at the pickup, but they squirted out before the missile hit. Pilot pursued the squirters and blew the shit out of a building where they'd taken cover. When the dust settled, he went in with a recon team to assess the situation. Turns out there were a bunch of families and kids living in the building he'd just shot to shit, refugees from another village who moved in when they heard everybody else was gone. Probably thought it was safer than living in tents.

"The pilot completely lost his shit. I mean, who wouldn't, right? The doctors kept him under observation for two weeks, trying to decide if he should be returned to the front line or moved back. He kept saying he was fine. Worked his ass off to pass every test they threw at him. Finally they checked the little box that says *Fit for duty* and he was sent back to the field. But the second they gave him back his weapon, he blew his brains out, which had apparently been his plan the whole time. He couldn't live with what happened, so he busted his butt until he could get his weapon back and end it."

Dylan took a long drag on the blunt. "Was he right to do it? Shit, I don't know. Not my call to make. For me, the most important thing I could do was to come home alive. He felt otherwise."

"That was his choice, and he made it."

"But that's the point. Blowing his brains out wasn't inevitable. He didn't kill himself suddenly, out of nowhere, because he was upset. He had two whole weeks to think about it and change his mind. It didn't have to happen. He *chose* that way. I chose another way. So when you ask me what I think about all this . . . I guess my answer is that sometimes when I hear you all talking, it feels like nobody's choosing anymore. It's just a given that you're going to do this, and that's that."

"Well, yeah, I mean, the only reason we're all *here* is because we think this is the right thing to do. Anybody who believes suicide is wrong wouldn't be on the bus in the first place, so you're only hearing one side."

"I'm just saying that it doesn't *have* to happen. You can still choose another way, right up until the last second."

"All those choices have already been made, Dylan. The choices you're talking about are the ones that got us here. Just because you didn't see them happen in front of you doesn't mean they didn't happen."

"I get that, I do. I just wish there was another way."

"Even for me?" I asked, batting my eyelashes.

He laughed. "I suppose."

"But Karen for sure?"

The laugh faded away. "Yeah. Karen for sure."

"Have you talked to her about it?"

He stubbed out the blunt. "Not sure if I should."

"Never hurts to ask."

"You don't think she'd get upset?"

"I've seen how she is with you, Dylan. She won't be upset. I don't think any of us would object to talking about our choices. Shit, why do you think people like us leave suicide notes? We're dead and we're *still* not done explaining. It's our way of saying, *And furthermore . . .*"

That got another smile out of him. "So do you believe in God, or an afterlife?" he asked.

That settled it. We were definitely at the stoned part of the conversation.

"No on both counts. I think the whole afterlife thing is just the bullshit we grab on to when we get old because we're afraid of dying."

"Not sure that's true."

"Come on, even you have to concede that one."

"Not really," he said. "See, everybody I ever knew who was old and dying—my grandparents, a couple of teachers I had when I was a kid, the drill instructor who trained me and came down with brain cancer—were okay with it at the end. They never talked about being afraid to die. They talked about how great it would be to see their old friends again, about how they were looking forward to being reunited with their parents, husbands, and wives on the other side of this life. When somebody dies, we miss them, and that feeling never really goes away. We just keep on missing them. The longer you live, the more of people you miss, until the idea of dying is less about *Oh, shit, I'm afraid* and more about *I'll finally be able to see all my friends again . . . everyone I've missed so much.*

"So no, I don't think it's the fear of death that makes us believe in an afterlife. It's our love for everybody we ever lost."

I'd heard Mark say there was more to Dylan than what he showed on the surface, but I never quite bought it because he was just the bus driver, you know? Turn right, turn left, drive straight, green means go, red means stop. Not a lot of thought involved, right? But I was wrong; the well went pretty deep.

"You're smarter than you look," was how I decided to say it.

"Thanks a lot," he said, laughing.

"No, seriously, I'm not saying you look like a knuckle-dragger, but you could definitely be like that guy's best friend."

"Lisa?"

"Yeah?"

"Please stop talking."

And for once, I did.

Hi, I'm Audio Recorder!
Tap the icon to start recording.

PETER ROUTH: As the new kid on the block I'm still learning the group dynamics of my fellow passengers, but full props to Vaughn for suggesting the Sheraton and to Theo for volunteering to sleep on the bus and keep an eye on things while everybody else crashes.

So why am I still wide awake at, hang on, what's the time, two a.m.?

At first I thought it was the sound of Karen and Dylan fucking in the next room, but I put up with that kind of thing all the time back at the dorm and it never bothered me. I'd listen to the moans, rub out a quick one, roll over, and go to sleep. Besides, they stopped fucking over an hour ago. Since then they've just been talking non-stop. Not even loud, really, except for a couple of points where Dylan sounded really pissed off about something before she shushed him, but not nearly enough to keep me awake.

But here I am. Staring at the ceiling and talking to my phone because something's been bothering me.

Whenever you tell someone you're getting a degree in psychology, they always weird out at you, like they're worried you're analyzing them the whole time. So you say hey, no, I'm definitely not doing that, so relax, but of course that's not true. You're constantly sizing people up because you just spent the last five or six years of your life learning how to do that and you want to get your money's worth.

And one of the things I'm really good at is being able to tell when someone's lying, and Mark was *definitely* lying when he talked about us meeting up tomorrow to decide what to do about the rest of this trip. He's already decided to give up. It was all over his face, the way he kept looking at everyone. And I can understand why he'd feel that way. If we keep going, we not only have to make it across Utah but also Nevada, and according to a quick Google search the laws there are also anti-suicide, which is funny given how many people probably kill themselves after losing everything at the casinos. The slot machines and the tables are allowed to destroy your life, but you're not allowed to take your life. If there's a better metaphor for capitalism, I don't know what it is.

Driving into Utah means we'll be out in the open and exposed. It's dangerous, so yeah, the smart move is to quit while we still can. So why not just tell us that and be done with it? Why lie about our having a say in the decision? Shit, it's his bus, he can do whatever he wants. Maybe he wants to make us feel like it's a group decision so he doesn't have to deal with an insurrection. Or maybe he's letting everyone get used to the idea of breaking up so that when he does say he's unilaterally decided to pull the plug, everyone's emotionally prepared. It's like the old cat-on-the-roof joke. A guy leaves his cat with his brother and— Shit. Who the fuck is knocking? Yeah, I hear you, just a second let me put my pants on, I don't want anybody going blind.

Hey, what's up?

DYLAN: You alone? We heard you talking.

PETER ROUTH: I'm doing a journal entry, why?

KAREN: We need to show you something.

PETER ROUTH: Okay, just let me turn this—

AdminMark

The worst thing in the world is waking up fifteen minutes before the alarm goes off. The window is too short to go back to sleep, and too long to want to get up yet. But I didn't dare risk closing my eyes. I need to be clearheaded for the breakfast conversation, so I dragged my ass out of bed to go over my notes one last time. Given how tired everyone is right now, I don't think it'll be hard to convince them that discretion is the better part of valor. We made a statement, we saw two of our own through to the end, escaped the police, and made it to sanctuary, so let's declare victory and split.

Once everyone's gone their separate ways, I can stash the bus at Denver Airport long-term parking, then fly back to Florida. After things calm down, I'll come back long enough to yank out the server and sell the bus, then I'm done.

The hardest part of going home will be facing my old man. We're talking about weeks of *I tried to stop you for your own good. I knew you'd get into trouble and fuck this up and come back with your tail between your legs asking for help.*

Once I'm on the other side of *that* particular slice of hell, the trick will be figuring out how to turn the material collected so far into something usable. The safest approach would be to alter any details that are too specific so nobody can come back at me later and say *Hey that's my life he's writing about!* and sue me. I have everyone's signed release forms, so I'm *probably* okay, but it wouldn't hurt to have an attorney vet the manuscript to make sure I'm clear of liability. Then I just have to come up with a satisfying ending. Until now, the book has literally been writing itself, but now I'll have to step in and create something, and maybe that's a good thing, make it my own book and not just something I inherited.

But there's plenty of time to figure that out later. First I have to get past the "it's done" conversation.

Here we go.

Hi, I'm Audio Recorder!
Tap the icon to start recording.

PETER ROUTH: Okay, here he comes.

KAREN: You getting this, Peter?

PETER ROUTH: Yeah, just started recording.

LISA: You hold him and I'll hit him. Little fucker.

VAUGHN: No need for that.

LISA: Says you.

MARK ANTONELLI: Hey, guys, what's up? I thought we were going to meet for breakfast. Is there a problem?

LISA: Yeah, the problem is that you're a fucking liar.

MARK ANTONELLI: Whoa, where's this coming from?

PETER ROUTH: From your own words.

DYLAN: They're right, Mark.

MARK ANTONELLI: I don't know what you're talking about.

KAREN: I printed this up at the hotel business center and gave everyone copies. Tell me again you don't know what we're talking about.

MARK ANTONELLI: Fuck.

SHANELLE: Yeah, fuck.

MARK ANTONELLI: I can explain this.

THEO: I don't think there's much to explain, Mark. It's all right here.

MARK ANTONELLI: How did you get this?

KAREN: Tyler found the files accidentally. But that doesn't matter.

PETER ROUTH: She's right. All that matters is that you've been using us this whole time.

MARK ANTONELLI: That's not true.

KAREN: No? Paragraph two of your proposal for Charter Publishing. Quote. None of the passengers will know that they're engaged in manifesting this book with me. Like the characters in *A Chorus Line*, who were based on the words and thoughts of real people, their diary entries and texts will form the foundation of a story that I can turn into a more conventional narrative.

SHANELLE: That's why you had us sign the release forms, so you'd own everything we said and—

MARK ANTONELLI: Wait, are you recording this?

LISA: Goddamn right we are.

KAREN: Paragraph one, page three. Obviously I have no intention of driving us off a cliff, but the passengers will not know that until we reach San Francisco. At that point, they will be debriefed about the project and given the opportunity to have their names removed, but it will still be made clear to them that I own the underlying material.

LISA: Wait, I want to read this part. For legal reasons, your publishing company cannot be a party to this while it is in process, but once the material has been gathered, edited, and framed into a novel, it can be submitted to you for publication clear of encumbrance. So please contact me if you would like to pursue the chance to combine the novel format with true stories that I believe will make this a very saleable and publicity-worthy—blah blah blah blah.

VAUGHN: Material. We're just material. That's what you said.

THEO: Or an encumbrance. I've always wanted to be an encumbrance.

DYLAN: Me too. I'm not even sure what an encumbrance is, but I'm on board.

PETER ROUTH: It's like baggage.

SHANELLE: Baggage? Fuck you twice, Mark. Is that all we are to you?

MARK ANTONELLI: No, obviously not.

VAUGHN: Nothing obvious about this, except your decision to not tell us the truth about why you were really doing this—

MARK ANTONELLI: I didn't want to influence the experiment.

LISA: The experiment? Oh, fuck me.

PETER ROUTH: And you really had no idea what he had in mind?

DYLAN: No. I assumed this was going to end with all of you doing just what Mark said you were going to do. That's why I emailed him asking for a letter saying I had nothing to do with that part of it.

KAREN: He's telling the truth. You should've seen his reaction last night when I told him. His email's still in the archive if you want to—

MARK ANTONELLI: Okay, look, can I say something?

LISA: No.

VAUGHN: It's all right, let him talk.

MARK ANTONELLI: You're right. This was never going to end in us driving off a cliff in San Francisco. You guys have to understand, I've been writing since I was a teenager. I wrote short stories, poetry, a couple of novels, and none of it ever sold. None of it. The rejection letters always said the same thing, that it was interesting but not compelling or important. And the part that killed me is that they weren't wrong. I was just an average kid from an average family in an average neighborhood with an average education. I didn't have anything to say that mattered.

I've been on-and-off suicidal since I was a kid. That part's also in the archive, and it's true. I used to wonder what to write as my suicide note. What could I say that would be worth somebody reading it? I couldn't think of anything. Do you have any idea how depressing it is to realize that even your suicide note is going to be interesting but not compelling? A document like that is only as important as whoever's writing it and why.

That's where I got the idea for this. Alone, by ourselves, maybe our stories don't mean much. But put a bunch of us in a room together and maybe the whole is greater than the sum of its parts. So I took a chance, and yeah, I lied to you, because I didn't think I had anything important to say about my life. But together, maybe we do.

LISA: Keep piling up the bullshit, I can still see the top of your head.

THEO: Look, Mark, I can almost understand where you're coming from. That doesn't mean I agree or endorse it, just that I sort of get it. Where you went wrong, where you went stupid, was by lying to us about where this was going to end. You could've done pretty much the same thing and just said hey, we're going to have this big Death Party, and what you do at the end of the trip is your own business.

MARK ANTONELLI: Would you still have shown up?

THEO: I don't know, and the thing is, we'll never know for sure because you went the other way.

SHANELLE: I'll bet Zeke would've shown up.

VAUGHN: I had no particular plans.

PETER ROUTH: I said I'd only get on board if this was really going where you said it was going. So would I have come on? No, not a chance.

THEO: Either way, you started this wrong. Only question now is, can we take that lie and turn it into something good?

KAREN: This whole thing may have started under false pretenses, but the moments we've shared since getting on the bus were real. What happened with Zeke, what Tyler did for us, the craziness at the mall, all those moments were about us and who we are. They were real, they mattered, and that's something to hold on to, so at least some good has come out of this.

MARK ANTONELLI: I agree. So tell me what I have to do to regain your trust. I mean, I'm guessing you've been talking about this for a while, so you must have some idea of how to keep this together or you would've just split.

VAUGHN: Regaining our trust is going to take a while, Mark. To be honest, I'm not entirely sure it's possible. But there is a path forward, at least for the time being.

PETER ROUTH: When you said you wanted to hear our thoughts about whether or not to stay together, you'd already decided to pull the plug, right?

MARK ANTONELLI: Yes. It seemed like the safe, sensible solution.

PETER ROUTH: Yeah, well, we're not doing that. We're taking over the bus. Also the server. We've locked you out of the admin account, so you can still add to your own file, but you can't change or delete anything or email the document to anyone without our permission. The only people with the new passwords and admin authority are me, Karen, and Theo.

MARK ANTONELLI: Okay, I'm kind of confused about what we're—

KAREN: We've talked it over, and since Dylan's lawyer friend says we should be safe while we're in Colorado provided we don't get into trouble with the law—

LISA: Why do you look at me every time you say that?

KAREN: —we've decided to stay together and keep going at least as far as the Utah border. At that point we'll assess the situation, see what our options are, and take a final vote on whether to give up or make a run for California, try to find that cliff you talked about and finish this properly.

THEO: That's the only way to redeem the lie, Mark. By making it true.

VAUGHN: If we can make it to San Francisco and do what we came here to do, I don't think any of us cares what happens to what we wrote. It's yours. Do whatever you want with it.

MARK ANTONELLI: So what do I do in the meantime?

SHANELLE: Nothing. From now on you're just another passenger, on probation, and we can boot your sorry ass off the bus any time we want and go on without you.

LISA: And if that happens, you won't report the bus stolen because you're going to agree on this recording that you're okay if we take off with it. You asked us to sign a waiver with you, so this recording is your waiver with us.

MARK ANTONELLI: You good with this, D?

DYLAN: I signed on to drive the bus. I'll keep doing that as long as somebody needs me to take them somewhere.

MARK ANTONELLI: And what if I say no?

THEO: Then we get off the bus right now and wipe the server. You get nothing, and this all ends right here.

KAREN: So are you in or out?

MARK ANTONELLI: Then I guess I'm in, with this, and with you taking the bus if it comes to that. For what it's worth, I'm sorry this went down the way it did. You're right. I should have told you the truth from day one. To try and explain what I did and why in more detail, when I first had the idea I thought I could—

LISA: Okay, great, listen, I'm about to pass out from lack of food, so I'm going back inside to get something to eat. Anybody wants to come with me, let's go.

THEO: I think they're still serving breakfast for another half hour.

VAUGHN: I have to be honest, Mark, I'm very disappointed in you. It really didn't have to be like this.

MARK ANTONELLI: I know, and I'm sorry, I just—

END RECORDING

Karen_Ortiz

I don't think Mark really understood how close he came to getting kicked off the bus, but that seems to have gradually sunk in as everybody froze him out the rest of the day. He'd come up to one of us and start talking, like he was trying to make amends, as if none of it had happened, and we'd walk away while he was still talking. I've never been a big believer in shunning people, but it'll be worth it if he learns something from this. It's certainly better than getting his ass dumped by the side of the road while we drive off, and honestly, some of us still want to do that. As someone who grew up watching old episodes of *Lost in Space*, I don't see how we can justify keeping our own personal Dr. Smith aboard the *Jupiter 2* on our journey through the stars. They should have pushed him out the airlock by episode two. And so should we.

Mark

This is the third time I've tried to write this, and frankly, after that ambush on the bus, I don't know if I should even try. I don't know where I fit in. It's not my story anymore, I have no control over it, they're in charge now, I can't even access the files. I considered saying the hell with it and getting off the bus, but technically I still own this crate and I'm not sure I want to let it out of my sight until absolutely necessary.

Besides, there's a part of me that still wants to see this through to the end, whatever that end happens to be. So I guess I'll stick around for now.

Did I screw up? Yeah, probably, but it's easy for them to sit in judgment after the fact and say, *You could've done this better.* I didn't have the benefit of foresight when I put this whole thing together. I did the best I could. They can say *Most of us would've shown up anyway even if you'd told the truth from the beginning* all they want, but they don't actually know that's true any more than I do, so I don't think it's right to blame me for hedging my bets, or for them to say this whole thing was a lie. It's not. I showed up, I had the bus, I stocked it with water and drinks and chips, I took in everyone as promised, and until everything went sideways we were still on course for San Francisco. The only difference was in what would have happened after we got there.

So yeah, I think they're overreacting, but since nobody's interested in my point of view, I'm going to stop defending myself. The situation is what it is. I'm just going to sit quietly in the back until we get at least as far as Denver and see where this goes.

And from here on out, everybody can buy their own goddamned chips.

SunnyShanelle

"Can I talk to you for a second?"

I was about to get on the bus but when I turned and saw Vaughn's face looking ten kinds of serious I stepped back. "Sure, what's up?"

For a man who seemed ready to say something important a second earlier, he took a long time to find the first set of words that'd get him there. "I like you, Shanelle," he said. "I like you a lot."

"I like you too, Vaughn."

"I know, and that's . . ." He didn't say, *That's the problem*, but I could see that's where he was going, so I waited for the rest of it. *I decided it didn't mean anything when I took your hand, so let's forget that ever happened, okay?*

"The other day, you said I was a good man. But I'm not a good man. I've done . . . well, I've done some pretty bad things."

"You were listening when I talked about all the stuff I did, right?"

"I was, and it made me think that it's only fair to let you know what I've done, and who I am, in case you change your mind about—"

"About holding hands?"

"About *anything*," he said. "So I'm going to give you access to all my journal entries. Easiest that way."

"You don't have to do that, Vaughn."

"I know. But I want to."

"So what parts should I be looking for?"

He hesitated, then said, "You'll know it when you get there."

"Okay, but if it turns out this is about you peeking up somebody's skirt when you were nine, I'm gonna be real disappointed."

He smiled back at me, but there was no humor in it. "You'll know it when you get there," he repeated.

Karen_Ortiz

Once we got back on the bus, I asked the others where we should go next, but everyone seems to have figured out that Dylan and I are Dylan-and-I, so they're okay with letting us make that call. So we took off down a road that runs west parallel to the freeway that's straight enough to keep us on course but will let us do a little sightseeing. No one's in a hurry to get to the Utah border knowing the decision that's waiting for us. We know it's there, the same way you know gravity's there, gently but constantly pulling you toward it, and we'll deal with that when the time comes.

For a long while there was nothing but the road. Nobody spoke much, emotionally exhausted by the confrontation earlier. Then we started seeing one seriously small town after another, most with less than a hundred people, that had grown up around a single business, like a post office, a train station, or a fertilizer company. The number of people who live there are equal to however many are needed to run that business, along with the churches, schools, bars, shops, and hair stylists needed to look after them, little self-contained islands of people surrounded by miles of small lakes and open land stretching clear to the horizon.

When I was a girl, I loved to lie on the grass in our backyard and stare up at the sky, digging my fingers into the grass and pretending the sky was the ground, and that if I let go, I'd fall toward it. That's what it's like to stand out in the open between these little towns. The sky is so ridiculously big and blue, and the land so wide and flat, that a few times I got dizzy and started laughing because it felt like I was going to fall up into the sky and keep on going forever. Dylan probably thinks I'm a little nuts, but really, would I be here otherwise?

In the past I kept my crazy thoughts to myself because other people didn't know how to handle them, but everybody on the bus has something broken sticking out of our skin, so they don't turn away. I like that they trust me and Dylan enough to leave the pre-Utah decisions to us. After so much drama, they're happy to not make any decisions for a while, and I don't mind doing it.

Falling into the sky is fun!

PeterWilliamRouth

This afternoon we rolled into Sterling, the first decent-sized town we'd come across since entering Colorado. It was right out of the 1950s, lots of square office buildings, generic stores, Brady Bunch suburban housing tracts, and a few historic buildings scattered around here and there. We'd just parked at the Wonderful House restaurant (yes, that's the name), one of those anonymous, boxy, strip-mall Chinese restaurants you always see near freeway exits, when we heard a police siren right behind us. Everybody froze. *Okay*, I thought, *here we go. Typical Routh bad luck.* Then the car made a U-turn and took off after somebody who'd just run a stop sign.

It worked out in the end, but I didn't like that feeling of helplessness. So after dinner, while everybody else took a walk to scope out the area, I headed across the street to do some shopping. We'd picked this part of town because it's two blocks from Northeastern Junior College, where most of us will blend in, except Vaughn, so I told him to just scowl at any students he came across. That should convince them he's a teacher and leave him alone.

There aren't a lot of things that scare me, but getting arrested is right at the top of the list because I'm a control freak and the law can take that control away and stick you inside a box where they can do whatever they want and you can't do shit about it. I don't care what Dylan's lawyer friend says, the idea that we're only walking around free because the person in charge of deciding who gets arrested doesn't feel like doing it right now isn't exactly reassuring. That could change in a second, because there's always somebody with a badge looking to hit their quota for the day, and we could help them with that really fast.

When I gave Tyler the wakizashi, I lost my ticket out if things go wrong. I had to find a replacement, but apparently there aren't many stores in Sterling that sell katanas. The most interesting thing I've seen so far is the husk of a carefully preserved F.W. Woolworth's next to a vape shop, and how's *that* for your latest update from the culture wars?

I found a hardware store and searched the tools department until I found the biggest X-Acto knife they had, the #11 Classic Fine Point, which had the longest blade and could cut really deep. I also liked that it's technically labeled the X-Life. Who doesn't appreciate dramatic irony?

No, it's not a katana or a wakizashi. It's not even a tanto, the little-girl sword Gogo Yubari used in *Kill Bill*. But it's big enough and sharp enough to get the job done fast in case any cops try to storm the bus.

After that, I went by the college and grabbed a coffee and an ice cream at the student cafeteria and walked around for a while. I'd intended to check out the rest of the town, but I was feeling a bit down, so I went back to the bus, grabbed my bag, and checked into the Sterling Motor Lodge. Usually all of us stay at the same hotel, but this time everybody went their own way. We definitely need a break from each other, even if it's just for the night.

The bathroom was one of those fluorescent let's-overlight-everything-until-it-hurts-your-eyes situations that make your face look pale and washed out. I stared at myself for a long time without really thinking about anything, just looking past my eyes at whatever was on the other side, when my brain said, *What are you waiting for?*

If the cops show up, maybe you'll have time to X-Life your ex-life, and maybe you won't. Maybe they'll grab you outside the bus or come to your room or who the hell knows, and you won't have time to take care of things, and you'll end up in jail and they'll put you on suicide watch so you won't be able to do what you have to do and everything after that is just suffering and embarrassment and judges and sanity hearings and hospitals and what the fuck are you waiting for when you can avoid all of that by just taking care of business right now?

It was a valid point. This trip wasn't turning out the way I'd imagined, and while it's still possible for us to make the journey into what it was supposed to be in the first place, that didn't change the fact that this whole thing could go sideways in a minute.

Screw it, I decided. *Let's get this over with.*

I stripped down, put the X-Life on the edge of the tub, and ran the water until it was almost too hot to touch. Funny how I'm okay with dying but don't want the bathwater to be uncomfortable. It has to be hot enough to make the veins and arteries expand so the blood can evacuate fast; cold water makes the veins shrink and everything takes longer.

I climbed into the tub and settled down. The water sloshed and rose right to the top but didn't spill. I'm tidy that way. Then I thought, shit, right now my blood's still inside my body, so the volume in the tub is stable. But once the blood starts to come out, won't that add to the volume and make the water overflow? I imagined the maid coming in to clean and stepping in pools of blood before running out screaming like a scene from *The Shining*.

Can't have that, I thought, and grabbed my iPhone on the sink and Googled *what is the volume of blood entering a heated tub*, but it's a pretty specific request and I guess nobody ever asked it before because the nearest data I could find only listed the speed at which blood leaves the heart. (Three feet per second. You're welcome.) To be on the safe side, I let two inches of water out of the tub.

With that done, I reached behind my shoulder, picked up the X-Life, and closed my eyes, enjoying the warmth until I was good and relaxed.

Okay, I thought. *Here we go.*

I didn't move.

My thoughts kept drifting back to the others on the bus. We promised to stay together until we reached the Utah border. They'd already been lied to once by Mark; did I really want to add a second broken promise to the list? There was no one to stop me from jumping the line, but the more I thought about it, the more it just felt *rude*, you know?

We've only known each other for a little while, but in that time we've been through a lot together. We're friends now, and I'll be honest, I haven't had a lot of those the last few years. This may surprise you, but I can be kind of a prick sometimes. And though it's pretty clear that most of the others felt that way about me when I first showed up, eventually we got past it. Kind of like *The Breakfast Club* with death, y'know? So like I said, we're friends, and that *means* something.

Fine, I thought, and put the X-Life on the floor, *let's ride it out a little longer. But just to be safe I'll keep the blade in my jacket pocket, close enough to be grabbed fast if needed. I can still make it work, even if the cops force their way in. Easy-peasy.*

As I settled into the tub, the little voice in the back of my head said, *That's a very convenient, very tidy justification for not doing what you know you should be doing, what you said you were going to do. Maybe you're worried about letting your friends down, and maybe you're not as committed to following through as you think you are. Maybe you're looking for a way out of looking for a way out.*

By now the water was starting to get cold, so I pushed the thought away, ran the hot water again until I gained back those two inches, grabbed a bath bomb from a tray on the side, held it high, and dropped it into the water like a grenade about to go off.

Boom!

Oooh . . . lavender . . .

SunnyShanelle

I read what Vaughn wanted me to read. Now I just need to figure out what to say to him, and how to say it. Because obviously he's waiting for me to say something, and the longer he waits the more he's going to worry. But I can't think about that right now, I can't think about anything, not after this—

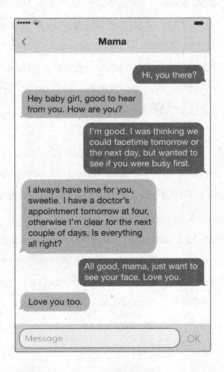

IamTheo

From: Theo THX1129@mich.edu
To: S stillhere2125@gmail.com
Subject: Hello, Love

I was thinking about you tonight, a not uncommon event, and wanted to reach out, literally as well as figuratively, but since the distance is greater than the length of my arm, I will have to settle for the latter.

After some false starts, or more accurately a false middle, the journey I talked to you about seems to be going as hoped for. I have met some fascinating people. We have laughed and cried and broken bread and sent two of our group ahead of us to scout the way.

I'm surprised by how flat the road has been. I've never been in Colorado before, so I imagined we would immediately be among mountains and rivers and peaks, because those are the images on all the posters they send out into the rest of the world as bait for the tourists. But so far there's nary a mountain or even a decent self-respecting hill to be seen.

After leaving Sterling this afternoon we planned to do some sightseeing, but so far there have been few sights to see, just clumps of houses, empty railroad cars awaiting cargo, industrial buildings, farms, and the occasional trailer park. Our impromptu tour guides, D and K, say we should be in Denver tomorrow, so perhaps then things will pick up a little. But none of that has any bearing on why I thought of you and what I wanted to tell you about.

As night fell, without a hotel or motel in sight, we pulled over to crash for the night. As usual, my mind was whirring with one thing or another and I couldn't sleep (a situation you know far too well), so I pulled on the jacket you gave me for my birthday and stepped outside to take a walk. In other parts of the world saying *I'm going to take a walk through an area I don't know all by myself in the middle of the night* is an invitation to homicide, but for some reason, such thoughts do not occur around here. There are no passing cars of strangers (well, except for us) and very few clubs or bars, just scatterings of houses and narrow roads that empty after sunset and the world goes to sleep. When there are only a hundred or so people to be found for miles in any direction, the odds of one of them being a serial killer unknown by the rest seem quite small, John Wayne Gacy and Charles Manson being the obvious exceptions, so I wasn't terribly worried.

The night air had that quality you only find in the middle of the country, brisk and cool but dry and so clear that it makes you feel like you can see farther than normal. Even the stars seemed unusually close and friendly. It reminded me of that night in Oregon when we hiked as far up Mount Hood as our tired legs could take us, and when we turned around, you gasped and said it was like looking all the way to the end of the world.

I hadn't meant to go very far, but once I hit my stride I kept walking for almost a mile. I was about to head back when I saw a little trailer park down a dirt road. Most of the lights were still on, and I had the strangest urge to see what was going on inside them. I think I wanted to take a mental picture of the people who were there, living their lives, oblivious to our passing (and, I suppose, our Passing) . . . a moment to experience all the little unimportant moments we were leaving behind.

I tiptoed through the trailer park and glanced in where I could, not to be voyeuristic, just to see if I could tell what was going on. The door to the first trailer was open, and a large, heavyset man inside was watching a reality show about a chef who tries to teach high school kids how to become cooks. Here was this man in his late fifties or early sixties, built like a football player or a professional wrestler, rooting for the kids to choose the right ingredients. "Not the saffron, not the saffron," he kept yelling as the audience cheered. "Nobody uses saffron in that." I found it oddly enchanting.

The next trailer was dark, so either no one was home or they'd already gone to bed. In the third, I saw a red-haired young woman, probably in her twenties, doing dishes and singing "Touch-a, Touch-a, Touch-a, Touch Me" a cappella from *The Rocky Horror Picture Show*. She was singing the hell out of it, so she'd either had a really good day, or was planning to have a really good night.

I started to approach the fourth trailer when I heard someone say, "Want to come sit?"

I turned to see a woman in her fifties sitting on some concrete steps that led up to one of the other trailers. I don't know if she'd settled in without my noticing, or if she'd been there the whole time, but from the Buddha-like way she had parked herself, a cigarette in one hand and a glass of whiskey in the other, you might've thought she'd been sitting there without moving for at least a year.

I said, "I'm sorry, I didn't mean to trespass."

"It's okay," she said. "You're the most interesting thing to happen here all day. Have a seat."

She scooted over and I sat on the step next to her. "I'm Cathy," she said. "You want a drink—?"

"Theo, and no, thank you. I hope you don't think I was being a creeper or something."

"Nope. Well, at first, maybe a little, but once I got a good look at you, I knew exactly what you were doing."

I smiled, wondering what conclusions she'd reached. "And what's that?"

She let the cigarette smoke out in a long, slow breath, then glanced back as if seeing straight through me. "Last looks."

It wasn't the answer I was expecting, and I guess she saw the surprise on my face because she said, "It was in your eyes, love. You were saying goodbye. I've seen it before. Saw it in my mom before she died, and with a couple of friends who went away. Even saw it in my own eyes a few times, though I never had the guts to follow through on it. But you? You're already gone, darling. It's all right there, plain as day. Might as well be on a billboard.

"When people get old," she said, "they get this hunger for travel. See the world! That's what all the brochures say, right? So they go, even though traveling means picking up your bags when you've got arthritis, then sitting in little airplane seats and train seats and God forbid bus seats for hours and hours when your hips are on fire, all to spend days with people you don't know and don't like, taking one last look around the property and collecting all the memories they can before they get evicted. Gives 'em something to hold on to when old age starts to yank out all the wiring in their brains. Nobody *really* knows where we go when the end comes, but we can at least take the time to see where we've *been*, so we go around memorizing as much of it as we can.

"That's what I saw you doing, and how I know what you're gonna do."

"You going to try and talk me out of it?"

She laughed up smoke. "Shit, no, darling. Like I said, you're already gone. It's like when you're watching the sun go down over the ocean, except the sun's already disappeared, all you're seeing is a reflection of the sun as it bounces off the sky. There's no point in trying to talk you out of anything because this is just your reflection. You're already on the other side of the horizon. Truth to tell, there are days I wish I hadn't let myself get talked out of going over the sea the last time I had the notion.

"When I was on the drill team back in high school, if you'd've told me I'd end up living in a place like this all by myself, shit, I would've laughed my ass off. Not so funny now, but I'm not ready to call it a night yet, either. Still a chance Prince Charming might come down that road one day."

She dropped her cigarette into the empty glass; it sizzled and went out. Then she set it down between us and looked back at me. "You got anyone special, love?"

I smiled again. "Yes, I do."

"They know what you're doing?"

"Yes."

"And they're okay with it? They understand the why of it all?"

"I think so. All I could do was tell the truth, and that seems to have been enough."

"Then you've known the best kind of love there is. Someone who isn't out to change you or confront you or argue with you, who just understands and lets you go your own way when you feel you have to go there."

"I agree. I'm very lucky."

We talked for a little longer, until it started to get cold. As I got up to go, she put her hand on my arm. "Got something to take with you," she said. I thought she was going to give me food or a handout, but before I could stop her, she'd already gone back inside.

She came out a moment later with a brightly colored postcard. "Something to remember me by," she said. On one side was a photograph of the Empire State Building, above the words *Welcome to the Big Apple!* The other side, where you would write the address and the message you wanted to send, was blank.

"Bought this from a collector at a flea market in Denver. I thought, one day I'm going to go to New York and send someone this postcard so they'll know I've been someplace amazing. But I never made it. So I'd appreciate it if you could take it with you. Take it someplace amazing for me."

I promised her I would. Then she hugged me, said good night, and stepped back inside the trailer as I returned to the road.

On my way back, I thought: Wouldn't it be interesting if I walked back and found that there *was* no trailer park, no one watching cooking shows or singing or smoking? The others and I are traveling a road between life and death, between here and there, and sometimes amazing things happen on roads like that. What if I just experienced Colorado's version of meeting the Buddha?

But the postcard is still in my pocket, so I suppose that's a pretty good argument for this not being an illusion. Unless it's a very clever illusion!

Sneaky old Buddha!

When I reached the bus, exhausted and ready for bed, I found that sleep was still eluding me. All I could think about was you, and what Cathy (if she really existed) had said. And I wanted to thank you: for being in the world, for being there for me when I most needed you, and for being my light and my strength when it came time to make this decision. Never judging. Never arguing. Just loving and trusting.

I love you. I love you so much. And I want you to know that I will miss you. I will miss you terribly.

Be at peace, love.

I am.

Theo

PeterWilliamRouth

From: Peter Routh GrailHunterZero@gmail.com
To: Everyone
Subject: Party!

Having successfully reached Denver, the halfway point in our journey across Colorado, with nothing between us and the Utah border but some national parks and roadside shops selling Native American jewelry, Vaughn booked himself a suite on the 40th floor and asked me to extend an invitation for everyone to meet for dinner and get totally shitfaced. He promises booze, food, music, more booze, snacks, chips, dips, those little cheese-stuffed celery things nobody eats because they're totally fucking gross, and did I mention a fuck-ton of booze?

If anybody wants to bring party favors (side-eyeing you here, Lisa), that's totally between you, your pharmacologist, and your deity of choice.

Vaughn would send this himself, but he said he screwed something up in his email settings and now every time he tries to do a group send, they end up going to some lady in Germany who has started to complain to the authorities, and we have enough problems as it is. And I choose to believe him.

Room 4012. The trouble begins at eight.

Be there or be cubed.

———————————————

Karen_Ortiz

Party!

Dylan and I could hear music blasting through the cracked-open door even before we pushed through. The place was jamming! I don't know where Vaughn found all the incredible food that crowded the kitchenette—Dylan said he probably ordered it from a local restaurant, because there was no way the hotel had that much crab and lobster tail and tacos and burgers—but OMG there was a lot of it. It was a corner suite, so we had a beautiful view of the city, and in the distance we could just make out the bright blue statue of the horse the locals nicknamed Blucifer, fire-eyed guardian of Denver airport.

We were the last to arrive, but this wasn't the kind of crowd to wait around before digging in. The Rolling Stones and Talking Heads (obviously Vaughn's choices) were blasting through the suite and the smell of weed was so strong that I was glad the windows didn't open, not for our sake but because any birds flying overhead would've been knocked out of the sky by the contact high.

Peter was in the kitchenette, looking out at the city and eating from a plate of food so full I was afraid it would spill at any second while somehow managing to balance a glass of champagne on the edge of the plate.

"Bacchanalia!" he called out when he saw us. "Freaking bacchanalia on the half-shell!"

"He's not wrong," Theo said, loading up at one of the food stations, then added, "For a change."

"Hey!" Peter yelled over the music. "I heard that!"

"Truth hurts," Theo said, laughing. "That's what it's *for*."

We continued into the den, where Lisa was dancing in the middle of the room, as usual not giving a shit that there was nobody dancing with her. "Make it louder!" she yelled.

"That's as louderer as it gets," Mark said, sitting on the couch next to Shanelle.

"Fuck hotel sound systems!" Lisa shouted, then instantly forgave everything when the Stones' "Mixed Emotions" popped up on the playlist. "Oh, fuck, this song is so me!" she said, and went back to dancing.

I was about to ask Mark where Vaughn was when he came out of the bedroom in a three-piece suit. "About time you got here!"

"Look at you, all fancy," I said.

"You like it?" he said, and gave me a turn. "I bought this ten years ago, only wore it twice. Figured I should get some mileage out of it while I can."

I realized I was grinning as he raised his glass to his reflection in the window. Until now Vaughn had always been the serious one, watching out after the rest of us, and I loved seeing him turn up the volume and let go.

Then suddenly Mark yelled, "Fuck! Shit!"

We turned to see him fumbling with his wallet. "Goddamnit!" he said.

"What's wrong?" Theo asked.

"My emergency credit card's gone! I keep it in the pocket behind my ID. I was putting my room card inside and I noticed it's gone! Shit!"

He headed for the door. "Sorry, I gotta take care of this before anybody else finds it and—"

"No, no, wait!" Lisa said, then rushed to her purse on the couch and pulled out the card she told me she'd *liberated* from his wallet the night she'd slept in his tub. "I found it on the bus this morning as we were getting off. I meant to give it to you earlier, but I got distracted."

Mark took the card and slid it into his wallet. "Jesus, thanks, that's a relief."

"My pleasure," Lisa said, and when she glanced my way and winked, I started laughing and couldn't stop.

"What's so funny?" Dylan asked.

"Oh, nothing," I said, shaking my head at Lisa. "Just glad his card's okay."

"Put on some neo-swing!" Lisa yelled. "Who's got neo-swing? Parov Stelar! Caravan Palace! Lazlo! Paul Borg! Let's burn this place *down*!"

Shanelle Bluetoothed her iPhone to the system and an electronic backbeat shook the floor.

"All right!" Lisa said, and grabbed Vaughn's arm. "Dance with me!"

"Why do women keep asking me to dance with them?" Vaughn said.

"Because you're an old fart and it's funny and we love you!"

"Fair enough," Vaughn said.

"Me too!" Shanelle said, and they hit the floor together.

Hi, I'm Audio Recorder!
Tap the icon to start recording.

PETER ROUTH: Oh, fuck, here we go.

LISA: Okay, everybody line up!

MARK ANTONELLI: What for?

LISA: Just fucking line up!

PETER ROUTH: Lucy is in the house.

DYLAN: Oh, shit.

THEO: All right!

VAUGHN: Who's Lucy?

LISA: Shit, I dropped the dropper.

MARK: So I guess it's a dropder.

SHANELLE: Just a variation on louderer, come up with your own jokes.

LISA: Here we go! Who's first? Peter!

PETER ROUTH: Hit me.

MARK: Me too.

LISA: Fine, whatever.

VAUGHN: Who's Lucy?

LISA: Molly's bigger, badder older sister. You liked Molly?

VAUGHN: Yes, very much.

LISA: You trust me?

VAUGHN: Shit, no.

LISA: Open up anyway.

PETER ROUTH: Go Vaughn!

LISA: Dylan?

DYLAN: Sure.

LISA: Karen?

KAREN: I don't know.

DYLAN: It's all right, I'll be right here.

KAREN: Okay.

LISA: Bam! Theo?

THEO: Absolutely.

LISA: You on board, Shanelle?

SHANELLE: Why not?

LISA: And ba-bam!

PETER ROUTH: Want me to do you?

LISA: I would definitely need Lucy first—

DYLAN: Bet you hear that all the time.

PETER ROUTH: Fuck you.

LISA: I can do myself.

SHANELLE: Yeah, we've noticed.

LISA: Hey!

END RECORDING

Karen_Ortiz

I've never used anything stronger than weed, so the idea of doing acid scared me enough that it never even got near the bucket list, but I knew Dylan would protect me if things got weird, so I went for it. At first I didn't feel anything, and I thought maybe Lisa was just bullshitting us about Lucy, but then it started to kick in.

Writing about what happened is like remembering someone else's dream. Random images blurring into each other. The lights of the city spiraling like a galaxy, my arms three times longer than they should have been. Everything was a smear of color and sound and sometimes I couldn't tell one from the other, and I kept thinking how Dylan had a soft green voice and Mark's was purple, and you can never entirely trust purple. When Dylan touched me, it felt like static electricity, a flash of energy where his cells touched my cells and whispered to each other in their own secret language.

And Theo! If liquid could become a person, sit on a couch, and be effortless and present, there and not-there, it would be Theo at that moment in that place.

After a while I had to go to the bathroom, and it seemed to take forever to cross the room, walking past Vaughn and Lisa and Peter and Shanelle dancing, and the window where I didn't dare look out at the blue horse in case he might be looking back at me. By the time I got inside the bathroom and closed the door, it felt like an hour had gone by.

Once I remembered how clothes worked, I sat on the toilet and closed my eyes, only to snap them open again because I wasn't sure how much time had passed or which bathroom I was in.

Moving carefully and deliberately, I flushed, dressed, and washed my hands in the sink. But when I looked up at the mirror, it wasn't my reflection staring back at me.

It was the Spider.

For a second I thought I should be afraid, but I wasn't. Somehow seeing it outside me made it seem smaller. Pain is amorphous, invisible; it doesn't have a face, it's just there, as big as the world. But now the Spider was the same size as me.

And I wasn't afraid.

This time it was the Spider who was afraid.

I live only through you, it said inside my head. *If you die, I will have nowhere to stay, and I will die too, and I don't want to die.*

Tough shit, I thought back. *Should've thought about that before you made every day a fucking nightmare.*

I was protecting you from the world. I kept you close, and made for you a cocoon of tears.

You hurt me.

I was singing to you in the only language I know.

Bullshit. You'd say anything to save yourself.

Yes, I would. Is that so wrong? I am trying to save us both. I am made of your nerves, your neurons, your flesh, your blood, your muscles, your bones. I/ we knitted them together into webs, into a thought, into a word, into a Spider. And if I am made of you, then whose face are you really looking at in the mirror?

"Fuck you," I said, out loud this time, and closed my eyes as tight as I could, mentally stitching my face back onto the reflection.

When I opened them again, the Spider was gone.

As I stepped back into the suite, Dylan came toward me. "You were in there a long time," he said, "I was starting to get worried. Are you okay?"

"I'm all right," I said, and surprised both of us when I leaned against his chest and whispered up at him, "I love you. You don't have to say anything about it or do anything. You don't have to respond, you don't even have to acknowledge that I said anything. I just want you to know. I love you."

"I love you too," he said, and I think he was as surprised and pleased by that as I was. Then he put his arms around me and pulled me to him, hard.

And this time the Spider had nothing to say about it.

———————

IamTheo

Gray dawn was starting to come through the windows by the time the last of the acid wore off, and we'd fallen into that very familiar post-trip dorm-room tradition of talking about the Big Things. Also the stupid things, like, *What's the strangest place you've ever had sex?* and *Did you ever get so drunk that you threw up and shit yourself at the same time?* That one in particular was a lot of fun, but I'm not sure the answers bear repeating. Most of the other questions were light and easy.

Then this happened.

"Predestination or free will?" Peter asked, and everyone groaned.

"What the fuck?" Lisa said from her position on the floor. Exhausted by dancing all night, she had retreated into a fetal position beneath the coffee table, and her voice drifted up to us as if we were holding a séance. "How do you go from 'Let's classify different kinds of farts' to freaking predestination?"

"I was just thinking—"

"Okay, mistake number one," Shanelle said.

He kept going anyway. "Most of the people who believe that everything is predestined, that it's all God's will, are also against suicide. Now, I don't believe in predestination, but just for the sake of argument, let's say that predestination is a real thing. That means everyone in this room was *meant* to check out early, so why would anyone who believes in God have a problem with that?"

"It's not that black-and-white," Vaughn said. He'd lost the jacket and tie and was curled up in a chair across from the big sofa where most of us were sitting. His eyes were still jackpotting a little from his time with Lucy, but that just made him more eager to dive in. "I was a church-going man for a long time, and predestination is for big-picture stuff; free will is for small-picture stuff."

"But don't they interweave?" Dylan asked. "I mean, the guys who killed JFK or Gandhi were working off individual free will, but what they did changed the world."

"Then the pastor would argue that that's predetermined."

"But if those guys *had* to do it, if they were *destined* to do it," Mark said, "then they didn't have free will, did they?"

Vaughn rubbed at his face. "Shit, Mark, how the hell should I know? I'm not God. I'm just saying the point isn't as cut-and-dried as Peter's suggesting."

I finished the last of a glass of white wine and dove into the fray. "I think free will is all about purpose, about doing what we were meant to do while we're here. Some people might say that by taking our own lives, we're defeating that purpose by cutting it short."

"Unless doing this *is* our purpose," Karen said. Dylan was sitting next to her on the couch, his arm draped around her, but he let the cushion take most of the weight. "Maybe this whole thing, the journey, the journals we're leaving for the world, maybe that's what we were put here to create."

"So you're saying Mark is doing God's work?" Dylan asked.

"Fuck! My! Life!" Lisa yelled from beneath the coffee table, her voice echoing through the room like it was coming from the bottom of the Mariana Trench. "Dylan, if you give this asshole even one inch of credit for any of this, I will crawl out of here and kick your ass."

"Sitting right here," Mark said.

"Also an asshole," Lisa said.

"Okay, enough with the heavy questions," Dylan said. "Let's go back to the funner ones."

"Did you seriously just say 'the funner ones'?" Peter asked.

"I did, and by the way, fuck you."

"The man's a trained soldier," Mark said, "so I'd for sure fuck off if I was you."

"Who asked you?!" several of us said at exactly the same time, and it turned out to be the funniest thing ever.

"Copy that," Mark said.

"Okay, next question," I said. "Pizza: Plain or with toppings? For me, it's bell peppers."

"Nope," Peter said. "Put anything on a pizza and you can't tell how good it is or isn't. It's gotta be just plain-plain-plain."

"Were you a monk in a previous life?" Dylan asked.

"Maybe."

"Mushrooms and sausage or I go home," Karen said.

"Bell peppers, onions, and olives," Shanelle said.

"I don't care," Lisa said. "If it's round, has cheese on it, and it's a pizza, I'm eating it."

"Pineapple," Mark said, and there wasn't one of us surprised to hear it.

"Sausage and pepperoni," Dylan said. "Vaughn? How about you?"

"At the risk of agreeing with Peter, I think plain's the way to go."

Peter glowered at him. "What do you mean, 'At risk of agreeing with Peter'? When did *I* become the goat? I thought that was Mark's job."

"Still sitting right here," Mark said.

"Still an *asshole,*" Lisa called out.

"Okay, lightning round," I said. "You can wish for just one thing, but it can't have anything to do with why we're here. Quick answers only. Ready, and . . . go!"

"Superpowers," Peter said, "flight and invisibility."

"Shit, he stole my answer," Shanelle said. "Um . . . to meet everyone in the world and hear their story and make them feel better about themselves!"

"So, Super-Psychologist!" Vaughn said.

Shanelle nodded. "Exactly!"

"To be president of the United States for twenty-four hours," Dylan said, "just so I could look at the UFO files."

"I want to be able to dance like a ballerina," Karen said.

"A big-ass pineapple pizza," Mark said.

"Mark and his fucking pineapple pizza getting thrown off the balcony," Lisa said.

"I'd want to see the aurora borealis," Vaughn said.

"A visit to the Library of Alexandria before it burned down," I said. "For all those lost secrets and incredible stories."

By now everyone was tired and starting to glaze over, so I was about to suggest we call it a night—or a day, since it was now fully tomorrow—when Vaughn stood and tapped on his glass for attention.

"I don't know if making a toast is something you bunch still do," he said, "but I'd like to propose two of them. The first one, I don't think you're going to like. The second . . . well, we'll have to see.

"I think we can all agree that Mark leaves a lot to be desired as a human being. His intentions when he started this were wrong, and by misleading us, he hurt us. But on the other side of that great hurt is the fact that he brought all of us together on this journey, and I would not trade having that time with you for anything on this good Earth. So I would like to suggest that we forgive him for his transgressions— just a little, and just for tonight—and raise a glass to thank him as our host and the inspiration for our travels. To Mark Antonelli!"

Some of us hesitated, but as much as we hated to admit it, Vaughn was right, so we raised our glasses. "To Mark!"

Vaughn kicked the coffee table. "To Mark!"

"YeahwhatevercanIgotosleepnow?"

"As to the second toast," Vaughn said, refilling his glass, "this one's a little more personal.

"When I got on the bus and you saw me, you probably went *Oh shit* the same way I went *Oh shit* when I saw *you*. I'd assumed my fellow passengers would be a bunch of old farts like me who'd come to the end of the line because I couldn't imagine . . . well, I couldn't imagine *you*. So I don't think either of us quite knew what to make of each other. But the more I talked to you, the more I *listened* to you, I began to see the beauty in you . . . in *all* of you . . . and I have been moved and humbled by it. I wish you could see yourselves as I do.

"I was married for longer than all of you have been alive, and for most of that time I thought I knew what love was," he said, and I noticed a glance between him and Shanelle as he said it, and wondered what it meant. "But it took me until now, until *you*, to understand what that word really means. We've got a big decision waiting for us when we hit the Utah border. Once we make that decision, there may not be a lot of time for talk, so I want you to know now that I am proud and honored to be among you, that you are beautiful, and that I love you all.

"To you!" Vaughn said, and raised his glass. "To *us*!"

"To us!" we said, even Lisa, and as we threw back our drinks, I could see that I wasn't the only one whose eyes welled up at Vaughn's words. I don't think many of us had ever been called beautiful before.

"Now get the fuck out," Vaughn said, "so I can get some sleep."

As the others filed out, I hit the bathroom because I'd had a lot to drink and there was no way I could make it back to my floor without courting catastrophe.

When I emerged, everyone was gone except for Lisa, who had fallen asleep beneath the coffee table, and Shanelle, who was kissing Vaughn.

Good for her, I thought as I tiptoed toward the door. *And good for him. I'm glad they found each other.*

VaughnR

I was trying to figure out how to drag Lisa out from under the coffee table without getting too personal when I saw Shanelle standing next to me. "You're beautiful too, you know."

"I appreciate the sentiment, but I am way too old and ugly to be beautiful."

"Not true," she said. "You know what makes you beautiful?"

"Natural style and charisma?"

"When you look at me, I don't feel like you're looking at a black girl, or a fat girl. You're just looking at me."

"Who you are is all that matters."

"And that's what makes you beautiful."

And she kissed me.

When we came up for air, I took a moment to study her face. "Are you really sure you want to get involved with someone like me?"

"Why wouldn't I?"

"Because of what happened with Carolyn."

"I saw what you wrote, Vaughn, and it doesn't change a thing. You've done nothing but feel bad about what happened ever since it happened, and as far as I'm concerned there's no reason for it."

"Shanelle—"

"Let's pretend for a second that you didn't do it. How much longer do you think she would've hung on?"

"I don't know . . . one doctor said weeks, another said maybe a couple of months."

"And knowing that, you really think what you did was so bad?"

"My point is that I did it."

"And *my* point is I don't care. I know who you are *inside*, Vaughn, and you're just what I said you are, a good man. You cared for her and put up with her bullshit longer than anybody else would've *ever* done. You had one moment of weakness in a lifetime of trying to do the right thing."

She leaned in and kissed me again. "You're a good, kind man, Vaughn, and I've never had sex with a good, kind man before. Someone who saw me for exactly who I am, and liked me just the same."

"I'm just not sure this is the right time."

"This is as right as we can make it, and we are all out of time, right, wrong, or whatever. This moment is all we have, and I want to have that with you, right now."

Then she kissed me again, very softly, and pulled me into the bedroom. And we made love.

And when I started crying, and couldn't stop, she held me until I could.

And she healed me.

Then she went to sleep in my arms, and I stroked her hair and studied her face for what felt like hours. Just looking at her.

Beautiful. My God, so beautiful.

Mark

I knew this moment was coming, but that didn't make it any easier when the hammer fell.

I came down from my room this morning to find everyone else already on the bus except Dylan, who was waiting outside. "End of the road, boss," he said.

"So soon? I was hoping we could stay together for a little longer."

"They want to go the rest of the way alone. Like Vaughn said last night, they appreciate you getting everyone together, but from here on out, it's about them and what they want to do when they decide to do it."

"What about you?" I asked. "If I'm not involved anymore, then you're technically off the clock. You don't have to go any further."

"Yeah, we talked about that. Lisa and Peter said they can drive if I want to get off the bus, but I said I'd stick around for a while, see where it all goes."

"Also, Karen," I said.

He nodded soberly. "Also, Karen. Whatever time is left, I'd like to spend it with her."

"I understand," I said, and repeated it a few times as I tried to decide what to say next. When they took over, I wanted nothing more than to walk away and let them go off on their own and crash and burn for all I cared. Now, I was surprised to realize that I would miss them terribly. "Listen, I know you need to get going, so tell the others I won't cause any problems for them about borrowing the bus. I won't get in the way."

"I appreciate that," Dylan said, and extended his hand. "Thanks for giving me the job, Mark. It's been one hell of a ride."

"One hell of a ride," I said, and shook it. "Good luck, D."

A few minutes later I watched as Dylan put the bus into gear, made a long turn in the circular hotel driveway, and headed out. Theo and Vaughn in the back waved goodbye.

And then they were gone.

I went back inside, extended my stay for another day, and took the elevator to my room to write this since I can still upload to the cloud even though the bus is out of range. Not sure what I'll do next. Wait to hear what happens, I guess. Either way, I've decided that this will be my last entry.

It's all down to them now.

PeterWilliamRouth

After we left the hotel, Karen moved up front to be near Dylan while Shanelle and Vaughn sat together a few rows back. I was pretty much by myself on the other side, across from Theo, who was spread over two seats to write, while Lisa crashed out in one of the bunks, all of us quiet, lost in our own thoughts. I don't want to say it's because ditching Mark and heading for Utah made things real, because it's been real for a long time, but there's *real* and there's *more real*, and this was the latter. So I shut the door to what I was feeling and turned my attention out the window. Living more inside my head than in my body is something I learned to do early on. My dad was a drunk, violent and racist, an awful human being in every way you can imagine. The sampler platter of evil. I used to come home from school to find him passed out on the sofa, blitzed out of his mind, or worse still, find him awake and beating the hell out of my mom. If I said anything about it or tried to stop him, he'd turn that rage around on me, so I learned early on how to take the violence, hide the bruises, and make it all go away inside.

But every day as I walked home from school I'd get more and more anxious the closer I got, never knowing what version of the monster was going to be waiting for me. Sometimes I'd have this overwhelming urge to turn around and run until I reached a place where he could never find me. But I knew what would happen to my mom and me if I even tried it, so every day I shoved down my emotions, fought the urge to flee and walked through the front door.

By the time I hit college I prided myself on being a brainiac, for being more about thinking than feeling, for staying calm when everybody else freaked out, and for being able to rationally talk myself out of anything that went wrong. The only problem is that after you spend years shutting down the bad emotions, you realize one day that you've also shut down all the good ones. Yeah, I wasn't sad anymore, but I wasn't happy, either; I wasn't afraid every minute like I'd been in the past, but joy was just something I read about or saw in other people. I'd built a wall around my heart that was so thick and so high that even I couldn't get over it to the other side.

It's no secret that some of the others on the bus aren't impressed with my reasons for wanting to end it. They think it's just an intellectual decision, not an emotional one. (This of course means accepting the premise that an emotional decision to commit suicide is more rational than a rational decision, which is just being emotional, and that doesn't make *any* kind of sense.) They don't understand that rationality is all I *have*, so you can imagine my surprise this afternoon when after all these years I finally discovered real, true awe.

The Arapaho National Forest west of Georgetown was the first time any of us had seen trees and mountains that big, and we couldn't get enough of them. I must've looked like a grinning idiot as I craned my neck out the little bus window for a better look, but the tops of both were way past my line of sight. The others were having the same problem, so after Theo checked the map for a place to stop, we pulled over into Silverthorne, between a forest to the north and Dillon Bay to the south.

Everybody piled out except Shanelle, who was taking advantage of a good cell signal to FaceTime with her mom, and we walked around for almost an hour just *looking* at everything. The sky was crazy wide and deep blue, and the wind was so fresh from all the trees and the water that it knocked us back on our heels a little. Even Lisa didn't know what to say; she just kept looking from forest to mountain to lake, muttering *So cool* over and over.

Dylan said this was as good a place as any to break for lunch, so once Shanelle was done with her call we got a bite on the patio of the Red Mountain Grill so we could see the water. I couldn't get enough of it.

The world is so wide, I thought, *and my remaining choices so narrow.*

Talking about death and dying has always been easy for me, because in some ways it was easier than living. But now that death is nearly here, now that it's *real*, a part of me is afraid to go forward. But I've come too far to go back. I'm committed to the choices I've made.

Pushing down the thought and the panic made the world suddenly seem very far away, as if it had nothing to do with me anymore. It's too big for me. My world is the bus, and where it's going, and what happens when we get there.

I was afraid to go home, but going home was inevitable.

I am afraid to go forward, but going forward is inevitable.

And with every breath, I fight the urge to flee.

Karen_Ortiz

After lunch we got back on the road, and by five we were in Fruita, Colorado, the last town with any decent motels before the Utah border. Dylan said he picked the Balanced Rock Inn because it was walking distance to a drugstore, a couple of bars, a park, some fast food places, three banks, and two churches. Something for everyone. But mainly I think he liked the name.

When we checked in, Dylan said he was going to take the room across the hall from me rather than sharing the same room. Now that we were close enough to pick up the Utah PD on the police scanner, he wanted to get up early to get a sense of what's in front of us without having to wake me. I told him I love that he's considerate, but I'd happily trade a few hours of sleep to lie against his warmth, so we're back in the same room for the night. I don't think we have many more nights together, and I'll fight for every one of them.

In the end, we *both* lost sleep when Dylan got a midnight email from his lawyer friend. Would post more, but just really exhausted now. More later.

VaughnR

After we got into the room, Shanelle seemed distant, almost sad. I asked if everything was all right and she said she was just tired, but I could tell there was more going on inside. I thought maybe it was something I'd done, so to make up for any accidental stupidities on my part I went looking for food while she took a nap since the motel didn't have room service. At a City Market two blocks away I loaded up on salads, turkey, ham, snacks, beer, and bottled water. And yes, I was that old guy you see wheeling a stolen grocery cart down the street because there's too much to carry.

The room table was pretty small, but I managed to cover it with enough food to feed a small South American village for a week. She laughed when she woke up and saw it all, but when we sat down for dinner she barely touched any of it. By now I was sure that she was going to say that what happened between us was a mistake and that we should move into different rooms. Instead she asked if we could go lie down together for a while.

I was married for over forty years and I *still* have no idea how to read women.

With both of us still dressed, she spooned on the bed with me tucked in behind, her head resting on my arm. I assumed she just wanted to take a nap, but then I felt tears on my arm.

I tried to nudge her back around so I could see her, but she wouldn't roll over, like she didn't want to face me. "What's going on?" I said.

"Nothing," she said, but the tears kept coming.

"I've seen nothing, and this ain't it. What's going on, sweetie?"

"I can't do it."

"Can't do what?"

"When I talked with my mom today," she said, the words tumbling out, "she was just so happy to see me, and we laughed about a million things and I told her I was seeing somebody and she was so pleased to hear it, all she asked was, *Is he good for you?* and I said, *Yeah, he's so sweet, he's the best thing to happen to me in a long time,* and she teared up, she was so thrilled that she didn't need to hear anything more, she just kept saying she loves me, so much, over and over.

"And I can't do it, Vaughn. I can't finish this with the rest of you. If I do, it'll break her in half. She'll never get over it. She'll blame herself for the rest of her life."

"But it's not her fault."

"Doesn't matter. She'll never believe that. She'll agonize over every conversation we ever had, everything she ever did or said, or didn't do or say, looking for the one thing that she can point to and say, *It's all my fault.*"

She finally turned to face me, her cheeks covered in tears. "I didn't know how to tell you because we're all in this together. We said we were going all the way, and I don't want to let you or the others down, but I can't do this to her, Vaughn. I just can't, and I'm sorry."

"You're not letting me down, Shanelle. Far from it. I'd accepted that you were going to end it with the rest of us because that was your choice and I had to respect it, but I hated the idea of a light as bright as yours going out so soon. If you want to get off the bus, there's not one of us who'd complain about it. Especially me.

"You said I was the best thing to happen to you, Shanelle, and that means the whole world because you're the best thing to happen to me. Until I met you, I thought I'd have to walk off the earth alone."

"But you are!"

"No, I'm not. I've got the others now. More important, I've got you, right here inside me, and nothing can ever take that away. If anything, knowing you'll still be in the world after I'm gone will make my part of it easier."

"You don't have to go," she said. "If I'm staying behind, you could too."

"Can't, sweetie. I appreciate everything you said about how I shouldn't blame myself for Carolyn, and some of it may even be true. But I did what I did and my soul says there has to be a reckoning, there has to be balance. Besides, I'm not a good prospect for any kind of long-term relationship. At my age, it's only a matter of time before my dick falls off and my brain turns to oatmeal."

She laughed through the tears. "That's a terrible thing to say!"

"Maybe, but it's true. I don't have a future, Shanelle, but you do, and the idea that you'll be out there somewhere living it is the happiest thing I've ever heard.

"I *want* you to get off the bus," I said, and I realized I was crying now too. "I want you to *live*. For me, for your folks, for the others, for *yourself*. I want you to chase your dreams and live your life. Run as far and as fast as you can, and never, ever look back."

"You're sure you're not disappointed in me?"

"The only thing that would've disappointed me is if we made it all the way to San Francisco, and just as we went over the edge of that cliff you turned to me and said, *On the other hand . . .*"

And she laughed and kissed me, and we made love for the last time, and it was tender and gentle and sad and beautiful.

It was the whole world.

It was everything.

Thank you for this, I thought at the universe after she fell asleep. *Thank you for Shanelle, and thank you for getting her to change her mind. I can go easy now.*

Let her be happy. Please, God, let her be happy.

PeterWilliamRouth

Well, that was unexpected.

We'd just gathered in Dylan's room to see if he had any updates about our situation when Vaughn told us that Shanelle had something to say. Half in tears, she explained that she'd changed her mind about going all the way with us, that she was going home, and that she hoped we'd understand.

The whole room cheered. Good for her, I thought. Nobody should go on the rest of this trip unless they're 100% sure they're doing the right thing for the right reasons.

It was Theo, of course, who said it best. "Shanelle, I think anyone who can stay in the world a day or a week or an hour longer than we can needs to do it. I can't, but I love and honor the knowledge that you can. You have no idea how happy this makes me."

Of my own uncertainty, I said nothing.

When she was ready to go, we hugged her and said all the expected things, like *Don't forget us,* and *Go kick ass,* and *We're proud of you.* Then we escorted her to the cab that would take her to the Denver Airport. Before she got in, Vaughn handed her the bag of cash. At first she didn't want to take it, but he insisted. *It's not like I'm going to need it,* he said. *I wanted to do some good with it. Well, now's my chance. Please. Take it, for the college fund if nothing else. Become that Super-Psychologist, Shanelle. Do it for me.*

Still crying, she nodded, took the bag, and hugged him so hard I thought she'd snap him in half.

Then she got in the cab, waved one last time, and drove out of our lives.

IamTheo

Maybe it's the curse of having a writer's eye, but even before Dylan started talking I could tell something was wrong, so I was glad of the diversion as we said goodbye to Shanelle.

"We have a problem," he said after she'd left. "Last night I got an email from my attorney friend Jamie, who's been in touch with a guy he knows in the Assistant District Attorney's office in Provo. He had to push pretty hard for information because this guy didn't want to risk losing his job for talking about internal decisions, but Jamie was finally able to piece together where we stand and what's been going on while we've been on the road.

"As Jamie suspected, the Nebraska police contacted the Utah AG and told him what happened and what we're trying to do, and now he's got a serious hard-on about us. He's afraid that if we finish this the way we want to, it'll inspire copycats to pick up busloads of people who want to commit suicide, or who *say* they want to help as a way to lure vulnerable people into situations where they can be exploited or killed. So he's decided to make an example of us, to discourage anyone else from doing the same thing.

"He started by raising hell with the Colorado AG's office, demanding that they pick us up before we crossed the border into his backyard. Colorado told them no, same as he told Nebraska, because he doesn't want the heat. But there are rules requiring cooperation between state law enforcement agencies, and when he said no, the Utah AG threatened to take legal action, so they compromised: Colorado would *technically* continue to ignore us, which saves their ass politically, while providing Utah with any information they had that would help them arrest us if we entered their jurisdiction. So now the Utah AG has detailed descriptions of us, the bus, at least some of our names, the license plate number, and, worst of all, location data from the traffic cameras."

"Wait, you're saying they know where we are?" Peter asked.

"Only roughly. Most of the cameras are on the freeway and in the big cities; the farther we went off the beaten track, the fewer times we pinged the system, so they know our general vicinity but not our exact location. One other thing in our favor is that they have no idea when or even *if* we still plan to cross the border. We could do it tomorrow, the day after, next week, or never, and Utah can't afford to have squad cars waiting around for us indefinitely.

"So I spent this morning on the scanner listening in on the Utah Highway Patrol to try and get a sense of what the odds are. The good news is that I only heard a couple of calls from dispatchers to units responding to calls along the border reminding them to keep an eye out for us, so overall it seems pretty quiet, but that could change in a second.

"Here are the variables," Dylan said, and for a moment I could imagine him as he was back in the army, giving a briefing to other soldiers. *We have to cross the frontier before the enemy knows we're there. The odds aren't great. Here's the breakdown.*

"One: there aren't a lot of roads in this part of the world, so from where we are, the only way into Utah is the 70 unless we want to go almost a hundred miles south, then take back roads across terrain where we can't go very fast, and even those run out so sooner or later we'll still have to get on the 70. All the alternate route does is take more time, and the longer it takes for us to cross the state, the more we're at risk; the faster we go, the better the odds we make it to the other side before they can catch us.

"Two: even though I don't think there are any police units parked on the other side waiting for us, the Highway Patrol still has our plates, which means they've almost certainly programmed the traffic safety system to flag us the moment we're picked up on camera.

"Three: once we cross the border, there's not a rest stop or a gas station for over a hundred miles, so we have to make sure the bus can go flat-out without stopping for at least that far.

"And four: because there *is* so much open ground between us and the next big city, even if the traffic cameras do manage to ping our plates, it'll take them a while to get anyone on our tail; how quickly they can respond will depend on where they've deployed their forces. If we move fast, we could be miles away from where they think we are by the time they get the call.

"So given all of those variables, unless anyone has a better idea, I suggest we avoid the back roads and stick to the 70—that way we can at least put the pedal to the metal. Speed is the only friend we have right now."

"How long do you think it'll take to cross Utah?" I asked.

"It's a bit over four hundred miles, so if we get on the road super early, before heavy traffic, and drive nonstop, we could reach the other side in about five hours. It all comes down to how quickly they ID us, how fast they can react, and how many cars they can mobilize in time to cut us off."

Five hours. Under other circumstances it would be an easy drive, but with what was waiting for us on the other side of the border, five hours sounded impossibly long.

"What if we put mud on the license plates, obscure the numbers?" Peter said.

"Traffic cameras look for obscured plates all the time—we'd still get flagged."

"Yeah, but we wouldn't get flagged as *us*, only as one more car with dirty plates. Might buy us a little more time before they put it together."

"Possible," Dylan said. "Wouldn't hurt to try."

Vaughn crossed his arms, weighing the information. "Assuming we make it out of Utah, what happens then?"

"There's a little strip of the 70 that runs through Arizona," Dylan said, "maybe twenty, twenty-five miles long. I'm not sure that the Utah AG would reach out to coordinate with the Arizona AG given that we'd only be in the state about an hour. And even if he did contact them, the Arizona police might not want to get involved with this mess since we're going to be in and out fast. So if we do get that far, it might make sense to stay off the main road long enough to catch our breath, refuel, and figure out our next move from there."

"You mentioned odds," Vaughn said. "Mark said you're a demon at the casinos. If you had to lay down a bet, what do you think the odds are of us reaching Arizona?"

Dylan looked down, and his eyes were tired. "If everything goes right, I'd say 50/50. It's *possible*. But if the cameras catch us early, and there's even one police unit near the border when we cross, we're screwed. We'll be in the middle of the desert with nowhere to hide, and there's no way we can outrun an interceptor. Everyone on the bus will be arrested. It's that simple."

Nobody spoke; the news took the wind out of us.

Finally, Dylan broke the silence. "You all agreed to stick together as far as the Utah border, then figure out what to do from there. Now that we're here, and now that you know the latest on where we stand and what we're up against, I suggest you take some time to weigh all the facts before making your final decision. That'll give me time to go over the bus, top off the radiator, check the tires, tighten all the bolts, and make sure it's ready to go if you decide to make a run for it. I also want to buy some extra cans of gas so we won't have to make any stops along the way. So let's meet at the bus at 4 a.m. and you can let me know what you want to do."

"One last thing," Vaughn said. "You said you wanted to make sure that *we* won't have to make any stops, but if we decide to go for it, you don't have to come along, you know that, right? We're more than able to take it from there."

"He knows," Karen said, and threaded her arm through his. "We can take it from here."

Dylan nodded in agreement, but there was something very different behind his eyes when he did it.

VaughnR

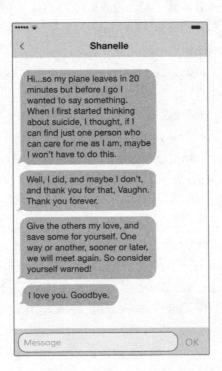

PeterWilliamRouth

If this was going to be my last night on Earth I didn't want to spend it sober, so I walked down a few blocks until I found a tavern on Mulberry that was still open. It was a little hole-in-the-wall kind of place with a bunch of motorcycles parked outside. None of them were Harleys and they were all pretty well looked after, more daddycycles than choppers, so I figured they catered more to the suburban biker crowd than Hells Angels.

Sure enough, most of the customers were on the older side, and were more interested in drinking beers and telling stories on each other than starting anything. I sat at the bar and ordered a beer and a burger since they were about to stop taking food orders so the cook could go home. They must not get a lot of newcomers in this part of town because everybody wanted to know who I was and when I got into town and what I was doing there and how long would I be staying? I didn't want to get into it, so I told them I was on my way to Utah when I hit car trouble and had to stop for the night.

"Goin' to Utah?" one of the guys said. "In-fucking-*tentionally?*" Everyone seemed to think this was hysterical, so I guess they didn't consider Utah a garden spot.

He got up from the table and leveraged himself onto the bar stool next to mine. He was a big guy, with a buzz cut, a round face, and the kind of build that looks like baby fat with an attitude. "Name's Dave," he said and extended a meaty hand.

"Peter," I said, and shook it. "One of those bikes outside yours?"

"The Yamaha. Been all over the country in that baby. You ride?"

"Not anymore. Used to, but I traded it in for something with a roof when I got into college so my textbooks wouldn't get washed away."

"What're you studying?"

"Psychology and philosophy."

"Philosophy?" he said, loud enough for the others to hear. "Well, that's debatable, isn't it?"

Apparently he was the comedian-in-residence. We all gotta have hobbies. Still, he was amicable and happy to see a new face, and we talked and bought each other drinks and were the last ones in the place when it closed down at midnight. I was still mostly sober, but Dave had started drinking long before I got there, so he was pretty wobbly as he walked toward his bike. He dropped his keys twice trying to get them out of his pocket, and staggered back each time he tried to pick them up, yelling, "Little rascals, come back here!"

I picked up the keys. "You shouldn't be riding. You'll end up wrapped around a tree."

"Love has strange ways," he said, and laughed.

"Seriously. I'm gonna call you a cab."

"Okay, I'm a cab. Now give me my keys."

"Not a chance," I said. There was apparently just one cab company in town, with only a few cars, but one of them was in the area, and ten minutes later, I shoved Dave into the back of the car, gave the driver twenty bucks, and watched the taillights fade away into the night. As I started walking back to the motel, I realized I still had his keys in my pocket. By now the tavern was closed, but there was a mail drop in the front door and—

And I'm not sure why I did it.

Maybe it was a desire to escape, an act of rebellion against the walls closing in; maybe it was those nine beers, or maybe I lost my mind for a minute, or maybe I got ambushed by the Let's Do Something Really Stupid gene that every guy my age knows far too well, but before I realized I was doing it, I straddled the bike, slipped in the key, and roared off down the street.

I hadn't been on a bike in a long time, so I told myself I was just going to take it around the block, but as soon as I hit the road I kept going. I pointed the bike south until I hit Rimrock Drive, which led through the canyons. There wasn't a stoplight in sight, just one hairpin turn after another bordered by hills and empty land, so I opened up the Yamaha to see what she could do. The speedometer showed fifty, then sixty. I leaned into the curves as they flashed at me faster and faster.

This is insane, part of my brain thought. *Slow the fuck down.*

Seventy.

I balanced side to side as fast as I could move, riding the white line to flatten out the curves.

Eighty.

I leaned low into the wind, heart racing, grinning at my own terror. *We're on a stolen bike hitting Mach seven on a road we don't know with more sharp curves than a sorority. Enjoying the ride?*

Eighty-five.

I yelled at the night. Incoherent. Raging. Heart pounding. *Alive.*

I hit a straight stretch of road and throttled up. Defying the night. *Daring* the night. *Fuck you! You want me? Take me now! I'm right here! Come on, you black-robed pussy, take your best shot!*

Then: movement on the road ahead.

Shit!

I hit the brakes. The bike skidded and bucked but held to the road, then shuddered to a stop.

Two deer stood twenty feet ahead, looking at me like, *Yo, what's up? We're just passing through*, one of them said to me with his eyes.

Yeah, me too, I thought back.

Then they turned and walked across the road, skittering down the side of the hill before disappearing into the shadows.

With the moment broken, my adrenaline levels dropped and rationality returned. *What the hell are you doing, this is full-tilt stupid.* It wasn't the first time I'd had that thought while screaming down the road, but until now I hadn't exactly been paying attention.

Keep up this kind of behavior and one of these days you'll get yourself killed, I thought, and laughed at the voice in my head.

I turned the bike around and headed back. I didn't blow out the speedometer this time, but I still kept the bike above sixty because why the fuck not? As I got closer to the tavern, a truckload of questions began scratching at the back of my head.

If I hadn't stopped for the deer, how far would I have gone? Would I have kept going and never come back? I mean, sure, I've been talking a good game about killing myself to everybody, but was I really committed to following through? When I decided not to end it in the bathtub, was it *really* because I didn't want to abandon the others, or was I just afraid to follow through?

I didn't know. I still don't know. Shit, maybe I'm not *supposed* to know for sure if I want to live or die or keep going or check out until the moment comes for real. Does anybody know until that second? Ever? Really?

When I reached the tavern, I parked the bike where Dave had left it, dropped the keys in the mail slot, and walked back to the motel, my face burning from the whipping the night air had given it.

As I came up the driveway, I saw Lisa sitting outside, smoking a blunt. She nodded at me but didn't say anything, so I figured best to leave her to her thoughts.

Last rides.

Last rites.

I tell myself, *Okay, I'm good, let's get this over with.*

But the questions keep right on asking themselves.

Hi, I'm Audio Recorder!
Tap the icon to start recording.

LISA: Hey, moon! Hey, God or whatever! Yeah, you! I got a question for you.

This whole time, did you think it was funny?

I mean, you had all these millions of combinations for the DNA thing, you could've done anything you wanted. You could've made me perfect, or given me cystic fibrosis or hemophilia or cancer or green hair . . . not sure if that last one's actually an option, but with enough genes I bet you could've pulled it off . . . something where I could've popped out of my mom and a doctor would've done a blood test and said yeah, it's this or that, so you're gonna have to prepare yourself and here are some pamphlets and your bill.

You could've done any one of those things, but you didn't. Instead you put a time bomb inside my head so I'd think everything was fine, until one day when it's like, okay, we're gonna jumpstart your hormones, oh, and surprise, you're going to lose your mind for the rest of your life. Have fun!

Did you think it was funny? Did it make you laugh? Or am I just being an asshole? I mean, you're out there designing butterfly wings and sending comets on these amazing trajectories, painting nebulas and goldfish and peacocks, so I guess you're too busy to talk about the things you screwed up, like putting the knees of flamingos on backward, and herpes, and me. Well, fuck you.

I want to know if it was worth it. For you. To do this. To me.

I want you to climb down out of that fucking sky and tell me what you were thinking, and why, and what it's supposed to mean, because from here I don't see it. Seriously. I don't see it. Was I put here just to piss people off? To be an annoying bitch? Is that it? Is that all I am to you? Because that's all I ever was to anybody else.

Can you name one good thing I did that anybody will remember? No. Because my circuits are fried. Because I was too busy being Crazy Lisa and after ten minutes even I couldn't stand her. All I ever wanted was just one chance to do something that mattered. But it never happened, and it's too late now.

So why was I even here? I didn't ask to be born. I didn't get a vote. Nobody checked with me. I had no control over it.

Well, now I do. I may not have had a voice in how I came into the world, but I sure as shit have a voice in how I leave it. And I'm going to use it to spit right in your face.

Karen_Ortiz

We'd finished making love an hour earlier, but Dylan was still wide awake, like something was racing through his head and he couldn't shut it off. "Four o'clock comes early," I said. "You should try to get some sleep."

"I will," he said, but it was clear that sleep was off the menu. "Can I ask you a question?"

"Of course."

He started, then stopped. "Let me back up so I can set this up."

"Not going anywhere," I said.

"I was thinking about the whole suicide thing—"

"I don't want to talk about that right now, not on our last night—"

"I don't either, but it's important," he said, and sat up a little. "See, I think the reason people kill themselves—"

"*One* of the reasons. We're all different, we don't lie down in rows."

"—is because they think they're never going to be happy again, that every day is going to be miserable and awful and lonely and painful and they might as well check out because there's no chance they'll ever be happy."

"Okay, fair. So?"

He looked at me with eyes so intense I could feel them burrowing right through mine and scratching at the other side of my skull to see what was back there. "Are you happy, right now? With us?"

"Dylan, come on, don't do this."

"I'm just asking. Are you happy . . . with me, and us, right here, right now?"

"Of course I am. I love you. I never thought that would happen to me, or that it could happen this fast, and maybe it's because I *don't* have time, but . . . yes, I love you and I'm happy when I'm with you."

"What about tomorrow?"

"You mean the vote?"

"No, leave all that aside, I'm just talking about us. Do you think there's a chance, just a *chance*, that for ten minutes tomorrow you could be happy with us being together, like this?"

"Dylan—"

"Five. Five minutes. Do you think you could be happy for five minutes?"

"I don't know. Maybe. Why?"

"Because if it's possible, then maybe you should think twice about tomorrow."

"I have. I thought about it a thousand times before getting on the bus, and a hundred times since."

"Even so, I'm asking you not to go, Karen. I love you. Don't leave me."

"Don't do this, Dylan. It's not fair."

"I know, and I don't care, not if there's even a small chance that you might be happy tomorrow, or the day after, for just five minutes—"

"We don't know that."

"We don't know that you *won't*, either. Can't we just live in that space? Live in the ambiguity?"

"You Googled *ambiguity*, didn't you?"

"Karen, c'mon, I'm asking you—"

"I know you are," I said, and touched his lips. So soft. And his eyes were softer still, held-back tears reflecting light at the edges even as he refused to let them out. "Let me read you something."

I leaned over the bed and fumbled around in my purse until I found my phone and called up Notes. "It's a Zen proverb I found online the day I answered Mark's ad, almost like it was a sign.

"'Empty-handed I go, and yet the spade is in my hands; I walk on foot, and yet I am riding on horseback: when I pass over the bridge, lo, the water flows not, but the bridge is flowing.'"

I glanced up to see him looking at me like a goldfish that couldn't understand why the magic food hadn't appeared in his bowl. Totally didn't get it. Tabula rasa. It was cute and charming and funny, but I didn't dare laugh.

"I don't get it," he said, stating the obvious.

"It means that sometimes intent takes over from everything else. I've committed myself to what I have to do, and I'm at that point now where even if I try to stand still, the bridge is flowing, and it's going to take me where it's going to take me."

"It's a stupid poem."

"It's Zen, it's not supposed to make sense. Also: a proverb, not a poem."

"I don't care."

"Totally get that," I said, and touched his face. He closed his eyes and rubbed his cheek against my cupped hand.

"I love you, Dylan, and as much as being in love with you means to me, it doesn't change what's inside me. Could I be happy tomorrow, or the day after, or the day after that? I don't know any more than you do. Maybe. Maybe not. But I know for an absolute *fact* that the Spider is going to be there for all of those days and the ones beyond. I can't live with that anymore. Please don't ask me to keep trying. I'm tired and I just want to go to sleep and be done with it."

"What am I supposed to do without you?"

"Live. That's all. Just live."

"I don't know if I know how."

"You'll figure it out," I said, and curled up against him.

There were two hours left before four o'clock.

And in those two hours, we lived a lifetime.

VaughnR

So how did you spend your last night on earth, Vaughn?

Watching infomercials for Snuggies.

It was dark as pitch, no moon, when I went outside at 3:30 and found Theo tending a fire in an old rusted grill behind the motel. "What's for breakfast?" I asked.

"Words."

Then I saw Theo's notebooks in the grill.

"Why are you burning them? I loved the parts you read."

"Thanks. I wrote them for myself, and anybody I chose to share them with. They served their purpose. The stories are done, so I'm sending them on ahead of me. You want to say anything over the cremation?"

I started to shake my head because I'm not really good with words at times like this. Then I remembered the rhyme Carolyn used to sing when we talked about meeting the end side by side, with love and courage, and while that didn't quite work out the way either of us expected, maybe this time it would.

I cleared my throat, crossed my hands in front of me, and said, "Together we will go, together we will go, heigh-ho the derry-o, together we will go."

A moment passed. Then another.

"That's it?" Theo said.

"It's all I've got."

Theo laughed. "Well, I've heard better, but I've also heard a lot worse. Thank you for the requiem, Reverend Vaughn."

Then I looked up from the fire and saw the others gathering outside the bus. "We should go."

Theo agreed, and raced toward the bus like somebody just offered free barbecue.

PeterWilliamRouth

Dylan closed the door and switched on the air conditioner. It wasn't hot outside, but I was seriously sweating. Then he got up out of the driver's seat and turned to us, his eyes heavy with the weight of what we were about to decide.

"The gas tank's loaded to the max, I picked up the extra fuel cans, and the bus is as ready as I can make it, whichever way you decide to go. Like I said, it's a five-hour drive. Maybe you can get to the other side before the cops know you're there. And maybe they'll nail you ten minutes after you cross the border. Either way, it's your call. What do you want to do?"

Theo stood at the back of the bus. "Can I say something?"

"Sure thing," Dylan said.

"The police are after us for what we did helping Zeke to go on ahead of us. If they arrest us, they'll stick us in a box and take away our freedom. And I think we can all agree that that would be bad.

So let's say we give up, pack up our bags, and go home. None of that changes the fact that sooner or later, we're going to do whatever it takes to follow Zeke and Tyler out the door because that decision was made before any of us even *heard* about this trip. And if the police find out what we're going to do before we have a chance to do it, guess what? They'll stick us in a box and take away our freedom. The only difference I can see is that at least here we have each other.

"Our lives and our bodies don't belong to the police, the church, our families, or the government. They want to force us to stick around so we can keep on being good little consumers or good little soldiers because that serves their purposes and their profit margin. They think they can control what we do with our bodies because we *belong* to them, we're their *property*. Well, I say we're nobody's property. Yeah, we could just end it right here rather than going all the way to California but it's the *principle* of the thing. Our lives belong to us, *we* decide what to do with them, no one else. So if we're going to end up in jail or an asylum either way, then let's finish what we started and make a run for it, ride this out right to the end. That way whatever happens, it's *our* choice, not theirs. *Never* theirs.

"We also need to recognize that we're not just talking about the decision to keep going into Utah, but also all the decisions that'll have to be made once we're in the middle of whatever's waiting for us. Things are going to happen fast and there won't be time to take a vote about what we should do about it.

"So if we decide to keep going, I propose that we don't stop once we're on the other side, not for anyone or anything, no matter what. If they want us that badly, if they want to keep us from doing what we believe is right for us, then let's make them work for it."

Then Theo sat back down, and we fell quiet for a minute. None of us had wanted to hear those words, but all of us needed to hear them, to understand the actions that might be required on the other side of the decision we were about to make.

We don't stop, not for anyone or anything.
No matter what.

"All right," Dylan said, breaking the silence. "Unless anyone has anything else to say, I guess it's time for the vote. All in favor of making a run for it, raise your hands."

He looked over at Karen, but she didn't meet his gaze as she put her hand up.

"I'm in," Vaughn said. "Like my old man used to say, in for a penny, in for a pounding."

"Lisa?"

"Shit, yeah."

"Peter?"

And suddenly I'm thinking about Shanelle, and wondering what she's doing right now. It's stupid early, so she's probably still asleep at her folks' place, maybe even planning to sleep in extra late because of all the emotions of the last few days, and when she does get up, she'll come downstairs and her folks will have breakfast waiting for her, and all I can think of, the only thought I can focus on, is that I'd like to have breakfast, right now, I'd like to have eggs and bacon and toast and coffee and orange juice, the kind with lots of pulp, just so I could taste it and have those few minutes and all I have to do is say no, shake my head just enough so they can see me do it, just stand up and walk off the bus, such a small thing, that's all, just stand up and put one foot in front of the other just for a minute, one minute so I can get something to eat, something to taste, something to—

"Peter?" Dylan asked again.

"Yeah," I said. My voice wavered, so I tightened it up. "I'm good. Let's do it."

"Okay," he said, then repeated it softly and with finality, like he was letting go of a part of himself, and maybe he was. "Okay."

And I was the first to see the look in Karen's eyes as he got behind the wheel.

Hi, I'm Audio Recorder!
Tap the icon to start recording.

PETER ROUTH: As expected, trouble in paradise.

KAREN: You can't do this.

DYLAN: Karen . . .

KAREN: Get out from behind the wheel, okay?

DYLAN: I signed up to do a job.

KAREN: Bullshit. Somebody else can drive, we already agreed—

DYLAN: I didn't.

KAREN: Dylan, if you go with us and this goes wrong—

DYLAN: Where you go, I go.

LISA: Except right now we're not going anywhere, so can we save the drama for your mama?

KAREN: I know what you're doing. You know I don't want anything to happen to you, so you're trying to pressure me into changing my mind.

DYLAN: I didn't know changing your mind was an option.

LISA: The gas pedal's that long flat thing by your right foot.

KAREN: Damn it, Lisa.

DYLAN: They want to go, you want to go, so let's go.

KAREN: You'll get arrested with the rest of us, or worse. If something happens—

DYLAN: What happened is that I love you. You can't ask me to just walk away from that.

KAREN: That's exactly what I'm saying, Dylan. This isn't fair.

LISA: What's not fair is wasting time when we're supposed to be on the road before dawn, and making us listen to your bullshit. At least take it the fuck outside.

KAREN: Why are you being such a bitch?

LISA: Genetics. Deal with it.

DYLAN: She's right, let's talk about this outside.

KAREN: Fine, whatever, thanks for your support, Lisa.

LISA: You're welcome!

PETER ROUTH: Nicely done.

LISA: I have my moments.

VAUGHN: What are you guys—

LISA: How far are they from the door?

PETER ROUTH: Standing by the luggage bin.

LISA: Okay, here goes.

PETER: Buckle up!

END RECORDING

PeterWilliamRouth

Welcome to Utah.

We're thirty miles in. Passing Thompson Springs. Lisa's still driving as Theo monitors the police scanner and Vaughn tracks the GPS for exits in case we need to get off fast. So far, so good.

Fifty miles.

Sixty.

We debate getting off on an exchange going north from the 70 to Green River so we can tuck in out of sight to see if any police units show up on the freeway looking for us, but there's no way to know what we'll run into if we drive into a small town and get bottlenecked. The smart thing is to keep going while we're on a roll, so we do.

Eighty. Still clear. Starting to think we have an actual chance.

Ninety.

Shit.

Hi, I'm Audio Recorder!
Tap the icon to start recording.

PETER ROUTH: Where? I can't see them.

LISA: Right behind us. Just came off the on-ramp.

VAUGHN: No need to panic yet. Theo, can you hear them on the scanner?

THEO: Just a— Yes. They're running our plates.

LISA: Fuck!

PETER ROUTH: What's the nearest exit?

VAUGHN: Only city's Salina. Thirty miles. Before then it's all just access roads and fireroads.

THEO: They've ID'd us. Here they come.

(UNRECOGNIZABLE SOUND)

LISA: Shit!

PETER ROUTH: We've got to get off the freeway, try to lose them.

LISA: Where?

VAUGHN: I don't know!

THEO: They're requesting backup.

VAUGHN: Hang on, checking the map.

LISA: They're right on my ass!

VAUGHN: Fireroad one forty-one. Half a mile. But the on-ramp only comes off the freeway going east.

LISA: How am I supposed to get to the other side, we've got guard rails.

THEO: Only at the curves. On the straightaways there's just the wire barrier and we should be able to—

LISA: Okay, I see it! Hang on!

(UNRECOGNIZABLE SOUND)

LISA: Which way?

PETER ROUTH: There! Make a right! Over there!

LISA: Jesus, could they make this road any smaller.

VAUGHN: It goes all the way up the mountain to Kinneys Peak, then forks off into a bunch of smaller roads on the way down the other side. If we can get far enough ahead, we can lose them.

LISA: Okay, got it.

VAUGHN: What are they saying?

THEO: Can't get a signal, canyon, too many trees.

LISA: Christ, this is steep, wheels keep slipping, bus wasn't made for this.

PETER ROUTH: Keep going.

LISA: Not a lot of choice, Peter.

THEO: Caught a little. They're sending cars up the fireroad on the other side.

VAUGHN: The sixteen.

THEO: They're trying to get to the top and box us in. If they get there first—

LISA: Going as fast as I can in this heap.

THEO: I know.

PETER ROUTH: Shit, that's a drop.

LISA: Yeah, it is. Theo.

THEO: Yeah.

LISA: Tell me about it.

THEO: About what?

LISA: The silver city.

THEO: What?

LISA: You said it was somewhere right around here, right?

THEO: I don't . . .

LISA: Theo?

THEO: Yeah . . . yes, it is. There's a secret entrance, right near the top of the peak.

PETER ROUTH: Okay . . . okay . . .

LISA: You know where it is, so just tell me when to turn.

THEO: Okay, I will, I . . .

PETER ROUTH: I'll take the scanner.

VAUGHN: Shanelle, if you're hearing this, I love you.

LISA: Keep talking, Theo. Tell me about it.

THEO: The silver city is old, so old that no one knows who built it, or why, or when.

PETER ROUTH: They're getting into position to cut us off.

VAUGHN: Is it beautiful, Theo?

THEO: More beautiful than anything you've ever seen.

PETER ROUTH: They're up ahead laying down spike strips.

LISA: How far?

PETER ROUTH: I don't know.

THEO: And the sunsets . . . the sunsets are . . .

VAUGHN: There! Police cars! Up ahead!

LISA: Theo? Where do I turn? Where's the entrance?

PETER ROUTH: Fuck you! Fuck you! You lose!

LISA: Theo!

THEO: There, it's there. Do you see it?

LISA: Yeah. Yeah, I see it. It's everything you said it was, Theo. It's beautiful.

VAUGHN: God. God, forgive me, I'm sorry, Carolyn.

THEO: Here! Turn here! Right here!

LISA: Here we go!

(UNRECOGNIZABLE SOUND)

(UNRECOGNIZABLE SOUND)

(UNRECOGNIZABLE SOUND)

END RECORDING

Karen_Ortiz

The news called it an accident. The police said the bus was driving erratically, and when the police tried to stop them, they made a run for it, going up into the hills before losing control and going off the fireroad. Easier that way. Cleaner. It absolves the police and the AG of guilt and leaves out the reason why they were in Utah in the first place and why they were trying to get away from the police. They think that covering up the truth will guarantee that no one else gets any ideas about doing the same thing. After all, none of them survived the crash, so there's no one to challenge the official story.

Except there is. It's all right here, in the cloud server.

And in five minutes, everyone's going to know the truth of who we were, what we did, and what *really* happened. Vaughn, Peter, Theo, Lisa, Zeke, Tyler . . . they were beautiful and I miss them and they earned the right to have their stories told.

But uploading the file to the internet also carries some risks.

"Are you sure this is what you want to do?" Dylan asked last night. We'd gotten a ride back into Denver with a trucker who dropped us off at the Airport Marriott. "Putting all this online will seriously piss off the Utah AG. He could come after you."

"Fine, let him."

"So you're totally cool with letting this out into the wild?"

"I am, and not just because I want people to know what happened. It's because of something Theo wrote."

I opened the archive and pulled out the quote. "*'The first way people kill themselves is a kind of spontaneous combustion. It comes out of rage or shock or sudden deep depression and catches you by surprise, and before you even realize you're doing it, you're reaching for the gun or the knife or the pills. It's as if something inside you gets too sad or too angry to survive anymore and it explodes, taking you with it. I think it happens most often to the very people who don't think they could ever kill themselves, because they're not paying attention when their switch gets flipped in the middle of something awful.'*

"Theo's right. The reason so many people are vulnerable to suicide is because they think it could never happen to them, so they don't know what to look for, what feelings could lead to making that decision. But the archive is full of all of us talking about why we decided to check out early, the whole thought process is right there, so anybody reading this will know *exactly* what it feels like to make that choice from the inside out. For some people maybe it'll be like a flu vaccine, giving them a little piece of the real thing so it immunizes them, so they'll know what that impulse feels like when it comes, and maybe they won't be as vulnerable because now they can recognize that feeling for what it is instead of being ambushed by it. And maybe they won't make that jump, or at least they'll know enough to wait and think about it some more.

"That's why out of everyone on the bus, I feel the worst for Peter. None of us knew he was having doubts. If we had, we would've done everything we could to talk him out of it, because nobody should've been there who wasn't sure that this was what they wanted to do."

"Wouldn't have worked," Dylan said. "You know how he was. Push him left and he'll go right every time."

"I know, but seeing his last entries, I think that if they'd just been able to keep going, sooner or later he would have gotten off the bus. You can see him starting to question whether or not he's really doing the right thing. But when the police came after them, it forced his hand. They pushed left and he jumped right. And now that I know what was in his heart, I wish he hadn't.

"People need to understand that," I said. "They need to see not just what led to our decisions, but that it's possible to turn back, as Shanelle did, instead of getting so walled up behind their decision that they don't see the possibility of backing off, as with Peter. They need to see that there's always a choice. So I need to get this out there, to tell the truth. *Our* truth."

Dylan nodded quietly, then said, "It's your story, so it's your call. I'll back your play."

So I guess we're doing this.

And in case the Utah AG or someone else decides to come after us, I've changed a few names and email addresses for safety. I'm not Karen, Dylan's not Dylan, and Shanelle's not Shanelle. As Theo said, if anyone wants to come looking for us, why make it easy, right? Mark is still Mark, but he expected that. I've researched a bunch of sites where I can upload the material, and narrowed it down to the ones where it has the best chance of being noticed. It's kind of like throwing a message in a bottle into the sea. *This is who*

we were, and what we did right, and what we did wrong, and why, and
what we think it all means. But really, it's down to you to figure it out.

As I write this, Dylan's off getting some coffee and doughnuts
while we wait for our plane. Through the window the blue demon
horse stares up at the sky like he might gallop into the clouds at
any second. Seeing him reminds me of the party in Vaughn's pent-
house, and I smile at the memory.

The night before Lisa drove the others off the planet, Dylan said
that as long as there's even the *possibility* of being happy for five
minutes today, or the next day, or the one after that, then it's worth
hanging on. He thinks it's like vitamins, that just five minutes of
happiness per day is the minimum basic requirement we need to go
on living. I don't know if I agree with that, but I'm going to try it,
even if that means going back to war with the Spider.

All I *do* know for sure is that for these five minutes, I'm happy
being with Dylan. I want to see if love is big enough and bad enough
to beat the Spider.

If not, if I still can't take it and decide I want out, there's always
another cliff waiting for me. Dylan promised he won't try to stop
me because he knows I'll just do it without him, and he'd rather be
there when it happens than let me go alone.

I can always do this tomorrow if today is not enough.

And today, right now, this moment is coffee, and doughnuts,
and Dylan, and a plane flight to someplace I've never been before.

What happens after that? I don't know.

Does anyone?

UPLOAD FILE TO PUBLIC SERVER?   Y/N
Y
BEGIN TRANSFER?   Y/N
Y

ACKNOWLEDGMENTS

This book would not exist without the assistance and guidance of: Ed Schlesinger, editor at Simon & Schuster, who stepped up when it mattered, along with his team of Editorial Jedi, including Maggie Loughran, Jennifer Bergstrom, Jennifer Long, Aimee Bell, Alison Callahan, Sally Marvin, and Eliza Hanson; also, my tireless agents, Emma Parry and Martin Spencer; my attorney Kevin Kelly, who has been looking after me for over twenty years; and my assistant and guardian angel, Stephanie Walters. My thanks and appreciation to all of you, and to the friends and First Readers whose observations kept me honest.

Together We Will Go is an examination of the
intense feelings that often underlie suicidal ideation
and depression. If you sometimes find yourself experiencing
similar feelings, and wish to speak with someone
who understands, please contact
the National Suicide Prevention Lifeline
at 1-800-273-8255.